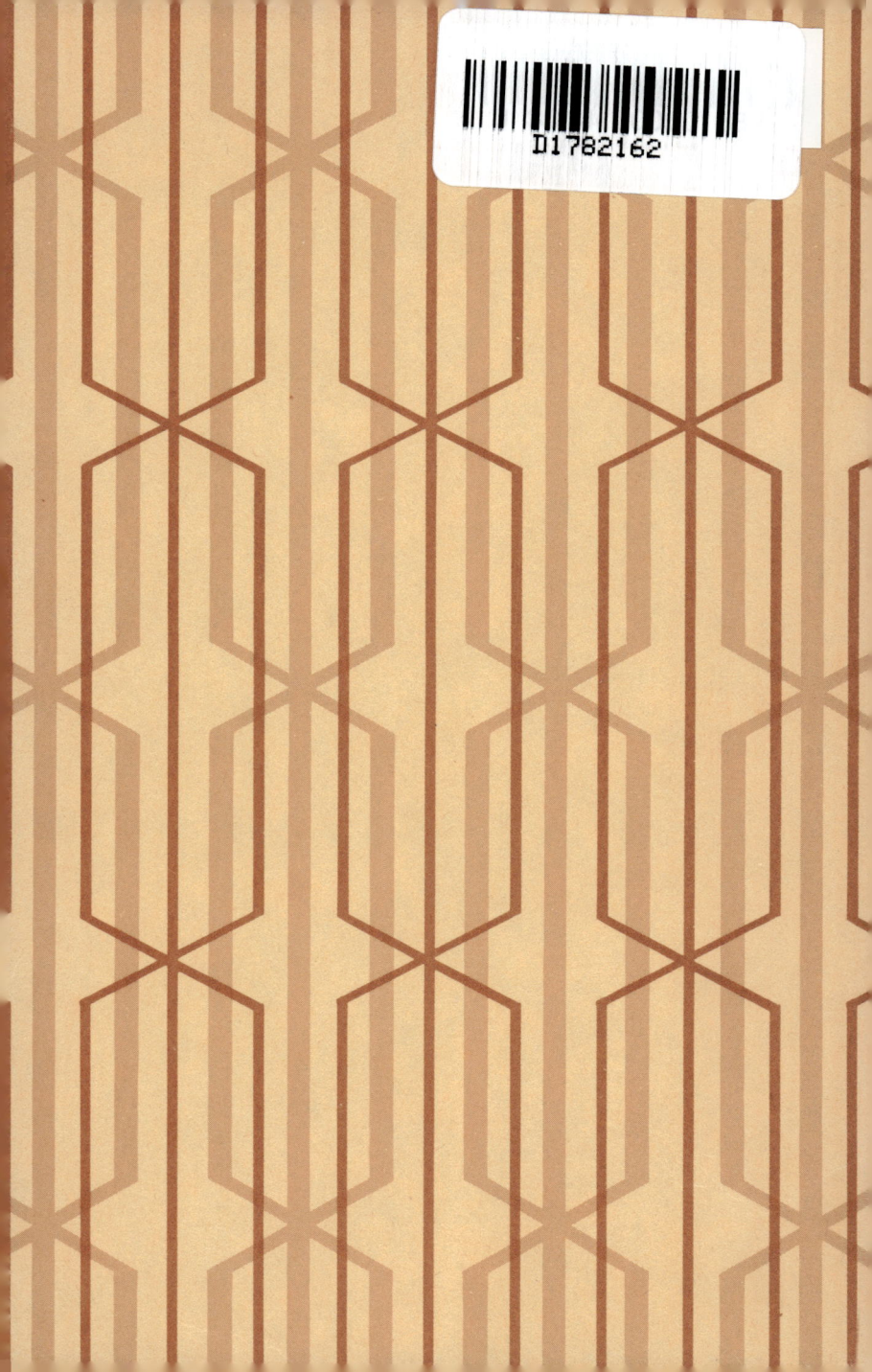

GALLOPS

GALLOPS

By DAVID GRAY

Two Volumes in One

Volume I

Short Story Index Reprint Series

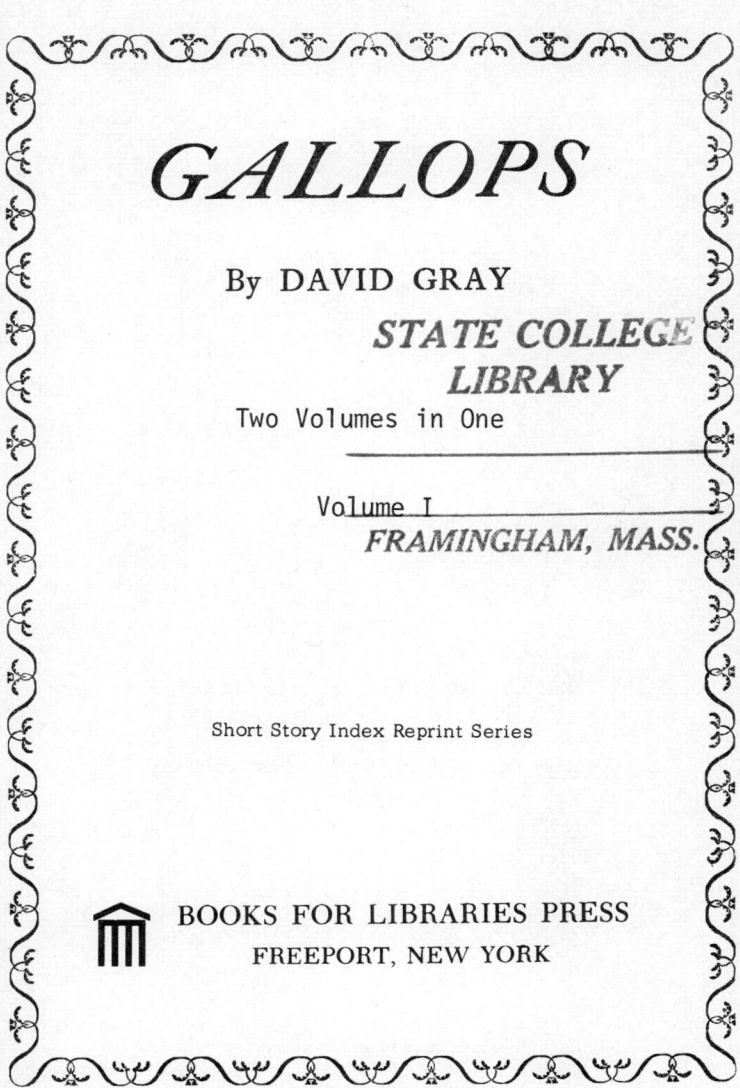

BOOKS FOR LIBRARIES PRESS
FREEPORT, NEW YORK

Vol. I First published 1898
Vol. II First published 1903
Reprinted 1969

Standard Book Number: 8369-3003-7

LIBRARY OF CONGRESS CATALOG CARD NUMBER:
73-75778

CONTENTS

	PAGE
THE PARISH OF ST. THOMAS EQUINUS	1
BRAYBROOKE'S DOUBLE-EVENT STEEPLECHASE	21
HOW THE FENCE-BREAKERS' LEAGUE WAS "STUMPED"	37
THE RIDE OF HIS LIFE	53
THE TRANSFIGURED PAIR	67
THE POPULARITY OF TOMPKINS	85
CHALMERS'S GOLD PIECE	101
THE BISHOP'S MISSIONARY MEETING	121
HIS FIRST RACE	133
CARTY CARTERET'S SISTER	159

THE PARISH OF
ST. THOMAS EQUINUS

I

THE PARISH OF ST. THOMAS EQUINUS

THE bishop settled himself in an armchair, crossed his short legs, and gave a sigh of relief and comfort. Through the open window he could see the hills across the valley and the two spires of Oakdale village. There was a gleam of silver in the bottom-lands where a bend of the river revealed itself. Out of doors the air was hot with the afternoon sun and murmurous with insect noises, but the large drawing-room was pleasantly darkened and cool. The bishop felt that he had earned peace, and meant to enjoy it. With half-closed eyes he watched the tea-things brought in and the two slender young women seat themselves by the table. Mrs. Alden Adams began to make the tea.

"Did you have a good time?" she asked the bishop.

"Yes," said the bishop; "I suppose so. It was rather extraordinary, however.—Two lumps and a little cream," he added.

"Extraordinary?" Mrs. Adams echoed inquiringly as she passed the cup.

"I think I may say *very* extraordinary," he replied in an injured tone.

Miss Colfax stopped in the middle of a stitch—she was embroidering something.

"I suppose the rector bored you to death," she said. "I hope you ordered him to stop advising the farmers to put up wire."

"Wire? Wire what?" asked the prelate, as if he were hearing of a new heresy.

"Wire fences, of course," the girl replied. "You can't jump wire."

The bishop seemed at a loss. "No," he said; "I suppose not. I don't want to. But, my dear young woman, I haven't seen the rector."

"Why," said Mrs. Adams, who was trying to snuff the lamp under the kettle, "I thought you and Willie had gone to the rectory in the victoria."

"That's what we were going to do," the bishop answered, with a resentful note in his voice; "but we gave up the victoria and your horses. The ones we did take made other arrangements."

The girl looked up from her work. "An accident?" she inquired.

The bishop hemmed. "I should hardly call it an accident. An accident is something contrary to probabilities." Both women looked puzzled. "My young friend, Mr. William Colfax," he went on, "informed me, as we were about to start, that the horses harnessed to the victoria were such 'rum skates'—pardon me, those were *his* words—that he would prefer to take me with some of his own."

"I am glad he was so thoughtful," observed his sister; "it isn't often that he is."

The bishop scrutinized the girl. She was earnestly embroidering. The corners of his mouth twitched.

"It *was* thoughtful," he continued. "He had a high red cart and a tandem. Two grooms held the horse in front, and there was another at the head of the wheeler."

The girl dropped the work in her lap. "I think Willie's manners are improving," she said simply. "He hasn't been so civil to anybody stopping in the house since he let Carty Carteret ride Manslaughter. He must like you."

"But I don't think," Mrs. Adams objected, "that a tandem is the proper thing for a bishop to visit one of his rectors in—not the first time, anyway."

"I may say," observed the bishop, "that this thought occurred to me also."

"Oh, stuff, Kate!" the girl interposed. "We're not in town. You're ruffled because Willie said your victoria horses were skates—and they are."

The bishop avoided a discussion of this question. "It may be," he said, "but I should have preferred them to the tandem. William said that he believed his horses were safe, or if they were not we should find it out. Before I was quite in the cart the front one pawed one of the men, and they let go of him."

"What could you expect?" said the girl. "He'd never been put to harness before."

"William mentioned that fact after we had started," the bishop continued. "At the Four Corners we met a steam threshing-machine, and the leader took the road in the opposite direction from the village. Then they both ran away." He paused to allow his words to take effect. The bare fact seemed to him impressive enough. He reflected what a terrible picture the newspapers might make of Bishop Cunningham in a runaway, and he considered how he could soften the information for his wife.

"They must have taken the Hemlock Hill road," Miss Colfax said thoughtfully. "How far did they run?"

The prelate looked annoyed. "Really, I can't say," he replied. "I don't know the country, you know. At first your brother thought we'd stop for the groom— we had lost him at the threshing-machine. But the horses pulled so that he asked me if I didn't think we would better let them go and enjoy it while it lasted." He swallowed some tea, and glanced from one to the other of the women.

"You couldn't have been very far from the Galloways'," Mrs. Adams suggested uncertainly, as though she were expected to say something. "We dine there to-night, you know. Pretty road, isn't it?"

"Is it?" said the bishop, dryly. Both women laughed. "I dare say, I dare say," he went on; "but I was thinking of something else than the scenery. We stopped the horses at the foot of the hill, and William said that if I didn't mind putting off going to the rectory he would go in and trade the leader to Mr. Galloway. He said that it was no use bothering with such a puller; and I quite agreed with him, though I wished he had come to that conclusion sooner."

"Willie had promised to let me hunt Albion," said the girl, regretfully.

"Never mind, dear," exclaimed her aunt; "you can have Alden's Thunder. I think he's afraid to ride him himself. But you missed seeing the rector," she added, turning to the bishop; "that was too bad."

Miss Colfax laughed. "You didn't miss much, and you did have a good drive. Of course it wasn't very long, but while it lasted it must have been rare. I've never had a tandem run with me." The prelate looked at her wonderingly. "But," she continued, "I don't see how Willie could have made much of a trade, with Albion so wet and hot."

The bishop's eye lighted up. "Yes; that was rather extraordinary."

"Extraordinary?" his companions repeated together.

"How, extraordinary?" Eleanor asked. "And you said you had an extraordinary afternoon, too. I don't see anything extraordinary about it." Sitting erect, with her hands in her lap, and a shaft of sunlight burnishing her hair, she was very beautiful, and as the bishop looked upon her his expression softened.

"My dear young lady," he explained, "I am a stout, elderly person, and for twenty years I have gone about in a brougham drawn, I may say, by a confidential horse. I have had to do only with the things which are the duties of a city clergyman. I have been a bishop but six months, and this is my first introduction to Oakdale, which my venerable predecessor sometimes alluded to as the parish of St. Thomas Equinus. Some things about it seem a little new, you know—yes, I may even say extraordinary."

The girl looked at him reprovingly, as if she suspected him of joking.

"I suppose," said Mrs. Adams, "that you are not

much interested in hunting, and all that. I know a man —Mr. Fairfield, the architect—who feels just as you do about it. He says this is the dullest place he ever got into."

"I shouldn't call it dull," protested the bishop.

"Well, I'm glad of that," she replied gratefully. "I should hate to have you bored. I hate being bored myself."

Miss Colfax yawned as if at the mention of the word, and put a slim and very white hand to her mouth. "You haven't told us yet what Willie got for Albion," she said lazily.

"I am not quite certain whether I know," the bishop replied. "It was somewhat complicated."

"Why? Wasn't Charley Galloway at home?" asked Mrs. Adams.

"Oh, yes. We met him in the drive, and William asked him at once if he could detect anything wrong in the leader's wind. He said he had galloped him six miles to find out. That was one of the things which struck me as extraordinary."

"You didn't think Willie was so clever, did you?" asked the girl.

"No; I didn't," said the bishop. "There were several other interesting occurrences, however, before the bargain was concluded. Mr. Galloway offered us refreshments, and then invited me out to see his horses jump."

"Only his green ones, I suppose," said the girl, with a shade of contempt—"lunged in the runway."

"Was that it? There was a kind of lane with a high fence on both sides, and barriers erected at intervals. The stable-men shooed the horses over without any one on them. Then, for my particular benefit, Mr. Galloway ended by sending a Jersey cow over. You know I am the president of a Society for the Prevention of Cruelty to Animals!"

"Really!" exclaimed Mrs. Adams, as though she found it hard to believe.

"It's odd the way he loves that cow," observed Miss Colfax. "He says he'll match her against any cow in America."

The bishop nervously gulped down his tea, and set the cup on the table. "I think," he said, "that, if you will allow me, I must call Mr. Galloway a very extraordinary young man."

Mrs. Adams laughed. "He must have had that waistcoat on," she said meaningly to her niece.

The ghost of a smile softened the bishop's mouth. "I think it likely," he said. "It was red, yellow, and black."

"There's blue in it, too," Miss Colfax added. "I

made it myself. Kate is a little envious because it's more effective than the one she made for Willie. But please tell us how the trade came out."

"At first it seemed as though there wasn't going to be one. Mr. Galloway wasn't sure that he cared for a steeplechaser, or that he had anything to barter."

"Yes, of course!" the girl exclaimed. "It's always that way. Go on, please."

"But finally he brought out a big sorrel horse which he called Lorelei."

"Lorelei? Lorelei?" repeated Miss Colfax. "How was she bred?" The bishop sat up with a start. "Oh, never mind!" she continued. "Probably you didn't ask. What cut of horse was it?"

The bishop shut his lips tight, settled himself again, and folded his hands.

"I mean," said the girl, "was it a harness horse or a jumper?"

A mental conflict was going on inside the prelate. Was it meet for a bishop of the Church to submit to all this? But the tea and the easy-chair and the girl's gray eyes were mollifying his indignation, and his sense of humor was reasserting itself.

"A jumper, I think," he answered in a resigned way. "Mr. Galloway said she could jump an enormous height—ten feet, if I remember correctly." The aunt and niece exchanged glances. "He said he had just got her from Long Island, and didn't want to part with her, only she was too slow to race, and he had plenty of hunters."

"What did Willie think of her?"

"He asked me if it didn't look as though her front legs had been fired—I think it was fired."

"Probably had been," Mrs. Adams interpolated.

"Well, Mr. Galloway was indignant about it; and I said I shouldn't venture any opinion—in fact, I said I hadn't any, which was the truth."

"How odd!" said Miss Colfax, looking at him suspiciously.

"Not at all," her aunt objected. "Sometimes even a veterinary can't tell."

"They examined Albion after that," continued the bishop. "William—very honorably, I thought—admitted that he pulled a little." There was a twinkle in the prelatical eye. "But he expatiated on his wind and his endurance, and recited his pedigree."

"War-cry out of a Lapidist mare, second dam by True Blue, third by Longfellow," the girl repeated. "It's very good, isn't it?"

The bishop looked appealingly at Mrs. Adams.

"Yes; it's capital," she said reassuringly.

"Do you mind giving me a little more tea?" inquired the bishop. "But," he went on, "Mr. Galloway said that he couldn't think of exchanging on even terms. He suggested that William should throw in a dun-colored pony and some kind of a cart."

"The pig!" exclaimed Miss Colfax.

The bishop laughed. "William seemed to be of that opinion. He intimated that if I wanted to convert a Jew I had the opportunity. I thought it was wiser for me to withdraw, so I went to see the Jersey cow."

"Well, how did they settle it?" asked the girl.

"As far as I could understand, they arranged a balance by extending the scope of the negotiations. Your brother secured Lorelei, a pair of cobs,—cobs, I believe,—a brood mare, and some chickens."

"Charley's game Japs, of course," said the girl, half to herself. The bishop looked puzzled, but disregarded the interruption.

"Mr. Galloway got Albion," he explained, "another horse named Jupiter, the cart, the dun-colored pony, a fox-terrier, and a lady's bicycle. It was very ridiculous; don't you think so?"

The women seemed not to hear the question. They were considering the terms of the trade.

"It was characteristic of Willie to trade your bicycle," said Mrs. Adams to her niece.

"I don't care," the girl replied; "I never use it.

Did he tell Charley about Albion running away?"

"Well," said the bishop, slowly, "as we drove off he did tell him that the horse pulled a good deal."

"And that was the second time he had told him," said Mrs. Adams.

"Yes. And Mr. Galloway advised your nephew to keep the mare's legs in bandages for a few days. He explained that they might be stiff after her journey on the cars."

"I have my suspicions about those legs," Miss Colfax remarked. "Charley is a bit too keen for a gentleman." She moved idly to the piano, and began to play. The bishop watched her with growing amazement. She played on, perhaps for ten minutes.

"That was very beautiful—wonderful!" he exclaimed when she stopped. She nodded, and swung herself around on the piano-stool.

"Do you remember whether the cobs were light chestnut?" she asked.

"I do not," said the bishop; and muttering to himself, he left the room.

THE Alden Adamses, their niece, and Bishop Cunningham found the usual party at the Galloways' that evening; but young Colfax sent word that he was indisposed. At the last moment the tip had come that there was to be a quiet cocking-main in the village. He considered the advisability of taking the bishop, who seemed to him to have possibilities worth cultivating, but decided that it might cause talk.

The bishop was rather confused by the fashion in which the people at the dinner addressed each other by their Christian names, or even more informally; but he sat next to Mrs. Galloway, who impressed him favorably. She was the daughter of a Philadelphia millionaire who was a pillar of the Presbyterian faith, and she had been married only a year. It was her first season at Oakdale, and the bishop experienced a certain feeling of relief in her company. The dinner was good, if the guests were somewhat noisy; and the bishop adapted himself to the conditions with the cheerfulness of a liberal churchman and a man of culture. Mrs. Galloway, he found, although a dissenter by birth, adopted her husband's religious preferences in the country; and she was so much interested in the bishop's project for a boys' gild in the village that he was encouraged to believe his first impressions of Oakdale incorrect. He felt again as though he were in a society which he understood; and, furthermore, the reliable victoria horses were in the stable waiting to take him home.

Miss Colfax, who sat on his right, appeared content with the occasional remarks which served her other neighbor, Jimmy Braybrooke, in the stead of conversation, and left the prelate for the most part to his hostess. As the dessert was served, however, he became aware that Miss Colfax was talking down the table to Galloway about the afternoon's horse-trade; and this conversation attracted Mrs. Galloway's attention also.

She heard her husband say, "Oh, yes, Lorelei will jump anything." There was a lull in the talk, and the words came distinctly. She looked up.

"Lorelei?" she repeated half aloud. Then, raising her voice: "Charley Galloway, you don't mean to tell me you traded that horse to Mr. Colfax? If you did, you will take her back. You told me yesterday she was broken down and not worth twenty-five cents."

A roar of laughter broke from the men—all except the bishop. He was regarding Mrs. Galloway with silent admiration. Yet, as Varick said afterward, he must have missed half the joke, because he was unaware that the lady spoke with the authority which clothes the bank-account of an establishment.

Galloway, the unblushing, was for once discomfited, and the laughter rose again. Just then the footman whispered something in his ear, and he hastily left the room.

"I trust there has been some mistake about this," remarked the bishop, benevolently.

"He ought to be ashamed of himself," said Miss Colfax. "Willie would never have done such a thing. It's dishonorable."

"Excuse me, Miss Colfax!" said Mrs. Galloway, flushing.

"Goodness me!" the bishop murmured. Then in his professional voice he began an anecdote that figured in his favorite sermon; but, to his relief, Galloway entered the room again, and all eyes were turned upon him.

"He's been writing Willie a check," Varick suggested in a loud whisper. But he took no notice of Varick. He remained standing, one hand on the back of his chair, his napkin in the other. A smile puckered the corners of his mouth.

"I am informed," he said pleasantly, "that Tim, my stable-boy, has broken two legs, and that Albion, the horse I got from my friend Colfax to-day, has broken one. I ordered him tried on the steeplechase course, and he ran through the liverpool. They shot him. And Tim's mother, who is Mrs. Galloway's laundress, is going to prosecute me. She says I had no business to put the boy on such a horse."

"Albion? Albion?" said Captain Forbes. "Is that

the horse? Well, he *has* rather an ugly reputation. He ran through a jump over in Canada last year, and killed his jockey."

Another burst of laughter made the candle-flames tremble, and an unholy smile grew upon Mrs. Galloway's meek little mouth. It was a smile that made the bishop shudder and turn away his head. He glanced at Eleanor Colfax. Her face was expressionless. Her lips moved, but in the hubbub only he and Braybrooke heard.

"I am very sorry," she said, "that the little idiot broke his legs; but he probably pulled the horse into the jump. He can't ride, and never will be able to learn. Mr. Galloway should have known better than to trust him with the horse."

"That's exactly it," Braybrooke assented, while the laughter of the others still rippled on.

"Bless me!" said the bishop to himself, "this is extraordinary—most extraordinary! I beg pardon!" he exclaimed, recovering his senses and rising hastily, for the ladies were leaving the room.

During the rest of the evening Bishop Cunningham, the practised diner-out, opened not his mouth. When he eventually reached the haven of his bedchamber, he took up his diary, as he had done nightly for fifty years. Then he paused. The events of the day passed before his mind's eye like the unordered memories of a play: the red dog-cart, the tandem, the foppish youth who calmly guided the runaway horses and proposed they should enjoy it while it lasted; Mr. Galloway, his waistcoat, the jumping cow, and the peculiar incidents of the horse-trade; the tea-table, and the two fair young women.

The bishop had come to know many curious things about women, for he had known many women as the father confessor does; but he said to himself that these were a new sort. The picture of the girl rose before him as she looked when she stopped her wonderful playing to ask about the chestnut cobs. He thought of her gentle gray eyes, and then of her words at the dinner-table when she heard about the boy's accident. "Has she two souls," he murmured, "or none?" From Eleanor Colfax his mind turned to Mrs. Galloway and the way she had smiled, and to her guests,—gentlefolk,—who talked of broken bones as one might talk of buttered muffins, and seemed to consider the legal doctrine of *caveat emptor* a pleasant matter of course in horse-trading. According to his habit, he labored to classify his impressions in the pigeonholes of his mind, and to index them, so to say, in his diary. How long he labored he knew not, but his efforts were vain. His thoughts came and went in a hopeless jumble, and the page lay blank before him. Suddenly he heard the tall clock in the lower hallway sound its prelude of muffled arpeggios, and then two low, throbbing strokes. He dipped his pen in the ink, and wrote hastily:

Oakdale, October the Twenty-fourth.—A most extraordinary day!

And below, as if in afterthought:

Hast thou given the horse strength? hast thou clothed his neck with thunder? (Job xxxix. 19.)

Then, with a sigh, he closed the book.

BRAYBROOKE'S DOUBLE-EVENT STEEPLECHASE

II

BRAYBROOKE'S DOUBLE-EVENT STEEPLECHASE

JIMMY BRAYBROOKE'S pony turned into the Hunt Club driveway, because it took a fancy to do so. The reins hung loose. Braybrooke was thinking about other things. Twenty minutes before, he had closed an interview with a certain girl which caused him more trouble than he had ever imagined there could be in the entire world. A lump ached in his throat, and there was a sick feeling lower down. It began to rain, and he took off his cap; the rain on his head was grateful. But it was all his own fault, he reflected; he had brought it on himself. Who was he, anyway?

He answered himself bitterly that he had never done anything but try to become a jockey, and hadn't succeeded even at that; his own stable-boys laughed at his riding. A comforting friend might have pointed out that to a youth of twenty-four with twenty thousand a year much may be forgiven. If such an idea entered Braybrooke's mind, it passed quickly out. This was not that kind of girl. She wanted a man who could be somebody, or at least could do something. He reflected miserably on the years in which he had steadfastly baffled his educators.

"I can read," he groaned, "and spell with a dictionary, and that's about the limit. I'm a poor lot."

The pony took the path that led past the smoking-room. Braybrooke heard the sound of voices, and mechanically dismounted. Crossing the stirrups through the reins, he turned the horse toward the stable and moved noiselessly to the open window. Through the slats of the blinds he could look into the room without being seen.

"And what am I offered for that good mare, Mrs. 'Awkins?" he heard some one bawl.

Mrs. Hawkins was his own mare. Varick was on the table, auctioning pools on the steeplechase that was to come off the next day for the great Oakdale Cup. They had made him auctioneer because he had a talent for imitating the speech of cockney touts. "Shut your eyes," Chalmers used to say, "and you'd think you were at Guttenberg in the old days."

"Do I 'ear fifty?" cried Varick, sarcastically. "Only fifty for that lovely mare, and Mister Braybrooke hisself to ride?" A roar of laughter followed the mention of Braybrooke. "Believe me, gents, she's the favorite

Mrs. 'Awkins—by Costermonger out of Lizer; and the only Mr. B. to pilot."

"I bid thirty cents," said Galloway, dryly.

"I say, isn't that a bit rough?" asked a quiet-looking young man. "If you don't mind, I'll make it five dollars."

"Bless your generous heart!" said Varick. "Do I hear six?" There was no response. "And sold for five dollars to Mr. Abercrombie."

"Who is a stranger," Galloway observed.

Abercrombie bowed his acknowledgments, and became the owner of Mrs. Hawkins's chances in the pool, which rapidly grew into a round sum.

"A good horse," Captain Forbes remarked to the purchaser; "but Braybrooke is a hoodoo."

The young man outside the window flushed.

"I am, am I?" he muttered. He went softly around the house and passed in. A volley of chaffing remarks greeted him.

"Your great race-horse is sold, O fortunate youth!" said Varick.

"Perhaps," said Braybrooke, quietly, "some of you fellows would like to bet. I'm backing my mare even against the field."

There was no difficulty in getting men to bet.

"Keep your money, my son," said Chalmers, kindly,

putting his hand on the young man's shoulders. For answer he made another entry in his note-book. Finally he remarked that he stood to win the price of a steam-yacht, and the consensus of sound sporting judgment was expressed by Varick.

"Providence," he said, "has sent this rich youth into a community with impaired incomes and refined ideas of both horse-flesh and living. It would be ingratitude to pass him by."

For this, Mrs. Innis, his widowed sister-in-law, called him a horrid brute, which was merely more evidence that Braybrooke needed sympathy and common sense.

The verdict of the Oakdale Hunt on Braybrooke was neither biased nor harsh. He rode heavily, and badly for one who had ridden so much. His judgment led him wrong when he used it, and when he "went it blind," as he usually did, he was likely to perform foolhardy leaps and to commit surprising blunders. And, worst of all, he was truly unlucky. In the long series of steeplechases held by the Hunt he had usually ridden favorites, and had regularly managed to get them beaten. He seemed incapable of remembering instructions. Several times he had ridden to the right of flags he should have passed on the left; twice his horse had fallen; and once, to his never-ending shame, he had fallen off his horse. Two years before, he had actually come in first, but dismounted before the judges gave him permission, was duly disqualified, and saw the second man take the cup. Mrs. Innis herself admitted that it was hard to imagine any course but a deep rail-road cut over which it would be possible for Brooky to win.

Therefore, when the bugle sounded, and the nine horses paraded past the line of four-in-hands and traps, no one took much notice of Braybrooke, except to wonder in which particular stupid way he was going to lose the race.

"It's a pity," said Captain Forbes, who was not going to ride, and was on the Alden Adamses' yellow drag, "that the mare can't go over the course with a dummy up. She's uncommon fit, and she knows enough to win by herself; but it's a good deal to ask of a horse to have brains for two."

The tall girl on the box beside him turned her back, and began polishing the lenses of her field-glass.

As the riders came up for the start, Braybrooke knit his brow, and labored to recall the parting words of his trainer. Conolly had said:

"Keep her head far to the right at the brushed hurdle, sir. It's a bit higher there, but she's took a dislike to the hole in the brush on the left, and she'll refuse."

To Braybrooke those words were mere sounds. His eyes kept wandering down the line of four-in-hands toward the yellow coach. He shut them, and turned his head away. He called himself a fool. Then the mare reared impatiently, and he began to feel the excitement of the thing. He found himself repeating, "The hole—the brushed hurdle—the hole—the brushed hurdle," till the words lost all semblance of sense. The starter called out to him sharply. He turned back into line, and set his teeth.

The flag dropped, and nine eager horses broke away together. Braybrooke found himself galloping easily in the middle of the bunch, the mare well within herself. She drew ahead slightly, even under his heavy pull. It was plain that she was the speediest of the lot; the question was, could she stay?

The field strung out as it swept on to the first jump, for the cautious were willing to wait for a lead. In front with Braybrooke, and to his left, was Chalmers on Tomahawk; to his right was Willie Colfax on Canterbury. The three took the hurdle almost together. Presently Mrs. Hawkins began to draw away, and she was galloping so handily that Braybrooke let her cut out the pace.

"A mile of this will do for Tomahawk," Chalmers said anxiously to Colfax, who was still by his side.

"It's no place for this nag," was the answer. "Let Brooky go. He'll ride out soon. When he gets ahead he always feels lost." Braybrooke, however, kept steadily on, and flew the water-jump ten lengths in the lead.

The course led around the great meadow, over a broad ditch, over another hurdle, and then, with a curving sweep, on to the liverpool. Chalmers and Colfax still galloped abreast. Each believed that he had "the legs" of the other on the run in, and was glad that his opponent did not force the pace in order to stay with Mrs. Hawkins.

Braybrooke was now twenty good lengths in front, and, barring accidents, obviously had the race, for the mare was still rating along under a pull. But the knowing spectators who were following the race with their glasses had seen the same thing too often before to be anxious about their bets against Braybrooke.

"Two to one," said Chalmers, who was beginning to pant, "that he goes off at the liverpool."

"No takers," gasped Colfax, with a grin; but the mare never swerved as she raced at the ugly jump; she flew rail, ditch, and hurdle grandly, and was on again. A cry of admiration burst from Chalmers. Colfax saved his breath. He was shortening his reins and settling down in the saddle. It is absorbing to go at a stiff liverpool, twenty miles an hour, on a horse that is no longer fresh. Both cleared it, but Mrs. Hawkins was still fighting for her lead.

"Afraid we're done for," puffed Chalmers. Colfax nodded. The same idea was passing through Braybrooke's mind. "I've got 'em beaten this time," he murmured. He smiled and stood forward in the stirrups, fancying that he was "riding light." The course turned abruptly, and the brushed hurdle came in sight.

"Here's the hole," he muttered. There was a bitten-out piece in the brush at the left, and he began to ride for it. As he afterward observed, he ought to have discharged Conolly for mentioning the matter at all. When a person tells you about a hole in a fence while you are mounting, you would be an ass to inquire whether you were meant to profit by it; naturally, it would never occur to anybody that you were meant to avoid it and to jump big.

Mrs. Hawkins began to pull off toward the right, but Braybrooke gathered her firmly and drove her for the low place with the spur. The trainer, who was at the finish with his master's glass, turned his back.

Then happened what is likely to happen when a thoroughbred horse is driven at something it does not want to jump. Throwing her head up angrily, Mrs.

Hawkins swerved sharply away from the hurdle and crashed into the wing on the side. Braybrooke, not anticipating this, continued on alone and took the hurdle at the low place. A hushed cry of apprehension ran through the distant crowd. The knowing ones laughed to themselves, and felt relieved about their bets. Braybrooke staggered to his feet, dazed but uninjured.

"Wonderful leap!" called out Colfax as, a moment later, he and Chalmers, still side by side, swept over.

Braybrooke reached his horse as she was disentangling herself from the remains of the fence. By some freak of chance the end of a splintered board had caught through the head-stall. With a vicious jerk of her head the band slipped over her ears, the throat-latch broke, and she tore herself free. Braybrooke gasped. He was standing beside a horse without bridle or reins. Varick, on Good Morning, slashed by him. He glanced at the horses in front, at the field thundering up behind. Then he pushed the mare's head toward the jump, and vaulted into the saddle.

"Get off!" he heard some one cry from behind. He only gripped the harder with his knees; but he knew what it meant—three jumps at the end of a race, with neither bit nor rein to steady a tiring horse.

Following Good Morning, Mrs. Hawkins bucked from a standstill over the brush at its highest point, and started after the leaders. The blood of twenty grandfathers and of the Godolphin Arab back of them was running in her veins. She was a race-horse, and she kept the track. In a few strides she went by Good Morning, and threw pieces of turf into that weary gelding's face, which disgusted him mightily and his rider more. Varick dismally thought of his long odds.

Colfax was about eight lengths ahead. The mare's wonderful pace held on. As they swung into the stretch she passed him. Chalmers was flogging Tomahawk, still three lengths in the lead. He thought Colfax was coming up. For a moment he held his own, and the cry "Tomahawk wins!" began to come from the carriages.

But Tomahawk had done his best; his tail was waving the distress-signal; and Mrs. Hawkins began steadily closing up. Such a burst had never been seen on the Oakdale meadow before. Twenty yards from the flags, Chalmers looked bewildered as he saw the mare's little head, innocent of harness, forge past his saddle. He forgot to flog Tomahawk, but it mattered little; Tomahawk was a beaten horse.

Braybrooke, sitting immovable as a statue, shot a clear length in advance, and passed between the flags, while the hysterical shouting that greets the winner roared down the line.

An excited crowd thronged the track, and a hundred pairs of hands stretched out officiously to catch the bridleless mare. She kicked one man on the knee-cap. After that they gave her room, and she followed the joyous Conolly toward the judges.

Then a tall, slender girl jumped from the box of the yellow coach and struggled through the crowd. The little mare was standing quietly, her flanks heaving, her nostrils flecked with foam. Her eyes were blood-shot, but there was a mild dignity in them—a look that said, "I have run a race." The girl made her way to the horse, shot a swift glance at Braybrooke, and flung her arms about his mount's dripping neck. The crowd faded out from Braybrooke's eyes, the hubbub died away in his ears. His senses were lost for the time in a great thrill which the look in the girl's gray eyes sent through him.

"You've spoiled your dress," he said.

Then the girl blushed, and drew back in the crowd. Scores of hands shook his, but it was as if they had not. He was the hero of the day, but the victory seemed strangely different from the thing he had imagined so often. He weighed in mechanically, and passing his hand across his eyes, followed the mare toward the trap where the blankets were.

"The fall must have shaken him up," he heard

some one say. Perhaps it had. The crowding figures seemed far off and strange. He put his face to the mare's sweaty neck where the girl's arms had been, and kissed it. Forbes smiled. "She's won his first race for him," he said to the man with him, who was a visitor. "Good boy, Jimmy!" he added to Braybrooke, and Braybrooke nodded absently.

The stable-boys put the blankets on, and asked him if he wished anything special done for the mare. He told them to spray her off knee,—she had rapped it going into the wing of the jump,—and they led her away. A stiffness in the region of his shoulder-blades gave warning that he himself was going to have a lame back. Conolly, who had lingered, noted his cautious experiments with the bruised muscles.

"They say you went over pretty fast, sir," he observed, "but I didn't see it meself. I turned me back, sir, when I see you making for the hole."

"Conolly," said Braybrooke, "if you hadn't mentioned the hole I should have jumped the high place and never got tangled up in the wing. But, then,—you probably think, whether you say it to me or not,—the mare wouldn't have lost her bridle, and I should have got out of the course as usual. I don't agree with you, but I think I'll have to raise your wages."

The man touched his hat impassively. "It's a great cup you've won, sir," he said.

"You're right," said Braybrooke; "it is."

And so it was. They christened it that night at the Alden Adamses' dinner. Varick made a mysterious speech, and named it the Great Double-Event Cup. But by that time everybody at the dinner knew what the second event was, so no one was really mystified, and Miss Colfax began to receive good wishes and "God bless you" glances before Varick gave his "double toast" and called on "the winner" to respond.

HOW THE FENCE-BREAKERS' LEAGUE WAS "STUMPED"

III

HOW THE FENCE-BREAKERS' LEAGUE WAS "STUMPED"

THE morals and practices of the Fence-Breakers' League had reached a point where they demanded and had received the attention of the officers of the Hunt. It is sound hunting doctrine to ride straight when the hounds are running, and to turn aside only for wire and wheat: for wire, because a man is supposed to consider his horse, whether he considers himself or not; for wheat, because in America foxhunting exists by the courtesy of free and independent landowners. But when the pack is not in cry the authorities hold it bad manners to endanger the fences by choosing the highest panels, and immoral to jump at all when there are open gates.

In the Oakdale Hunt there was a faction of unbalanced youth which violated these precepts, at first on the sly, then openly and without shame. It is a great pity that all the best sports should be subject to the same corrupting evil—the rivalry of the reckless. With polo and hunting it develops dangerously, and is usually cured only by some one getting seriously broken. When a master of fox-hounds notes "jealous riding" he begins to tremble for his puppies, which are in danger of being ridden down, and to prepare himself for an era of accidents and agrarian difficulties.

The Fence-Breakers' League exemplified this evil in its most virulent form. Their name had been given as a stigma, in the vain hope that it might shame them into mending their ways. They accepted it, however, as a distinction, proceeded to organize, to elect officers, and to institute weekly dinners, of which the less said the better. It was after one of these dinners that the great Moonlight Steeplechase was run.

Captain Forbes, with the interests of the Hunt at heart, undertook to remonstrate privately with Varick.

"This thing is causing no end of trouble," he said. "You have broken half the fences in the county, and the farmers are mad clean through. I can understand those fool boys acting in such a way, but I really am surprised that you should encourage them." Varick was thirty-five, and might have been a brilliant lawyer if he had not chosen to jeer at the earnestness of a utilitarian generation, and to become an indifferent horse-jockey.

"Forbes," said he, "you are a man whom youth overlooked."

"Bosh!" said the captain; "do be serious."

"You are beguiling me to disparage that generous disregard of consequences which gives life its poetry and hope. However, I couldn't stop the thing if I wanted to. You know as well as I do that boys who jump oak gates when no one is looking are not open to argument. Take Galloway. Galloway is unaffectedly insane about horses. He thinks and dreams of nothing else; and it is as much to him to take his black mare over something no one else will jump as it is for a doctor to find a new disease. He keeps a diary of all his fences over five feet, goes back next day with a tape, and, when possible, kodaks them too. He intends to publish a work entitled, 'Fences I have jumped.' Can I conscientiously urge him to renounce all that makes life worth while for him, and would he renounce it if I did? The rest of the crowd are all more or less on the same pattern—excepting myself."

"Well," said Forbes, who was getting impatient, "what are you?"

"I am an Epicurean philosopher. I jump things because I am afraid; and the pleasure I experience when I am over is worth an occasional spill. I also like to be thought something of a devil. Besides, you and Crawford"—Crawford was the M. F. H.—"take fox-hunting with such elaborate seriousness, and are such children of dogma, that I encourage schism and strife simply for the joy of it. Forbes, I might have been a great revolutionist—"

"You be blanked!" said the captain, and departed. This ended the effort to abate the Fence-Breakers' League by means of sweet reasonableness.

"The tomb yawns for them," said the M. F. H. when he heard Forbes's story; "and I am half sorry it has been disappointed so long. This Hunt is becoming intolerable for decent hunting-men."

Then the governors imposed fines for breakage till the club bank-account swelled to unrecognizable proportions; but the Fence-Breaker's League paid with cheerfulness.

"We are now indebted to no man," Varick explained; "and a great deal of money is not to be compared with the satisfaction of self-respect. The tedium of drawing blank coverts loses its terror when a man can hear his horse's hind feet trail through a board fence without a pang of conscience." And so the Fence-Breakers' League grew steadily more demoralized and demoralizing.

Said the master, finally: "I am afraid only sudden death will stop this nonsense. Of course it is prejudicial to the sport to have people killed, but in this case I think it would be best."

The following Saturday the Fence-Breakers' League were gathered in the club smoking-room, discussing the probability of a dull afternoon, while they waited for the hounds. On Saturdays there were bigger fields, and wretched one-day-a-week men who came down from town were sure to get in the way and crowd. Besides, it was too dry to expect good scent.

"This is the kind of afternoon," said Galloway, "when you insult a good horse by taking him out." A flabby young man who was not among the half-dozen of the Fence-Breakers' League agreed with him.

"On dry days," said he, "Crawford ought to give us a point-to-point for a sweepstake cup."

Galloway smiled, because this young man was apt to be taken ill before a steeplechase. But the talk stopped, for the M. F. H. himself unexpectedly entered, followed by a stranger.

"Here, Charley," said he, "I want you to know some of these fellows. When you get lost this afternoon, they will look after you." He called off the names of the group of men, while the stranger acknowledged the introductions with stiff nods. Just then a cracking of whips in the distance told the M. F. H. that the hounds had started from the kennels, and he hurried out.

The M. F. H. was absent-minded, and apt to introduce people in this one-sided fashion; and he often produced exceedingly queer persons, such as are rarely seen in a hunting-country. He had been at school in England, and had lived pretty much everywhere. Varick used to say that he had met chums of Crawford's all the way from the North Cape to Fiji.

The stranger who had thus been intrusted to the keeping of the Fence-Breakers' League was a short, insignificant-looking man, about fifty, with a red, smoothly shaven face and small white hands. Instead of top-boots and proper hunting-things, he wore tweed breeches, with gaiters, and a rough shooting-coat. This coat was peculiar. Its skirts were cut back so little that they hid the thighs, suggesting a frock-coat rather than a cut-away. When the man walked he limped stiffly, and two curious loops showed on his right breeches' leg just below the hip. They were like the loops sewed on the waistband of breeches to hold a belt.

It was obvious that the newcomer was something odd. It was also clear that he was not a hunting-man, for the M. F. H. had referred to his getting lost as a matter of course. Committing him to the care of the Fence-Breakers' League under these circumstances seemed a rather merciless practical joke, but the M. F. H. had a weakness for such jokes.

Galloway was next to the newcomer, and felt called

upon to make conversation; also, he was not without a healthy curiosity to find out who the man was.

"Pretty hot," Galloway began.

"Yes," said the stranger; "too hot to ride much."

"Your first time in the Oakdale country?"

"Yes."

"Brought any horses down?"

"No."

"Seen the hounds yet?"

"No."

"Pretty fair pack. Got ten new couples from the Earl of Reddesdale's kennels."

"Yes, I know."

"Had more rain in your country?"

"Yes."

"Too dry here for much sport."

"Yes; too dry, quite."

"Have something to drink?"

"Thanks, no."

"Excuse me, I will"; and Galloway beat a retreat to the lunch-room.

"Well," said Varick, who had followed him, "your friend is hardly garrulous."

Galloway scowled. "This," said he, "is the last time I shall try to make things pleasant for people I don't know. What do you suppose that fellow is?"

"Some little painter-man, I dare say; sticks his brushes through those straps on his trousers' leg. He probably feels bashful, and out of it, with so much horse all around. You ought to have talked art at him."

"Well," said Galloway, "I am not revengeful; but, all the same, I think I owe him one out of self-respect. If I get the chance, I shall treat that painter-man to a few thrills. Let's have another look at him." They went to the door of the smoking-room. The stranger was in a corner by the window, with a book.

"That's our copy of Tennyson," said Varick; "I know the cover. Perhaps he's a poet."

"If I can get him to jump," said Galloway, "I sha'n't care what he is. Still, a leaping poet would be especially worth encouraging. Hello! there's the horn." They hurried out to their horses, mounted, and followed the pack down the drive.

The day was too dry for scent, as had been foreseen. The field pottered about from one blank covert to another, and the members of the Fence-Breakers' League endeavored to work off their restlessness by such means as were at hand. They "larked" five-foot rails and regulation four-boarders, plain and with ditch accompaniments. They tackled all the stone walls that seemed worthy, and enjoyed themselves generally, rousing the envy of such as would have liked to imitate them but were afraid, and exciting the disgust of the mature. Finally the league resolved to pull out in a body, in order to express their censure of the M. F. H. for offering such wretched sport, and "to take a ride." Only the long-suffering farmers across whose lands the course of these Fence-Breakers' "rides" have lain can do them justice. The motto which Varick had bestowed upon the society was *Fit via vi*, and classicists translate it, "A way is made by force." But the M. F. H. said he preferred Willie Colfax's personal version, "Fits by the way," although either rendering was appropriate.

"Varick," said Galloway, "start the procession for the meadow bridge, and I'll get that poet chap to come along. Keep the road as far as you can, and don't jump anything till we get across. My conscience is clear, for Crawford has put him up on the Duke." This was the master's very best horse.

The meadow bridge belonged to a farmer who owned the land on both sides of the stream, and was chiefly used to take his cattle from one pasture to the other. The banks were too steep to climb, and the river was too deep to ford, even if there had been a path down to it. Beyond the bridge, and between it and the village, was a series of the stiffest, biggest post-and-rail fences in the country. A man who rode over this course needed a good horse and a big heart, or—what sometimes passes for the same thing—a big flask. They called it the "devil's run."

Galloway found the stranger, looking badly bored, on the edge of a piece of woods which the master was drawing. The breeze flapped his coat skirts back, and showed a stout strap passed through the mysterious loops on his right breeches' leg.

"Ruptured muscle, I guess," muttered Galloway to himself. "Perhaps I oughtn't to—" But he conquered his scruples and unfolded his proposition.

"Too late for anything to-day. Half a dozen of us are going to pull out, and I thought you might like to come along. Crawford's so mad at not finding that he's likely to stop out all night. Instead of going back over the iron bridge we'll cross three miles lower down. Pretty bits of scenery all along. Better come."

"Much obliged," said the stranger. "I think I will. This is slow." He started his horse, rising awkardly to the long trot, and Galloway rode beside him, gloating.

"Charming vista, isn't it?" he said, judging it best to give his conversation an artistic flavor. "I suppose you are fond of landscape."

"I want my tea," said the stranger. "Crawford overlooked lunch completely."

Galloway was somewhat taken aback. "Well, the

way we are going is a short cut," he observed. For the first time that day the stranger's countenance relaxed into something like a smile. "I've touched his stomach," thought Galloway; "he'll come."

They overtook the rest of the party and turned into the river road. Varick had explained what was on foot, and the Fence-Breakers' League hacked along as decorously as a riding-school class in the park. Here and there a wall, here and there a line of wicked-looking pickets, tempted Galloway sorely; but he conquered his desires. He even reproved Willie Colfax, who weakly suggested just one two-dollar competition over a lovely new oak gate. Had the M. F. H. been there, he would have doubted his senses.

The light of the short October afternoon failed rapidly, and it was almost dusk when they reached the bridge. Varick was riding ahead, and started out over the rather crazy structure. Suddenly he pulled up short.

"Here's a mess!" he exclaimed; "this thing is open."

The owner had taken up a dozen boards to prevent the cattle from crossing. Forty feet below was the water, looking dismally black. Galloway rode out, surveyed the situation, and came back swearing eloquently in subdued tones. There was no talk of jumping. A slip at the take-off, the least mistake, and horse and man would rattle down through the underpinning into the water.

"The devil!" said Galloway, soulfully; and he gazed at the distant lines of fence, and the village spires beyond them, dim against the sky.

"It's sure death," said Varick. "It's twelve feet, if it's an inch; and I am too old to die. We might as well get started back, for it's six miles around to the other bridge."

The stranger, who had inspected the gap, only half heard. He rode along side of Galloway.

"How far to the other bridge?" he asked.

"Six miles," replied Galloway, sourly.

"Six miles," he exclaimed. "Oh, I say, I should never get my tea!" Without another word, he clapped in his spurs, and shot out upon the bridge under full steam. A gasp of horror broke from the knot of men.

"You can't make it!" shrieked Varick. The Duke gave a mighty spring, and was over with something to spare. There was an instant's clatter on the boards, and the stranger was checking his horse in the farther meadow. He turned and looked back. Then he called out, with no change in the tone of his dry voice:

"Any one coming?"

No one answered. He pointed toward Oakdale, and called again:

"Is that the village?"

Again there was no answer, and he rode away. Without speaking, they watched him canter across the meadow, clear the first of the big fences, and fade into a small dark object in the twilight.

"The Lord deliver us!" said Varick. "Who is that man?"

But no one was any wiser than he, and there seemed no disposition to speculate idly. The Fence-Breakers' League had been "stumped," and by a man they had presumed to be an esthete. The disgrace was galling, and the mind of Galloway was filled with particularly bitter reflections. They started back, and presently saw Captain Forbes coming toward them. He was making for the bridge.

"You can't get over," said Colfax.

"Unless you happen to have a balloon," added Varick.

When Forbes gathered what had happened he laughed as he had not laughed in twenty years; and the Fence-Breakers' League listened, glum and angry.

"Have you ever heard of Charley Pelham, the Earl of Reddesdale?" he asked.

Now, every hunting-man knows the fame of the hunting Earl of Reddesdale, who rides with his wooden leg strapped to the saddle.

The Fence-Breakers' League kept silence. They were ashamed of themselves. Finally Galloway spoke.

"What can we do about it? Give him a dinner?"

"No," said Varick, glancing at Forbes; "disband."

"I second that motion," said Willie Colfax, gruffly; and the Fence-Breakers' League then and there disbanded.

THE RIDE OF HIS LIFE

IV

THE RIDE OF HIS LIFE

CORDILLAS Y SANDOVAL was an attaché of the Spanish legation, whom Varick invited to Oakdale to please Mrs. Varick and, more especially, her widowed sister.

"I believe I met him once at the club in Washington," Varick remarked. "I thought he was rather an ass; but we've plenty of stable-room. Does he hunt?"

Mrs. Innis, the sister-in-law, was afraid he did, (in a hunting-country men who do not ride are at a premium), but was uncertain about it; therefore upon his arrival the question was referred to Cordillas himself.

The Spaniard dashed Mrs. Innis's hopes. He asserted that he was "practised in equestrianism," and "worshiped horses."

"Yes, and I haf yoomp, too," he added. Then he branched off on the merits of his "fiery-eyed steed" in Madrid, which he was bound to believe would make an unparalled "yoomper," although, as there was no fox-hunting in his country, its ability had never been called out.

"I can see," said Varick, pleasantly interrupting, "that you are the man for us. I shall put you up on that good horse Thomas Dooley." There was duplicity in this, for Varick distrusted the horsemanship of all Latin foreigners; but the Spaniard suspected it not, and the sister-in-law discreetly held her peace.

Thomas Dooley, at the time when fate introduced him to Cordillas, was going on seventeen, and he knew more about getting across a hunting-country than men usually acquire in half a century. His ancestry was not discussed, but he had the best box-stall in Varick's stable, and would be gloriously pensioned when his time of service expired. Ten years back he had exchanged the plow for the saddle, as the result of a memorable humiliation which he put upon the entire Oakdale Hunt. One dismal, sloppy morning Dooley had appeared at a meet, ridden by a farmer's boy. Not long after the hounds had found, twenty angry men were sitting on as many sulky, discouraged horses in a deep-plowed field waiting for some one to break the fence in front of them. They were not soothed when they saw Dooley playfully switch his flowing tail over five feet of new oak rails, and disappear after the pack. Varick had been one of these men; and that same afternoon he possessed Thomas Dooley, who ever since had carried him with unerring judgment and ability.

As the years went by, Dooley came to be known as Varick's "morning-after" horse, and he never betrayed the confidence this title implied. Nevertheless, it must be said that, for a man whose nerves had not been outraged, Dooley could hardly be called an agreeable mount.

He was, by general admission, the plainest horse that ever followed hounds. His legs and feet were coarse, and he galloped with as much spring as if he were on stilts. The mighty quarters wherein dwelt his genius for getting over high timber were so much too big for him that he seemed to have got another horse's hind legs by mistake. He had a mouth no bit could conquer. He chose what he would jump, and how, regardless of his rider. Only the certainty that he would never fall made him venerated, and most persons who hunt resent the imputation that they need this kind of horse. If a man's heart is strong with sleep and November air, there is little satisfaction in being carried over the country by a machine.

When Cordillas made his first appearance on Thomas Dooley, it was noted that he rode with uncommonly long stirrup-leathers,—too long for hunting,—and sat as stiff as a horse-guard, bouncing dismally with Thomas's hard trot. The tails of his pink coat were unsullied by the loin-sweat of the chase, and there was no mark of stirrup-iron across the instep of his freshly treed boots.

"'E's quite noo," remarked the first whip, in an undertone.

"With Thomas," replied the huntsman, "'e won't be long noo."

The hounds found unexpectedly, and the advice Varick intended to give his guest was cut short.

"Don't try to steer him at his fences," he yelled; "it won't do any good." The next moment the rattle-headed four-year-old he was riding took off in a bit of marsh, and became mixed up with a panel of boards. Varick got up in time to see Dooley bucking over from good ground, his rider with him, although well on toward his ears.

"I guess he'll do; he's got to," said Varick, softly swearing at his muddied boots. He scrambled up into the saddle, saw his guest slide back into his, and together they swept on after the hounds.

For the most part Cordillas managed to remain inconspicuous, though he took a spectacular "voluntary" on the way back to the kennels. He tried to "lark" Dooley over a wayside fence, possibly for the benefit of Mrs. Innis, who was driving by in her cart. Dooley, knowing that the jump was needless, stopped at the fence and the Spaniard went over alone; but his heart

THE RIDE OF HIS LIFE 57

seemed to be in the right place, and he got up again, laughing.

The next time he went out, on a hint from Varick he shortened his leathers, thrust his feet home through the irons, and really did very creditably. He was good-looking, and had nice manners; and Mrs. Innis was so complimentary that by the end of the week he believed himself the keenest man in the field. But as he grew in confidence he also became aware of the reputation which his mount enjoyed. He began to hint to Varick that Dooley was not a suitable horse for him.

"If I only had my prancer here," he observed, one morning, "you would see yoomping." Finally he told his host point-blank that, however well meant it might be, to give him such a tame mount as Dooley was no kindness; it was a reflection upon his equestrianism.

Then said Varick, who was annoyed, "You may ride Emperor to-morrow; but I tell you plainly that he may kill you." For the moment, he almost hoped he would.

"Fear not," said Cordillas, and thanked him much.

Varick says that he did *not* forget to tell William to have Emperor saddled for Cordillas. The head groom refuses to talk about it, but shakes his head. Those who know William hesitate to decide between him and his master, so the truth is likely to remain hid.

At the meet next morning, Cordillas flabbergasted the stable-boy who assisted him to mount by slipping a bill into his hand.

"An' 'im a halien," said the boy, as he related the matter to William. "Then 'e pats 'is neck, an' sez 'e 'Ain't 'e a good 'un! Gawd! look at 'is fiery heye! This *is* a 'oss!' 'W'y, yes,' sez I; 'an' clipped yesterday, sir, which improves 'is looks uncommon. I might almost say, sir, one 'u'd scaicely know 'im.' Then 'e sez, 'Git up, Hemperor!' an' moves awfter 'em."

That day there was vouchsafed one of those "historic" runs which come usually when a man's best horse is laid up, or when he judges that the day is too dry for scent and stops at home. In the first covert the pack blundered on a fox, and burst wildly out of the woods, every hound giving tongue, and Reynard in full view, barely half a field away.

The men sat listening to the foxhounds' "music," half-eager bark, half-agonized yelp, with a fluttering of the pulses and a stirring of primeval instincts. The horses quivered and pawed, mouthed the bits, and tossed white slaver into the air. But the hounds had to get their distance; so the field held back, each man intently studying the far-off fence, and playing with the mouth of his restless horse. The excited Spaniard tugged on the curb, and his mount reared indignantly.

"Demon!" he shouted. A snicker rippled from the grooms in the rear.

"Good Lord!" exclaimed Varick. "He hasn't done that for eight years. Give him his head, man!"

At that instant the M. F. H. waved his hand, and the field charged across the meadow for the boards, over which the tail-end hounds were scrambling.

It was seven miles without a check to Christian's Mills, and the fox most of the time in view; then across the river, horses and hounds swimming together, and on again at a heartbreaking pace to Paddock's Gully, where they killed in the bottom. Three horses that went into the ravine were too pumped to get out again, and stayed there all night. In the memory of man such a run, without slow scent or check, had never been seen. It became the great after-dinner run of the Oakdale hunt; and when they brag of their horses, they tell how, twice in the twelve miles, eleven men jumped five feet of stiff timber without breaking a rail.

In the last mile Cordillas followed the insane Braybrooke over four strands of naked wire that turned the field aside, beat him into the ravine, and was first at the death. They came upon him half buried in the yelping, panting pack which fought for the mangled fox he held over his head.

"Beat 'em off!" yelled Braybrooke. The reply was a torrent of Spanish oaths. Then the huntsman rode up, and rescued Cordillas, plastered with blood and filth, but content. He patted his mount's dripping neck.

"How magnificent a horse!" he exclaimed.

"Carried you extremely well," said Braybrooke. "Never saw the old fellow do better, or show so much speed. Great gallop, wasn't it? Let's have a pull at your flask; mine's dry."

"To the run," said the Spaniard, as he received the flask back, "and your good health!" He clutched the mask in his other hand.

"You rode well," said Braybrooke. His respect for the Latin races had increased. "The blood's dripping on your coat," he added, as Galloway came up, but Cordillas only held his trophy closer.

THAT night Varick had a man's dinner. There were toasts and healths, and bumpers to the five-foot fences, and perdition to the man who invented wire; bumpers to every good horse and man who was out that day; long life to hounds, and good luck to all hound puppies. But the Spaniard was the lion of the evening, and toward midnight there were cries of "Speech!"

Cordillas rose cautiously, and stood facing the party, with a glass of champagne in his tremulous hand. He was touched, and his voice showed it. He thanked the company as a gentleman, as a Spaniard, and as a sportsman. He spoke in praise of his hosts' country, their women, and their bath-tubs. Then he got around to his prancer in Madrid, and settled down to horses. To an equestrian like himself, he said, whose bosom throbbed in sympathy with every fiery impulse of creation's most noble animal, the fox-chase was the sport of kings. To a distinguished company of huntsmen he might well repeat the words of the English poet, with which they might be familiar, "My kingdom for a horse!" Developing his theme, he asserted that, of the various kinds of horses, the hunter was the noblest. "And of all noble hunters," he shouted, "the noblest, the fieriest, the most intrepid, I haf rode to-day! I drink to Emperor!"

At that moment Thomas Dooley, the newly clipped, was sniffing a bran mash, stiff and sore with the weariness born of his day's exertions under Cordillas y Sandoval. As every one at the table except the Spaniard knew, Emperor had not been out of his stall.

There was a moment's hush. The toast was drunk in silence. The men looked at one another, and then a tumult of cheers burst forth which set the grooms waiting at the stables to speculating upon the probable condition of their masters. To Cordillas it was an ovation, and the climax of his triumph. The tears stood in his eyes. To the Oakdale Hunt it was the only way of saving appearances and their good breeding.

"Keep the racket going," said Forbes to Braybrooke. "Don't let him know any one's laughing."

"I shall die of this," gasped Willie Colfax; and he slipped under the table, gurgling hysterically.

What else might have happened no one can say, because Charley Galloway started "For he's a jolly good fellow!" at the top of his lungs. Mrs. Galloway, who was sitting up for him in her own house half a mile down the road, says she recognized her husband's barytone. Every other man did the best that nature permitted. The Spaniard was reduced to tears, and the party recovered its gravity.

"But what is going to be the end of this?" whispered Varick to Chalmers. "If he catches on he will have me out and kill me. And there's Mrs. Innis; oh, Lord! Reggie, you know everybody and all about everything in Washington; if you love me, get him back there."

Then Chalmers sent for his groom, and wrote some telegrams; and the following afternoon Cordillas came to Varick, sorely cast down, and announced that the minister had sent him imperative orders to return.

"I fear," he said, "those infamous Cubaños have caused complications which necessitate my presence at the capital."

Varick said that he was awfully sorry—but saw to it personally that he caught the evening train. As it moved off, the Spaniard stood on the steps and wrung his hand.

"My friend, possessor of that great horse Emperor," he said, "I thank you for the ride of my whole life."

"Please don't mention it," said Varick. "Don't speak of it!"

"But," he added to himself, "I am much afraid he will."

THE "TRANSFIGURED PAIR"

V

THE "TRANSFIGURED PAIR"

"I HAD always supposed," said Mrs. Innis, "that Eleanor Colfax would be married in her habit, with the groom and the ushers in pink, and her brother Willie blowing all he could of the wedding-march on a coach-horn. With her figure, she ought to have done it."

"It certainly was a great opportunity thrown away," said Varick. "A 'hunting wedding' would have got at least two columns in the newspapers, with portraits of the principals, probably life-size, surrounded by free-hand drawings of us all in riding-things. It would have been something to show our grandchildren. I suggested it to Brooky, but he began to talk about his changed life, his aims, and his duties, and finally pitched into me for wasting my genius upon the stable. He's the worst case I've known since my own."

"Well, you got over yours," said Mrs. Innis, flicking a grain of rice from his sleeve.

They were interrupted by the footman coming back after Braybrooke's hand-bag. He had dropped it on the veranda while protecting his bride from Willie Colfax's bombardment of rice and old shoes; for this new brother-in-law had played the evil small boy. The man hurried after the carriage with the bag, and the excitement died away.

It had been the most "matrimonial" wedding, as Varick put it, ever seen in Oakdale, which in the circumstances was hardly to have been expected. The bride wore her mother's wedding-dress and her grandmother's veil. The bridesmaids were four school-girl cousins, imported for the occasion, and hurried back to their books with scarcely more than a glimpse of the hunting-men, who had said, "How do you do?" very pleasantly, and then talked to each other about their horses. Similarly, Braybrooke had impressed four juvenile male relatives, who appeared in their first frockcoats; so that Willie Colfax, whom he couldn't help asking to be best man, was the one familiar figure in the wedding-party. "You and I," this youth remarked to the bishop, after the ceremony, "were about the only thoroughbreds in the outfit."

"You flatter me, William," said the bishop, with a twinkle in his eye. "I suppose I may expect another invitation for a tandem ride."

Now, the exact propriety with which this wedding had been conducted was the bishop's personal triumph, although, being a discreet man as well as a good, he did not boast about it. After his first visit to Oakdale, the year before, he had done a little earnest missionary work. A long-neglected needlework guild came to life again, the parish debt was paid, and the church got a new organ. The betrothal of Miss Colfax and Braybrooke had offered a chance for cultivating in the parish of St. Thomas Equinus a more serious public spirit. His experienced mind had taken due advantage of it, and the seed which he sowed brought forth beyond his expectations. To be sure, as he admitted to himself, it had fallen upon a virgin soil.

"Jimmy," said Miss Colfax, not long after they were engaged, "we owe a lot to the poor people in the village. I've made up my mind to carry out the bishop's idea for a boys' club." In consequence, every Thursday evening until they went back to town Braybrooke drove her to the gild-house, and played "Geisha" tunes on the melodeon; and the boys adored her so fervently that they forebore to guy him. The gibes of Varick and Willie Colfax he met with pity for their unregenerate state. He was filled with the idea of improving himself into a great and good man, worthy in a measure of Her, while it seemed to her that the bishop had opened her eyes to a beautiful and entirely new world of womanliness. They began to read the first volume of Gibbon together, and became known to the Oakdale Hunt as the "Transfigured Pair."

But her great plan was the wedding-trip. They were to go around the world, skimming the cream of culture in the temples and galleries of Europe, and reading the history of foreign peoples on the spot; and were to come back highly educated, and devoted to a new order of things, in which a fortnight's hunting at Oakdale was to be merely an autumnal incident. And so it was that, radiant with love and a satisfying confidence in the future, they had boarded the day express, with their trunks neatly placarded by Varick and Willie Colfax:

Property of Circumterrestrial Pilgrims of Moral and Educational Research. Handle Gently.

"Well," she said, as the train began to move, "it's begun." She settled herself with a sigh of content, and gazed out of the window. "It will be a whole year before we see the river again. Jimmy, I am so happy!" Braybrooke patted her hand.

"Look," she said, "there's the steeplechase course, and the brushed hurdle where Mrs. Hawkins refused."

He put his face to the window beside hers. In a moment the glimpse of the hurdle was gone, but the memories of that race-day almost a year before lingered in their minds. They glanced at each other; it was not necessary to speak. Presently the train swept around a bold curve, and Braybrooke crossed to the other side of the state-room and drew the curtains. He motioned toward the window across the narrow passage. "There's the pasture lot, and the horses," he said.

Turned out that very morning was her mare Queenston, and her second horse, the chestnut gelding with the white stockings, and the cobs she drove to her buckboard, and his hunters, Mrs. Hawkins and the rest, cropping the fresh grass which the recent rains had brought. As the train passed they lifted their heads and trotted in a troop toward the fence.

"Aren't they dears?" she whispered.

"And look," he said; "do you see the field beyond Morgan's woods? That's where we killed last November, and I got the brush I gave you."

"It's in my trunk," she said.

Morgan's woods faded out in the distance, and the country became new and strange. "Good-by, Oakdale," she murmured. Braybrooke smiled weakly, and tried to say something, but only gulped.

They had hit upon the highly original idea of stopping off for a few days at a place so near Oakdale that it would never occur to any one to suspect their whereabouts. Therefore, when they were greeted by a beaming hackman as Mr. and Mrs. Braybrooke, and handed into an aged barouche trimmed with white streamers, they were amazed and indignant. Of course they learned afterward that Willie Colfax had bribed the Oakdale station-agent to betray the place to which he had checked their luggage; but for the time being they could only wonder, and make the best of the embarrassing interest which every one about the hotel took in them.

There was a lake at this place, and a moon to shine upon it by night; and they passed three agreeable days discovering that never before could two young persons have been so fortunately married. On the fourth day Eleanor wrote to her aunt, Mrs. Alden Adams: "Both of us well and perfectly happy. We leave this afternoon." They posted this at the station, and set out upon their travels.

"I am so glad," she remarked, "that we have really started. We've got so much to do, and so much to see, and so far to go. It is going to be a wonderful trip. And it will be so nice to settled down at once to the kind of life we are always going to lead together—finding out all the greatest ideas that people have had, and trying to think them and live them ourselves."

She expressed these admirable sentiments with a certain note of defiance in her tone, as if she expected to be contradicted. Braybrooke glanced at her inquiringly.

"We shall have about five days of this sleeping-car before we get to Vancouver," he observed. "It's terribly stuffy." He fanned himself impatiently with a newspaper.

"And then," she went on, "we shall have three days before the ship sails, sha'n't we? We want to see Spokane and Seattle, of course, and run over to Victoria; and then—Japan and China! Isn't it splendid?"

"Yes, splendid," he said; "by the way, we must try to be decent to my uncle when we get to China. It will be a bore, of course. He's got his yacht there, and he's running some drag-hounds around Shanghai. He'll want us to go about with him a lot. Of course we'll be seeing temples, and buying bronzes and things; but I do think he'll feel hurt if we don't show him some attention. We might go out with the hounds just once, don't you think?"

"I don't see any harm in that," she assented.

"I forgot to tell you," he went on, "that I got a letter from him before we left Oakdale. Kingston, the horse he sent out to breed to native mares, is dead."

"What a pity!" said the girl. "Poor old Kingston!

He was Queenston's sire." She sighed. "Jimmy, was Kingston by Canadian Prince or Imported Autocrat? Willie and I had a bet about it, and I've always meant to look it up."

Braybrooke thought a moment.

"I forget," he said. He made a movement toward his hand-bag, checked himself, and colored.

"What's the matter?" she demanded.

"Nothing, dear, nothing; I was only trying to remember."

"Don't bother," she said; "of course it's of no importance. Suppose we read some Gibbon; we are awfully behind."

He fished the third volume out of his bag, found the place, and began to read aloud about Alaric and the sack of Rome.

Braybrooke read in a solemn, unpunctuated voice, and dealt with proper names and difficult words according to his first impressions. The results were sometimes curious, but she never corrected him. When he reached the account of the pillage of the splendid palaces she interrupted him: "We shall see some of those ruins when we get to Rome, sha'n't we? It's very interesting; but the car shakes so, I am afraid you ought to stop; you'll ruin your eyes."

He shut the book.

"I wonder," he observed, "if anybody ever read Gibbon on his wedding-trip before?"

She laughed. "I don't care. It's very improving; and, really, we must keep up, and do all the things we are going to do."

"Who said anything about not doing them?" he demanded.

"Why, no one, of course," she answered, and was silent. "Jimmy," she asked, after a long pause, "when do we get to Greece?"

"February or March, I think."

"Well, it has just occurred to me that Mr. Fairfield, the architect, is going to send us a book all about the Parthenon. He says it's the most wonderful building in the world, although it's mostly tumbled down."

"Yes; I've heard him speak about it," said Braybrooke. "When he was up at Oakdale, two years ago, he and Captain Forbes got talking about the horses on the frieze. Forbes says they must have been the greatest weight-carriers for their inches that the world has ever seen. Why, they only stood at most fourteen-one, and those fellows in the heavy cavalry, with their gear, averaged one hundred and ninety, anyway."

"They must have been a strain of Arab," she remarked. "It's always interested me to think how they bred up our big thoroughbred from such little stock.

And it wasn't very long ago, either. When was the Godolphin Arab brought to England?"

"I don't believe I remember," he answered; "but—" He started toward the hand-bag again, and stopped shamefacedly.

"Jimmy," she asked sharply, "what's in that bag? Get it!"

He opened the satchel, and handed her a volume. It was a part of the Stud-book. She looked at him seriously.

"I didn't know, you see," he said apologetically; "I thought we *might* need it, so I put it in along with the Gibbon. It makes the bag pretty heavy."

She turned her face to the window, and for a long time they sat in silence.

"Railway traveling is fearfully dull," he said at length. "Can't keep clean; can't exercise. I'm glad it's only five days to the coast."

She made no comment.

"Do you feel all right, dear?" he asked anxiously. "You're not ill?"

"I'm very well," she answered, without looking at him. There was another long pause.

"How would some lunch go?" he suggested timidly. "I'm nearly starved."

She shook her head.

"I'm not hungry a bit," she said gently; "but you get something."

He opened the basket, and tried some olives and a cold woodcock; but his appetite had vanished and he shut the hamper again. She seemed not to want to talk, and he fell to watching her as she gazed out of the car window. He had never seen her so quiet and subdued before. There was a sad, absorbed look in her face. It made her very beautiful, but it troubled him.

Was it usual for brides to act in this way on their wedding-trip? he asked himself. Didn't she love him, after all? Was she beginning to feel that she had made a mistake? He wanted to speak to her, and have the matter explained, but he was afraid; so he sat, miserable and full of fears, watching now her, now the passing landscape, until the fields and woods began to weave themselves into a sort of day-dream, and he almost forgot that he was on his wedding-trip, bound for the ends of the earth.

The autumn afternoon wore away, and still they rode on in silence.

Once she said: "Isn't it beautiful? There's no State so beautiful as New York. It will be a year before we see it again."

Toward dusk they entered a valley that suggested the Oakdale country. It was a region of good rail fences, with here and there a line of boards, and scarcely a strand of wire. There were broad bottom-lands, and beyond these a sky-line of gently rolling heights. From time to time a patch of blue on the flats showed where the river curved. The soft stretches of stubble-field, the reds and yellows of the woods on the distant hills, the long, dim shadows of the elms in the pasture lots, the sunshine fading into twilight—it was all like the end of an October hunting-day. He could almost hear the far-away outcry of the hounds; he almost expected to see them break from the next piece of woods. The clicking of the wheels began to run into the rhythm of a galloping horse and he imagined himself rating along on Mrs. Hawkins. He scanned the country as the next covert came into view, and was wondering what direction the fox would probably take, when he heard Her sigh. He glanced up apprehensively, and watched her. Then he almost laughed outright. She too was studying the fences, following them with her eyes till they passed out of view. A wave of great gladness swept over him. He knew now where her thoughts were. A great many plans came into his brain, and suddenly he reached a mighty determination. He watched her intently, chuckling to himself over the idea which had taken possession of him. All at once he heard her murmur, unaware that he could hear:

"That would be my place—the top rail would break."

"I suppose she's galloping her mare," he thought, and chuckled again. "Yes, dear," he said softly; "only Queenston wouldn't hit it."

She started, and colored guiltily. "You've been listening!" she exclaimed, and the tears stood in her eyes. "I don't love you as I ought," she said. "I thought I had put all those things away. But I've been thinking about Queenston and Oakdale, and the run they'll have tomorrow. I've got to tell you." She began to cry, and her head sank upon his shoulder.

"There, there!" he said gently. "I've got something to tell you, too. We're going back to Oakdale, and we are going tonight."

The weeping stopped. "Oh, Jimmy!" she gasped. "But we can't!"

"There are all kinds of people in the world," he went on, "and I guess we had better be our own kind. I fell in love with you when you were jumping the red gate out of the Four Oaks pasture, and it was a steeplechase that helped me out with you. Now, there'll be plenty of charity, and all that, at Oakdale, and we can read books and things evenings. But this globe-trotting isn't our distance. Besides, I am afraid I shall never make a good rater at culture; and, after all, it really is something to know a good horse. Nell, Oakdale is the place for us."

"But all we've planned out!" she sobbed.

"Let's own up we've drawn blank," he said. "Now, see here. The horses were only turned out four days ago, and they'll be fit to go tomorrow. A wire tonight will bring 'em up, and we will be there in time to ride. What do you say about it?"

She smiled through her tears.

"I was thinking of that, too," she said.

"It's the Deep Gully woods, and they will be sure to find."

Then Braybrooke sent for the conductor, and wrote a telegram three pages long. The conductor told him that the next stop was a very good place to dine, and that they could catch the up-train to Oakdale there at nine-forty.

"Then," said Braybrooke, "we get out of this in exactly half an hour."

His wife's maid was of the discreet order and raised no question, even with her eyes, when he asked her to get the hand-luggage ready as quickly as she could. Braybrooke was grateful for this. It is not pleasant to have even your wife's maid laugh in her sleeve when you start around the world and change your mind before you get three hundred miles. His spirits rose, and he was quite as perfectly happy as the bridegrooms of story-books when he led her down the car as the train drew into the station. He heard some very nice-looking people observe that the town they had come to was a funny place for a honeymoon, but he did not even blush. On the platform his face became grave. He turned to her.

"It's just occurred to me," he said; "they will guy us the worst way at the meet tomorrow. Do you want to change your mind?"

She pressed his hand, and with a happy look shook her head.

"But of course you will let me follow you?" she asked. "You won't be always telling me to keep back?"

He paused irresolutely on the step. He had not thought of that, and it meant a great deal—no more five-foot "larking," no more chancing it over wire. It meant a lifetime of sober, decorous jumping. Then he looked at her.

"What I jump, you shall too," he said; and stepped down to offer her his hand.

THE POPULARITY OF TOMPKINS

VI

THE POPULARITY OF TOMPKINS

"My dearest Mother," wrote Mr. Frederick Tompkins, when he had been at Oakdale a week: "The Varicks are awfully kind. They have a very good house, which Mrs. Innis—who is Mrs. Varick's sister, you know—seems to have a good deal to say about. I suppose this accounts for my being made welcome, although I am only her guest, and did not know any one else in the family. This is the greatest place I ever struck. I wish the governor would get a house here. I could run it, and get some of the men in our class to come up and stop with me, now that we are through college. You could come up for the steeplechases, and give a hunt ball. How does the idea hit you?

"Our Western hospitality isn't a marker on what they do for one here. I have been dined and lunched and furnished with horses in a way that is really wonderful, considering that I am a stranger. There is nothing much in the way of girls, but there is the smoothest lot of men I ever met. Mrs. Innis introduced me to the best of them, and I suppose they have showed me attention on her account. Monday morning, after I got here, there was a hunt,—not shooting, you know,—and Mr. Varick let me ride a horse called Sir Roger. He says that as perfect a type of hunter as this one is dirt-cheap at fifteen hundred, and I can well believe it. I just let him go, and was right in it from the start. Of course I had never hunted before—only after jack-rabbits at home, where there is no jumping; but Mrs. Innis told me it wasn't necessary to tell any one this, and that I would soon get the trick. She said just to let the horse alone and he'd do the rest, and he did. It was the greatest sensation I ever had in my whole life. Varick said that I had ridden uncommonly well, and that the horse was just suited to me. Of course I have always ridden out home with a curb and a loose rein, so I didn't bother his head, and let him pick his own jumping. Mrs. Innis said this was the best way to do with a well-schooled horse, unless you were a crack and had really good hands. She says that most men get falls because they think they know how to 'lift' their horses and 'foot' them at their fences. It is wonderful how much she has picked up about all this sort of thing, because she doesn't ride, and never talks horse the way some of the other women do. She also suggested that I should take whatever was said about hunting as a matter of course, which was clearly good advice. Mrs. Innis is a very charming woman. Monday she introduced me to a man named Galloway, and he asked me to come over to lunch on Tuesday and look at his string. He also offered me a mount for Wednesday. Varick told me I had better take it, as Sir Roger was pretty tired and had cut his frog. He was foolish once, and jumped on a pile of stones.

"Wednesday, on Galloway's mare Vixen, I had an immense ride. She got away from me once and jumped three strands of barbed wire, and I beat the whole field. Everybody is talking about it, and I am getting the reputation of being a hard goer. Galloway said that the price of that horse ought to go up five hundred after such a performance, but he's going to keep it at a thousand. If you hear of anybody in Washington who is looking for a regular clipper, tell him about Vixen; I should like to do Galloway a good turn.

"There is a fellow up here called Willie Colfax, whose cousin was in college with me. He has been very civil, and came over and got me Thursday morning, and took me for a ride 'cross country on a horse called Lorelei. They have a very good way here of sometimes bandaging a horse's legs to protect them from the thistles. Colfax had bandages on Lorelei. He said she is very thin-skinned on account of her breeding. It is a humane custom, don't you think? Lorelei jumped like a bird. She is the greatest bargain I have seen yet, and I almost wish I was buying horses. Colfax will let her go for five hundred; at least, I inferred so from some remarks he let drop. If Sis wants a good hack that can jump, the governor ought to consider this mare. Colfax was very flattering, and said he had never seen Lorelei go so well, and that it needed a hard goer to do her justice. You ought to be proud of your son!

"To-day (Friday) I lunched at the club with Captain Forbes, and looked over his string afterward. He has three very likely horses that he is willing to let go, as he has more than he needs. He is going to mount me to-morrow. There are a number of men here who have more horses than they need, and are willing to sell. They have been very kind in offering me mounts. I suppose they are glad to have them exercised.

"By the way, several people have spoken about the governor's starting fox-hunting out on the coast. He'd look queer riding to hounds, but it is a very captivating idea. Sound him about it.

"I have wired your New York florist to send four dozen American Beauties to Mrs. Varick, and the same to Mrs. Innis. I mention this lest I should forget to speak about it, and you should think the bill wrong.

THE POPULARITY OF TOMPKINS 89

This is a very long letter, and makes up for some short ones. Love to Father and Sis.

"Your aff. son,
"FREDERICK TOMPKINS."

When Mrs. Innis's friends asked her how it was that she had annexed this scion of the West, she replied that she was laying up treasure with the mammon of the Occident, and, moreover, that he was a very nice boy and admired *her*. She discovered him in Washington, where Senator Tompkins had established his family for the winter. Now, young Tompkins *was* a nice boy, and some day would be rich, and there were several mamas in Washington who considered Mrs. Innis's interest in him not less than shameful.

TOMPKINS sent his letter off to the post, and presented himself in the drawing-room to take tea with Mrs. Innis. He found Captain Forbes there.

"Hello!" said Forbes. "I was hacking over this way, and dropped in to see whether you were going to ride Rajah to-morrow. I understood you to say you would; but Varick said something about mounting you on a four-year-old of his."

"Well," said Tompkins, "I hadn't heard anything about the four-year-old. Of course, as I'm stopping here, I ought to ride Varick's horse for him if he wants me to; but I should like very much to have a go with the Rajah."

"All right," said Forbes; "I'll see Varick. Where is he?"

"In the smoking-room, I think," said Mrs. Innis.

The captain found Varick in very bad temper, making up his stable accounts. "Look here," said he; "it's low down of you, Varick, to keep this Tompkins chap all to yourself. He's a mighty attractive little chap, and he has a good eye for a horse, and I want him to ride some good ones, so I've offered him the Rajah. He says you haven't spoken to him yet about mounting him on that skate four-year-old, and he wants to ride the Rajah, but he afraid of offending you."

"Oh, hang him!" exclaimed Varick; "let him ride anything you say. This desperate altruism on your part, however, is something new. Get out of here, Forbes; I've been swindled on my hay."

Forbes went back, and told Tompkins it was all right about Rajah, and then rode away.

"Mrs. Innis," said Tompkins, after the captain had departed, "I've been having a great time this week. There is the best crowd of men here I ever saw. That fellow Forbes is a brick. There aren't many men who would lend their hunters to a stranger the way he's done."

"That's so," said Mrs. Innis, with a smile; "but then, Frederick, you are a very nice young man." He had asked her to call him Frederick.

"Oh, pshaw!" said Tompkins, and colored. "They're civil to me because I am your friend, that's all; they adore you."

"I wish I could believe that," said Mrs. Innis; "but I am sure it isn't so. I had Cordillas up here, and they were really horrid to him. But I don't suppose I ought to speak about that story, since you are going back to Washington."

Tompkins would have liked to hear that story, but he didn't say so; he held it unmasculine to be curious.

"By the way," asked Mrs. Innis, "have they said anything to you about starting a hunt out on the Pacific?"

"Why, yes," said Tompkins; "two or three of them have spoken about it. I think it would be a great thing, but I'm afraid the governor wouldn't vote for it. You see, it might hurt him politically."

"Did you tell any one that?" she asked.

"No," said Tompkins; "I didn't say much about it. I thought I would sound the old gentleman first. It might carry, after all."

"That's so," said Mrs. Innis. Tompkins stooped to pick up her handkerchief, and she smiled in a quiet little way that seemed quite for her own edification. The man who thought that he knew Mrs. Innis best called that smile her "*glad-i-at-or* smile," because it expressed what the cat said after she had eaten the canary. When he observed that smile he was always uneasy till he was quite sure that the victim was some other man.

The next morning Tompkins hunted Rajah, and had the time of his life. The Rajah was an old steeple-chaser with no particular mouth, and he rushed his jumps in a way that made mature persons who rode him wish to be at home in bed. Tompkins let him go, and the Hunt held back and gave him room. There is a saying that it takes seven croppers to make a horseman. Tompkins hadn't had his first one yet, and so there was no use in giving him advice.

"Confound that fellow Tompkins!" said the M. F. H. "He's been riding over my hounds all the morning. Forbes, tell him, if he can't keep that blooming runaway of yours back, to go home."

Forbes cast an injured look at the M. F. H., and counseled Tompkins to moderation. But when the hounds found, they went off at a very fast clip, and then Tompkins was in his glory. He led the field for seven miles, turning neither to right nor to left, and he was with the pack at the kill before even the hunts-

THE POPULARITY OF TOMPKINS 93

man. When the M. F. H. presented him with the brush it seemed that all the joy of the world was in his cup. He resolved that the governor certainly should take a place at Oakdale, and that he would hunt forever after. It was only natural, therefore, that an unmanly lump should rise into his throat when he read the telegram which was waiting for him when he got back to the Varicks' that afternoon. It said:

Letter received. You come home on first train.
FATHER.

THAT night, after dinner, Varick went to the club, and found a group of men playing pool.

"Hello!" said Forbes. "While I think of it, tell Tompkins—will you?—that I'm afraid the Rajah won't be fit to go on Monday. The fact is (of course you needn't say anything about it), his old tendon is as big as my wrist. The horse went marvelously. Really, though, that boy is a shocking pounder."

"I should say he was!" exclaimed Galloway. "Vixen threw a curb with him, and he rode so much out of Lorelei, just galloping her 'cross lots, that Willie has had to fire her again and turn her out."

"Really?" said Varick. "Well, he used up Sir Roger, too—jumped him on a pile of stones and cut his frog. But, I say, Forbes," he added, "Tompkins has gone; so it won't matter about the Rajah on Monday."

"Gone?" repeated Forbes. The other men regarded Varick incredulously.

"Yes; Washington on the eight-thirty."

"Well," said Forbes, "he's coming back, isn't he?"

"Not that I know of," said Varick.

"I guess he is, though," said Forbes. "The fact is, you see, I was told, rather in confidence, that he came up here to buy a string of hunters for his father. I understand that the old gentleman is going to run a pack of drag-hounds somewhere out West."

Colfax, Galloway, and Varick looked curiously at Forbes, and then at one another.

"I got the same 'steer,'" blurted out Galloway; then Willie Colfax nodded, signifying that it had likewise been imparted to him.

"That's very funny," said Varick; "for I heard something of the same sort myself. Forbes, do you mind saying whether Tompkins himself told you that?"

"No," said Forbes; "Tompkins didn't."

"Then who was it?" demanded Varick.

"I don't know that I ought to tell," he answered; "though I don't suppose there's any harm in it. You see, I wasn't actually told that Tompkins was going to buy, but it was put to me in such a way that I got that impression. I was asked as a personal favor not to sell him anything that wasn't the best—by Mrs. Innis."

Varick gave forth a long, low whistle, and in the silence that followed Galloway and Colfax moved thoughtfully toward different parts of the wall, and each pressed an electric button.

"I am afraid," said Varick, slowly, "that we have been 'up against it.' Ever since that Spanish chap rode old Thomas Dooley, and thought he was up on Emperor, my sister-in-law has been 'laying low' with Brother Rabbit. She won't believe that we lament the mistake."

When Forbes mentioned Mrs. Innis, the M. F. H., who had been practising billiard shots at the next table till his turn should come around, threw down his cue, and appeared to be choked by his emotions. A great light had struck him.

"This is almost too much!" he sighed. "Coming home this afternoon, for three miles Tompkins talked to me about the whole-souled generosity of the men of this Hunt—men who seemed to find delight in pursuing him with attentions and offers of horses. 'Why, Mr. Crawford,' said he, 'I never saw such a place! I believe I could stay here a month, and be mounted three times a week!'"

Just then the sound of women's voices rose in the hall. A party had come in for supper.

"Hello!" said the M. F. H., listening; "Mrs. Innis is out there now. This is too good to keep; I've got to tell her." He went to the door. It was a family sort of club, and ladies often went into the billiard-room.

"Don't you want to come in here and exult?" he said. "I'm not equal to the whole thing myself; and besides, it's your party."

Mrs. Innis turned, and hesitated. "What's that?" she asked.

"Why, you have caused the heathen to rage," exclaimed the M. F. H., "and they are making themselves very amusing about some horses they didn't sell."

"*Exult?*" she replied. "*Horses they didn't sell?* What on earth are you talking about?"

The M. F. H. took a long breath, like a man who gets a bucket of cold water thrown on him. Then he became matter-of-fact and mirthless. He knew Mrs. Innis pretty well.

"Oh, nothing much," he said; "just any old thing. By the way, next week I expect to have two chaps stopping with me, who are coming on to look about for hunters; and I shall be awfully busy just then, because Mrs. Crawford is going to have a lot of girls at the house. Can't you help me show 'em about a bit?"

THE POPULARITY OF TOMPKINS 97

Mrs. Innis looked at the M. F. H. as though she were wondering whether she could conscientiously comply.

"Why, yes," she answered; "I shall be glad to help you in any way I can."

"Well, they won't be much trouble," the M. F. H. added. "Men who are buying horses always seem to be popular up here. If you've never noticed it, I'll make you a present of the idea."

"You are very good," replied Mrs. Innis. "It is certainly a very ingenious idea. But you are always having ingenious ideas; you have an ingenious mind."

The M. F. H. bowed.

"Yes. The idea's ingenious enough; only there's the very deuce to pay if they don't buy, after all. Now take the case of your friend Tompkins. It's rather serious There are three or four chaps in here who are talking of having him arrested for fraud—"

"Why, Mr. Crawford!" exclaimed Mrs. Innis, incredulously; "you don't tell me that any one thought Mr. Tompkins came here to buy horses? He came here to see me. Of course, before he arrived, I thought it possible that he might want to pick up a hunter or so, and I asked the men I knew not to sell him anything that wasn't the best. But, dear me! the day he arrived he told me that his father had forbidden his buying horses of any kind, and so I never bothered about the matter again; it quite went out of my head." Then she looked at the M. F. H. with the faintest gleam in her eyes. "Please take this thing," she added.

He took her wrap and put it on a chair. "Why, of course," he said; "nothing could be more natural."

They could hear all this from the billiard-room.

"Crawford," called Varick, "are you going to play pool, or do you wish me to telephone for Mrs. Crawford?"

"Coming at once," replied the M. F. H.

"Varick," growled Galloway, who was thinking of Vixen's curb, "let's drop Mr. Tompkins and his popularity. It's your shot—hurry up and play!"

CHALMERS'S GOLD PIECE

VII

CHALMERS'S GOLD PIECE

"THERE goes a good chap," said the M. F. H., nodding toward Chalmers. The hunting Earl turned in the saddle, and looked. He was jogging alongside of the M. F. H., who was taking him into covert with the hounds. (This was only the proper courtesy to extend to so great a fox-hunter.) "He's back this morning from the Rockies," the M. F. H. added; "I'd like to have you know him."

"Beg pardon," observed the Earl, "but isn't he rather queerly turned out?"

The M. F. H., who was sounding his horn, laughed, and spoiled his note.

"Those *are* pretty awful riding-things. They belong to his groom."

"Not very well off—bankrupt or something?" suggested the Earl.

"Thunder, no!" exclaimed the M. F. H. "He's a terrible millionaire. You see, he got back a day sooner than he expected, and they hadn't brought his things down from town. He didn't have time to borrow any breeches, and he wasn't going to miss a run, so he put on the cords belonging to his man's new livery, and an old jacket. They are all running him about it, for he's usually rather smart. I dare say you've seen his yacht, the *Independence Day*, at Cannes. He prowls all over the place after big game, and he's one of the best men in America to hounds."

"Very interesting indeed," said the Earl. "I should like to meet him."

The M. F. H. looked back and tried to catch Chalmers's eye; but Chalmers was watching a young woman coming over a big panel of rails in a slashing way one doesn't often see. It impressed him, and he rode over to Varick, who was dismounted tightening his girths, and asked him who the strange girl was.

"Didn't notice her," said Varick; "but there are several new ones here just now. There's a professional from some London riding-school, looking about for high jumpers. Colfax is trying to sell her Lorelei at a low price and no guaranty. Then there's a Miss Crackenthorpe, a Philadelphia girl, stopping with the Galloways; and—" He stopped abruptly, and listened. Somebody was calling in the distance. It was indistinct at first; but then the breeze swelled lazily and brought a faint "Gone away! Gone away!" from the whip on the farther side of the covert. A moment later the pack picked up the hot scent, and set up a terrific yeow-yeowing.

"Hullo, they are off!" Varick exclaimed, and, mounting hastily, he galloped after the troop of excited men and horses.

An hour later—they had lost that fox, and were after a second one—Chalmers emerged from a big woodlot, and looked about him for signs of the Hunt. There was no one in sight. It is not pleasant to find one's self a minority of one on the question of inferring a fox's ultimate line from his circlings in the impracticable underbrush—unless, of course, one happens to be *right*, and has hounds, fox, and everything to himself, in which case he has an exclusive smoking-room story forever after. But Chalmers had neither quarry nor pack.

"Why, oh, why," he murmured plaintively, "do I never hit it right?" He strained his ears for the sound of the hounds; but there was only the rustle of the stray leaves that bobbed across the stubble on the wind. The region was unfamiliar and, in the desolate stillness of a November afternoon, unprepossessing.

"That wretched fox certainly has doubled back," he said to himself. "I'm out of it, and I'm afraid I'm lost, to boot." He felt hungry, and inspected a lone and crumpled sandwich; but he reflected that he would doubtless be hungrier later on, so he put it away. He was searching the dull horizon for the sun, from which to get his bearings, when he was startled by the crash of breaking rails.

He glanced around, and saw a woman coming a most appalling cropper over the fence between him and the wood-lot. The horse scrambled to its feet, trailing its rider head down, and broke into a gallop. The skirt of her habit was hooked over one of the pommels. It all happened as swiftly and inevitably as things happen in a bad dream. It sickened him, but the instant the horse started he had started after it. There was no time to follow the runaway and pull him up, for at any moment the woman might swing under his hoofs, or be dashed against a stone.

It came to Chalmers that the thing to do was to "cross." This was an experience which he had several times unintentionally provoked at polo. After his first thorough collision he came to before the match was over, and a famous No. 2, who was looking on, bent over his stretcher. "Next time when you see there has got to be a smash," he said, "don't let the other fellow hit you *behind* the saddle. It's just as well to let *him* have the spill." This means that a pony run down forward of the girths is not so likely to be thrown off his hind legs, and has a chance of collecting himself before he goes completely over. Chalmers remembered this. He had only fifty yards to ride, and he calculated his pace correctly. The bewildered horse which he was attempting to head off made no attempt to swerve, and they met fairly at right angles. Chalmers was conscious of a stunning shock and of being in a heap with two horses. He wondered where the woman was. As he got up he saw that she had been thrown clear and was lying motionless. A drop of blood was gathering from a scratch on her cheek. He noticed it hang an instant, and then trail down across her face. He was sure that she was dead. There was a numb feeling in his left shoulder, and mechanically he changed the bridle to his right hand. For a moment he stood dazed and silent. The woman's horse picked itself up and went off, and Chalmers still stood, wondering exactly what had happened. Then the woman sat up, and his senses came to him.

"Are you much hurt?" he gasped. His knees felt weak, and he leaned against his horse.

"No," said the girl; "I think I'm only shaken up."

Chalmers watched her anxiously. It was the girl he had noticed taking the fence before the run began. "Yes; it's the riding-mistress," he said to himself. It had just occurred to him that he had once met the

Philadelphia girl whom Varick had mentioned, and that she was quite a different person. Besides, this girl spoke with a markedly English intonation. She began to turn her head first one way and then the other, as if she were making sure it was really there.

"I'm afraid you've hurt your neck," he said. "Have you any pain—down your back?"

"No," she answered weakly; "but I can't get all those hoofs out of my eyes. It seems as if they were coming down smash! They're worse than I ever had before."

Chalmers had experienced the hoof phenomenon himself, and he knew that it made the first moments after a bad cropper extremely bewildering.

"Lie down a minute," he suggested.

She collapsed miserably into a heap, and began to cry softly. Chalmers turned his head away, and wondered what he ought to do. For a man of his age he had been confronted with some exceptionally trying situations, but with nothing upon this order. Besides, this was inwardly distressing. It would have been easier if she had sniffled and "taken on" hysterically; but she wept in the subdued manner of utter wretchedness. It was very pathetic.

"You poor little thing!" Chalmers murmured. That she was not little, but rather tall, with a classic type of face and a wonderful skin, back into which the pink was beginning to find its way, did not abate the strain upon his feelings. He let his eyes rest on her for a moment.

"It's inhuman to make a woman like that ride for her living," he muttered. "It's devilish!" His ideas about women in the hunting-field underwent a rapid revision, as is apt to be the case with men who have just seen their first bad side-saddle spill. "And it's only a question of time before she'll be killed. By Jove, she simply mustn't!" Now Chalmers meant this to be positive and final, for at that moment an idea struck him, which he hastily elaborated.

It was a simple solution of the matter. Chalmers had a sister whose fad was her hackney farm and her harness-horses. She drove four, and tandem, and all other possible ways; but she thought poorly of riding. She needed a confidential assistant (she had told Chalmers that), but a difficulty had confronted her in the prevailing sex of horse experts. This fixed it. He would wire Elizabeth; Elizabeth would wire Miss What's-her-name (he would find that out when he was properly presented) to New York, and the message would be repeated to Oakdale, as if Elizabeth didn't know she was there. Then, by an odd coincidence, Miss Chalmers would turn out to be his sister, and the girl's risks of sudden death thenceforth would be limited to smashed vehicles and that class of accidents from which she would have almost the same chance of escape as a man. Presently the girl stopped crying, and Chalmers left off the works of his imagination with a smile. It was diverting to arrange matters for a person whom one didn't know. She lifted her head.

"Will you give me your flask?" she asked. "I'm still a bit faint."

All Chalmers's things were on their way from town, and he hadn't a flask with him.

"I'm very sorry," he began awkwardly.

She sat up, and looked him over from head to toe with a swift glance.

"I beg your pardon," she interrupted. "I didn't think. I shall be quite well directly." She rose to her feet, leaving Chalmers somewhat mystified.

"Does your head trouble you?" he asked.

"No," she answered; "I really feel much better. But will you kindly explain to me how you came to be here? I thought I was jumping into an empty meadow."

Chalmers briefly explained that he had lost the hounds, and happened to be standing at one side when she fell, and afterward stopped the horse. The girl thought a moment.

"But your horse was down on his knees?" she said inquiringly. "I remember that."

"Well," answered Chalmers, "there was a bit of a collision."

"I think I understand," she answered. "That was a very brave thing to do!" Her eyes turned from his face, and Chalmers was somehow impressed for a moment that he was clad in ill-fitting cord breeches. Then she repeated impulsively, "A *very* brave thing to do!" He felt the red coming into his face.

"Nonsense!" he exclaimed. "The question is, How are we going to get home?" He looked after the runaway horse. It was already in the field beyond. They watched it take the fence and disappear over the brow of a hill.

"Well, he's gone," said Chalmers. He glanced at his own horse with the man's saddle, and then at the girl. Their eyes met, and he fancied by the corners of her mouth that she understood the situation.

"When I was a child," she said gravely, "I used to ride straddle always. I think we can manage it if you will shorten the stirrups."

As he stretched out his left hand the ache in his shoulder became a sharp pain, and the hand dropped.

"What's wrong?" she asked anxiously. "Is your arm broken?"

"No," said Chalmers; "if it's anything, I guess it's only the collar-bone. It didn't hurt, and I hardly realized it was cracked. It is of no consequence, anyhow."

"It is of a great deal of consequence," she answered. "I am very, very sorry! Let me make a sling." She unbuckled the curb-rein, and triced the arm up with the skill of experience as well as the woman's instinct for doing such things rightly.

"Grateful and comforting," he said to himself; "should be on every breakfast-table." Then he blushed at his own joke, and helped her up. Thus they set off in search of the turnpike, Chalmers leading the horse, and the lady riding astride. They got over a low fence, and through a gate across another field, and then they went into a piece of woods. From the other side of the woods a farm-house was visible, and presently, by winding through lanes and farm-yards, and by opening innumerable gates, they came out upon the highway.

"Well, this has been quite an adventure," said Chalmers. "I feel as if I were an 'Idyl of the King.' Those chaps used to go grailing and things with solitary maidens, didn't they?"

"Where did you hear about the 'Idyls of the King'?" she demanded.

"Hear about them?" he said, somewhat taken aback. "Why, I guess I must have read them."

"It is true, then," she said, half to herself, and as if she were making a note of it. "Every one reads books in America. I like that about America very much. I'm in favor of popular education. You see, I'm a great radical, and all that sort of thing."

"That's good," said Chalmers. It struck him that she was the right sort to get on with the people on Elizabeth's farm.

"Have you been long in America?" he asked.

"About a month," she replied.

"What do you think of it?" He felt uncomfortable at sinking to this, but he wished to know what she did think.

"It's very big," she said, "and very different—oh, quite different! The people are very odd, and the customs are strange. Have you ever been in New York?"

He said, "Yes," and chuckled.

"Every one travels in America, I've been told. In England they usually stop about the place where they were born. They rarely travel far, unless they go out to the colonies, you know."

"But you have been in London?" he asked, with a straight face.

She smiled. "Of course; I am very much in London," she replied. Then she asked, "Do you live here all the year?"

"So she's going to quiz *me*," he thought. "Well, turn about is fair play. No," he answered aloud; "I am pretty much all the time in New York and other places." As he usually spent the winter poking his yacht into out-of-the-way parts of the earth, he thought that this was specific enough.

"Really?" said she. "I suppose that most of the gentlemen who hunt here live in town—I mean New York. Mr. Varick has a town house there, I believe."

Chalmers said that he had. He wondered, though, why she seemed to associate him with Varick. He wondered if she took him for Varick's brother-in-law, Freddy Blake, who was stopping with Varick. He had been taken for him before.

The conversation languished, and for a long time they proceeded at the slow, measured pace of the walking horse. It began to grow dark. Presently they came to a farm-house which he recognized. He knew that it was only three miles from the kennels, so he felt encouraged. As they were passing the orchard a few old thaws dangled in the bare boughs which overhung the road. In the dusk they were scarcely discernible.

"Are those black spots apples?" she asked suddenly. "I've had no tea at all, and I'm famished."

"You poor child!" he thought. "I'm afraid they're frozen," he said. He hesitated. "I have a sandwich in my pocket, only it's a good deal mussed."

The girl seemed embarrassed.

"No, really!" she exclaimed; "but I can't think of taking it. It's your last one, you know."

"But you must," he insisted. "It's lucky I happen to have it. At the last check your friend Mr. Varick divided his lunch with me." He handed her the small silver box. "He gave me the box, too, years ago. I've known him since he was a boy."

"Oh, indeed!" she said. "How very nice! Really, you are very good!" She examined the contents of the box rather gingerly, but proceeded to eat them.

"This is very good bacon," she remarked as she munched; "and they usually have such nasty bacon in America."

Chalmers laughed. "I shall have to warn Elizabeth to make an effort in the matter of bacon," he thought.

They trudged along for a while, till suddenly the road curved and showed them the lights of the club-house glimmering half a mile ahead, and the village beyond.

"Where shall I take you?" he asked.

"I think," she replied, "that I will go to the club. My uncle will probably be there."

"Uncle!" Chalmers exclaimed inwardly. "Good gracious! Is she in tow of some horse-dealing relative?" It struck him that his arrangement might meet with some new difficulties. "Well," he thought, "I guess we can fix uncle, too. I have a farm myself."

The big lanterns on the gate-posts shed a cheerful light as they turned into the club driveway.

"It can't be much past six," he said. He noticed that she was fumbling for the invisible watch-pocket in her habit. "Just twenty minutes past," he added, holding his watch to the light. "We've made a very good pace—seven miles in two hours."

"I hope your arm hasn't pained you much," she said.

"No; it hasn't," he replied. They came under the porte-cochère, and stopped.

"I thank you very much for all that you have done," she said. "I shall tell my uncle and Mr. Varick about it." She slipped off with the support of his good arm, and extended her hand. The next moment Chalmers felt a coin in his palm.

"Oh, I say! I beg pardon!" he gasped. She paused on the steps, and faced him. He stood there speechless, with his arm outstretched toward her.

"Please take it," she said. "I know it's different in America, but you must. Of course one can't pay another for saving her life; I can only thank you for that: but you have been to a great deal of trouble, too. English gold is good everywhere, isn't it? It's all I have with me. But my uncle will be very grateful to you. You must come and see him tomorrow. Please have your collar-bone carefully set. Good night."

She turned and went into the club. The situation burst on Chalmers. He slipped the gold piece into his pocket, and started for the stables. He stopped before he reached them, though. He was sitting doubled over, on a bench by the roadway (it hurt his collar-bone less if he laughed doubled over) when a voice came out of the darkness:

"What's the matter there?" It was the M. F. H., on his way back from the kennels.

"Nothing," replied Chalmers, weakly—"nothing that I can tell you."

"Oh, is that you, Chalmers?" said the M. F. H. "I've been looking all over for you. Hurry up and make yourself presentable. You're dining with me at eight."

"I can't," Chalmers answered. "I've broken my collar-bone, and I hate to feed in company with one hand."

"It's too bad about your bone, but you've got to come. Your food shall be served to you all cut up, or you can have six courses of soup. But I don't see what's so mighty funny about a bu'sted collar-bone."

"No," said Chalmers; "and you won't. Telephone right off for the doctor—will you?—or I shall be late." He rose and went on toward the stables. Suddenly the thing struck him in a new light.

"A sovereign," he mused, "must be quite a lot of money for a riding-mistress to give as a tip. I never thought about that. I wonder who her people were?"

THE M. F. H. met Chalmers as he came into the drawing-room.

"Hullo," said he; "all comfy? I want you to know the Earl of Reddesdale. He's been here only a week, but he's disbanded the Fence-Breakers, and he's brought his niece with him, besides. Those are two praiseworthy acts. Because you have foolishly got spilled somewhere, you are going to take her in to dinner. Miss Hamilton," he added, "may I present Mr. Chalmers?"

Miss Hamilton turned, and said she would be much pleased. Then she glanced at Chalmers, and her eyes dropped.

"I think," she said, "that I have had that pleasure—this afternoon. Mr. Chalmers brought me home."

She touched the Earl's arm. "Uncle," she began, "this is—"

"This is very extraordinary!" ejaculated the Earl. "I thought a groom brought you back, my dear—one of Mr. Varick's men—"

"Oh, uncle!" the girl exclaimed.

When it was quiet enough for Chalmers to be heard, he announced that he had something to say. It seemed to him that the chaffing was a little trying for the girl, and he did a very noble thing. With certain reservations, he disclosed his hypothesis of the riding-school mistress, and drew the fire upon himself. He blushed a deeper red than Miss Hamilton, but it was not so becoming, for his pink coat killed the effect.

"Well, you see," he added ingenuously, "I got back only this morning, and I never saw a woman ride like that who wasn't a professional." Then dinner was announced.

"It was very generous of you to confess all that," she said, when they were seated.

"No," answered Chalmers; "it was only fair. My conscience would have troubled me if I hadn't. But as I have no mama to consult about receiving presents from young ladies, I think I shall keep that sovereign."

THE BISHOP'S MISSIONARY MEETING

VIII

THE BISHOP'S MISSIONARY MEETING

Mrs. GALLOWAY checked the horse to a walk, and peered into the darkness.

"I think this is our turn," she said, "and we are only half a mile from home."

"I must say, madam," observed the bishop, "that my spirit goes forth in thanksgiving. We have really had a most adventurous expedition."

For two hours the bishop had been ironing the loins of Mrs. Galloway's phaëton-horse with a hot flat-iron, a fatiguing occupation to which he was unused. It was nearly ten o'clock, and he had had no dinner. He was weary, and his soul craved the flesh-pots.

The bishop had driven forth, in Mrs. Galloway's care, to inspect the condition of the parish poor with a view to organizing a home-missionary movement. His rector at Oakdale seemed inadequate to the task; so the bishop, according to his custom, had decided to examine the field for himself. At the cottage of Mrs. O'Rourke, eight miles from the Galloways', the horse, which had been left unblanketed, developed mysterious and alarming symptoms. His hind legs appeared to be paralyzed. The bishop led him under a shed, and the eldest of Mrs. O'Rourke's nine, who was twelve years old, diagnosed his trouble as a chill in the kidneys.

"Youse git a flat-iron from ma, and iron him with brown paper where he's scrunchin' down. Linyimunt would be good, but I guess the flat'll fix him if youse keep at it. I'd do it meself, only I ain't that big."

Cuthbert O'Rourke ("These O'Rourkes is all of thim Or'ngemin, and there's no Patricks," said the widow) superintended, and carried out the hot irons. The bishop ironed, and Mrs. Galloway lamented and apologized. A smaller O'Rourke was sent to the village with a message to be telephoned to Mr. Galloway, instructing him not to wait dinner. Mrs. Galloway had invited a large company, which was to discuss the bishop's scheme and to subscribe money for carrying it out, so she naturally was exasperated. It was a quarter before six when the flat-iron treatment began; and at about eight o'clock Cuthbert assured the bishop, who was laboring by the light of a tin lantern, that the beast was well enough to travel. They started back at a slow trot, and what with the cold and the darkness, the pangs of hunger, and the apprehension of a return of the chill, the eight miles seemed excessively long. When they turned up the cross-road the bishop made an effort to confront the situation with Christian fortitude, and became almost cheerful.

" 'After the toils and perils of war, grateful is the feast,' " he observed. "This is a pagan sentiment, but one rooted in the subsoil of our human natures."

Mrs. Galloway was wondering what sort of feast would be forthcoming at that hour of the night, but she held her peace.

"It is truly noble of you, Mrs. Galloway," the bishop continued, "to assemble these people for a discussion of our project. I think I shall be able to state the matter strongly, and I doubt not that we shall receive generous support. I have been keenly interested in this parish, as presenting the problem of Christianity versus the well-to-do—the problem how to awaken a sense of higher responsibilities in a community of amiable barbarians. Do not misunderstand me: I use the word with the interpretation and authority of Mr. Matthew Arnold. And bear in mind, madam, I appreciate the usefulness of honest sport, and the physical manliness it engenders. But that is not all of life; and, unfortunately, I have observed in our sport-loving rich an indifference, a colorless moral attitude, toward the serious things of existence, which is almost more difficult to combat than actual vice. As I have intimated, this parish stands as a peculiarly suggestive type, and it is highly gratifying to feel that the small efforts which I have put forth are slowly but surely bearing fruit—are slowly but surely producing an interest in spiritual things. A year ago, I dare say, such an occasion as this would hardly have been contemplated."

"It really *is* gratifying," said Mrs. Galloway; "but I am afraid you will have a very poor dinner. It must be nearly ten o'clock."

"Well," said the bishop, " 'an egg and an olive,' partaken of in peace and with worthy discourse—that is a feast. Ah, here we are!" he added, with a sigh of relief. They drove under the porte-cochère, and stopped. A peal of uproarious laughter and a sound of stamping feet burst from the house.

"They must be still in the dining-room," said Mrs. Galloway. "Hold the horse, please, and I'll ring the stable bell. You couldn't find it in the dark."

Just then a loud voice within shouted:

"Hit him with the poker! Oh, harder! Make him feel it!"

Mrs. Galloway paused with her finger on the bell. The dining-room windows were open, but the heavy curtains were drawn. She could hear what was said, but could not see what was going on. There was a sound of dull whacks, and the noise of a scrimmage.

"Stop it! Don't, I say! Stop it! You're a brute!" This was in women's voices. Mrs. Galloway turned toward the bishop, speechless.

"Bless me!" said the bishop, anxiously: "this is very strange!"

She tiptoed toward the nearest window, and listened.

"Well, that's no go," some one said. "Try jabbing him with a fruit-knife."

"No; please don't!" cried a woman.

"Suppose he kicks?" said a man.

"If he's a gentleman, he won't kick in a lady's dining-room." This time they recognized Varick's voice.

"Suppose he does!" exclaimed somebody else. "Let him kick! We can't keep him here all night. Mrs. Galloway and the bishop are likely to blow in any minute. I want you to remember that this is a missionary meeting." There was another laugh.

"That was Charley," whispered Mrs. Galloway. "Do you suppose they've caught a burglar?"

"It may be," replied the bishop. "It's very strange."

"I'll tell you," said Varick's voice. "Try blindfolding him. Take a napkin." There was a general giggling for a moment. "Now hit him gently with a bottle."

"Come on there!" came in angry tones from Galloway. "You can't stop here forever. Get hold, you chaps, and push."

There was a sudden scuffle, and a sound like the tramping of heavy boots.

"Catch the candles!" a woman screamed.

There was a deafening crash of glass and china, and a hubbub of screams and exclamations. A dead silence followed, and then Galloway's voice was heard, unnaturally calm:

"Well, the dinner-table's gone!"

Mrs. Galloway stood petrified. A groom appeared and took the horse.

"What is going on in there?" demanded the bishop. The man moved into the shadow.

"I dunno, sir," he replied in a queer voice. He got into the phaëton, and the bishop and his hostess walked softly along the veranda toward the door.

"I am afraid something terrible has happened," said Mrs. Galloway, tremulously. "Suppose they have killed him?" She drew back, and the bishop went in ahead. They passed down the hall to the dining-room. With a little scream, Mrs. Galloway clutched the door-jamb.

"Thank goodness! Thank goodness!" she murmured. "I thought it was a burglar. Some water, please —quick!"

But the bishop gazed fixedly into the room. "Some water for Mrs. Galloway!" he called huskily.

A horse with a napkin knotted about his neck was in the middle of the room, by the wreck of the dinner-table. Varick was standing the candelabra on the floor, and relighting the bent candles. The others were watching Galloway, the women with their skirts wrapped about them, prepared for any new catastrophe. When Mrs. Galloway screamed, they turned and regarded her and the bishop.

"My dear," said her husband, "this is an unfortunate occurrence. We need not discuss it. As you did not come home, there was some talk between Colfax and myself which ended in his betting me that I couldn't ride Camelot through the house. Now he's in, and we can't get him out. He balked at the lights."

"I think," said Mrs. Galloway, "you had better send for the servants, and clean up this mess. Then I want you to hurry and get that horse out of the room. I told you the last time, when you brought Huron in here, that such things must stop."

"Oh, you've been practising this game, have you?" interrupted Colfax. "I don't think that was square. I'll leave it to the bishop."

"Only with Huron," said Galloway, "and he's sick. I've never had this one in."

"Charley Galloway," said his wife, "are you going to get that beast out of here or not?"

"Be reasonable, my dear," said Galloway. "I have been trying for half an hour to get him out. I tell you, he's balked."

"We might put a candle under him," suggested Varick. "There isn't much left to smash."

"Put that candle down!" said his sister-in-law, Mrs. Innis. "This isn't your house or your horse."

"Yes; do put it down," said his wife.

"I don't see what there is to be done," Galloway observed, "except to let him stop here till he gets tired. The rest of us might as well go into the smoking-room."

"Take that horse out of here at once!" said Mrs. Galloway.

"My dear!" protested her husband.

"*At once!*" said Mrs. Galloway.

There was an uneasy silence.

"Mr. Galloway," said the bishop, with some hesitation, "my brougham horse sometimes balks, and I always give him sugar. Have you any sugar?"

Galloway smiled scornfully, but found the coffee-tray and handed him the sugar-bowl. Galloway's smile said: "This is a harmless fancy which may divert my wife; but of course it is impossible to get that horse out of the house by any such nonsense." Varick's answering smile plainly implied: "Why, of course; preposterous, isn't it?"

"Now, my good beast," said the bishop, "here's some sugar." Camelot took two lumps with relish. The bishop patted his neck. "A nice horsey—a nice horsey," he said soothingly. "Here's some more. Come along now, and you shall get the rest of the bowlful." He chirruped softly, and the horse started. Holding the bowl in front of Camelot's muzzle, with stately deliberation the bishop led him through the hall, out upon the veranda, and down the steps. The company, hushed and at a respectful distance, followed, and halted on the veranda.

"Bishop Cunningham," said Mrs. Galloway, "I am very much indebted to you—very much indebted indeed. Mr. Galloway, will you be good enough to order us something to eat, and send for a groom to take this horse?" Mr. Galloway went into the house. "I am distressed, on your account, that this should have happened," she added to the bishop; "and, I admit, somewhat mortified on my own. I cannot help feeling that you must draw the line yourself against horses in the dining-room."

"Please do not speak of it," exclaimed the bishop, with a bow. "I beg of you to let the subject drop."

"You are *so* good!" murmured Mrs. Galloway. She gave a little choke; her nerves were beginning to assert themselves.

"What we all ought to do," said Varick, "is to give three cheers for the bishop, who is a horse-tamer and a brick, and leave this ruined home to its inmates."

"Hold up!" interrupted Willie Colfax. "Cheers are all right, but I want to make a speech first." He turned toward the bishop. "You see, sir, I have just won a hundred from Galloway because he couldn't get that horse out. You *have* got him out, and, considering the matter on the general principles of a sweepstake, you ought to get the hundred. I don't suppose you want the money yourself, so I am starting your missionary subscription with it, and as much more added to fat up the pot. Now, the rest of you fellows, remember you are at a missionary meeting, and do the right thing." And they all did.

HIS FIRST RACE

IX

HIS FIRST RACE

YOUNG Hatfield sat up in bed, and began groping for matches and the candle. He struck a light, and looked at his watch. It was half-past five. He drew a long breath, and tried to recall the nightmare from which he had just escaped. He had been riding furiously, over a vague, gray, boundless country seamed with immense fences. The dream at first had been confused and misty, but gradually it had turned into a situation where he was alone and helpless, on the back of a mad runaway. Then as he galloped faster and faster toward an enormous fence, the vision grew clear and real—frightfully real. The horse hit, the fall came, and he was awake, but the crash of breaking rails still jarred in his ears. His heart was thumping with the dream-horror that had come as his horse's head and withers sank under him. He was breathing hard and his knees felt weak. He had believed that he was dead.

To throw the impression off, he slipped out of bed, and pushed open the shutters. The pines about the

Oakdale clubhouse were sighing. Down the valley a southwest wind was herding successive ranks of low, wet clouds. In the first glimmerings of dawn the distant hills were only a darker shadow across the horizon. The gray fields in front of the club sloped dimly, and were lost in the mists on the bottom-lands. Hatfield stretched his arm out, and opened his hand to the wind.

"They'll race," he muttered; "there's no frost." He cuddled his hands in his pajama sleeves, and shivered. Then he closed the window, and jumped into bed.

Hatfield had left Forbes's dinner about two o'clock; therefore he needed sleep, but he knew that it was out of the question. His brain was in that stage of nervous alertness which results from champagne and much coffee, followed by an evening of Scotch and soda. His dream weighed upon him; there was a prophetic vividness about it which he could not put out of mind. He argued that the horse he was going to ride had run many steeplechases, and had never hurt any one. Forbes had told him that, when he offered him the mount. Then an inner voice suggested that this was the more reason for avoiding that horse. Every horse will fall some day. His mind brought up instances of men killed in the hunting-field when mounted on their best. He had known an Englishman killed in that way the winter before. At the end of an hour he felt certain that he was going to be killed, or at least badly hurt, and he tried to be calm about it. He was not superstitious, but presentiments nowadays have a scientific recognition, and he felt sure that a presentiment had come to him. He imagined how he would look in his coffin, and he wondered whether his mother would come over, or whether they would send him to her. His mother lived in Europe. Then he fell to thinking about the Girl who, at that moment, was asleep at the Alden Adamses', a mile up the road. He wondered if by any freak of thought-transference his dream had come to her.

Suddenly it occurred to him that he was not obliged to ride. He might be taken ill, and afterward give up hunting altogether. He was ashamed and angry, but he could not put the idea out of his mind. It came back, tempting him with plausible excuses. A little before seven he got up and dressed. Then he took a writing-case from his trunk, and wrote three short notes. Two of these he sealed with his ring. One was addressed to his mother, the second to the Girl who was stopping at the Adamses'. The third was open, and addressed to Forbes. The possibility that, after all, he might be making an ass of himself had occurred to him, and what he wrote was bald and matter-of-fact. He hoped against conviction that he was making an ass of himself. He had much to live for. He had planned things which it was hard to imagine he was not going to fulfil. He put the envelops in his writing-case and went down-stairs to wait for breakfast.

Hatfield was twenty-three, and was spoken of as a boy who might amount to a good deal if a comfortable income and half a dozen other pitfalls of youth did not destroy him. Horses were a new fad. As a child he had ridden his pony, but going 'cross country was a fresh experience. When the Girl went to the Alden Adamses' for November, Hatfield had bought a couple of hunters and gone down to Oakdale. He had been out four or five times with the hounds, and the game had ensnared him. His views of life forthwith changed. It seemed only worth while to become and to be known as a "hunting-man." He pinned his stock the way Braybrooke pinned his; he affected Galloway's practice of carrying a cutting-whip instead of a crop; he copied Forbes's seat—that is, until Whitney Corlies came down; after that he modeled himself upon Corlies. He realized that he was a beginner, and was discreet in his opinions; but he was impatient to acquire a standing. If Corlies had suggested flying the river, Hatfield would have gone at it without hesitation. When Forbes had offered him the mount for the steeplechase, the night before at dinner, he felt that his chance had come.

Forbes knew that Hatfield was green, but he had observed that he rode with his heart in it; and, moreover, there was no one else to put up who could make the weight. He had written to Carty Carteret, offering him the mount, and the day before had received a telegram of regret. Carteret wired that he knew the Rajah, that his accident policy had expired, and that he owed it to his beloved parents to decline. The fact was that Carteret wanted to hunt that day in Philadelphia. The telegram nettled Forbes, because he was sure the horse could win. There were exactly eight other gentlemen at Oakdale each privately holding similar views about his own horse.

When Hatfield went into the breakfast-room he found Corlies there.

"He's around awfully early," thought Hatfield. But Corlies's ways were not as other men's. Neither did people ask him personal questions. He nodded to the boy.

"Better take your coffee with me," he said.

"I'd like to," Hatfield answered as calmly as he could. It was a distinction to breakfast with Whitney Corlies. What Corlies did not know about horses, and what he could not do with them, were not things of consequence. He was a lean, finely proportioned man of forty-five. Everything he did he did well and easily. All his life the world had run after him. What he thought about it no one knew, for he rarely spoke. Men as well as women thought him handsome. Meissonier might have painted him as a colonel of cavalry. He was unmarried, and there was a romantic story about him. Once Hatfield had asked Mrs. Innis about it. She looked surprised, and told him that she didn't know the details.

"So you're riding the Rajah," said Corlies, as the boy sat down.

"Yes," said Hatfield. "I've never been on his back, and I've never ridden a race before. I'm afraid I shall make rather a mess of it."

"He's a brute at times," observed Corlies. He spread out his paper, and proceeded to take the top off his egg. Presently he spoke again:

"It's going to be wet. Have you got a braided rein?"

"No," replied Hatfield. "But perhaps Forbes has."

"He doesn't believe in them," said Corlies. "I'll have one sent down for you. Your horse bores. I rode him once." The Rajah was an English horse. When he was six years old, and sound, Corlies had ridden him in the Grand National.

"Thank you for the rein," said Hatfield. "It was

very good of you to think about it." He was pleased, because he knew that Corlies paid few attentions to men. Besides, he had experienced the difficulty of bringing a bolter's head around with an ordinary wet bridle-rein. What he had heard about the Rajah was not assuring. A horse that bored was likely to get his head down, and run into a jump without rising. He knew of a man who had been hopelessly crippled by such an accident.

Presently Corlies rose. "Don't you want to see the paper?" he said. He pushed the sheets over the table. "You'd better find out whether Forbes has had the mud caulks put on. He's careless about such things." He nodded and moved off.

MOST of the men who were going to ride, and a number who weren't, lunched at the club that day. They made a party around the big center-table. It was noticeable that those who were going to look on seemed to be having the best time. They talked most and ate most. The others talked less, and pecked at things with a great show of appetite; some of them drank liberally. Willie Colfax, who sat next to Hatfield, was lunching mainly upon a magnum of Bass.

"Better have some," he suggested politely, for the fourth time.

"No," said Hatfield; "I don't think I'll drink anything. To tell the truth, I don't feel like eating much, either."

Colfax grinned.

"Don't feel much like gorging, myself," he remarked confidentially. "That's why I've got this." He nodded toward the magnum.

"Are you really feeling that way, too?" Hatfield asked. Colfax had ridden many steeplechases.

"Why, of course," he replied. "It's nothing to be ashamed of. It's just excitement. None of them are really feeding," he went on, waving his hand toward the men who were dressed to ride. "They're just putting up a bluff—that is, all except Corlies. He's colder than ammonia-pipes. I say, Charles," he remarked to Galloway, "have some game-pie. It's hearty, you know. You're a little short of weight."

Galloway laughed.

"Pass it to Hatfield," he said. "If he's riding the Rajah, it'll be his last meal on earth, and he ought to make the most of it."

"Oh, shut up!" snapped Forbes. "I'm sick of hearing you run down my horse. Why have you always wanted to buy him?"

"To feed to the hounds," said Galloway, sweetly. "But if he's all right, why don't you ride him yourself? Why are you always looking for foolhardy boys?"

Forbes declined to reply.

"Don't pay any attention to him," he said to Hatfield. "He knows we have the legs of the lot, with the possible exception of Corlies's mare. We're going to win."

"Do you really think so?" asked Hatfield. "You know," he added, "I'm afraid I'm a hoodoo."

"Nonsense!" said Forbes.

The chaffing went on, and Hatfield fell to studying the faces of the men he was going to ride against. They seemed to him discouragingly unconcerned. He felt drawn to Colfax, who admitted that food had no fascinations. Yet, if these men were free from apprehension, there could be no real risk. Three of them were married—happily—and had families; they were not indifferent about existence. This was a logical argument, but it carried no conviction.

"When you've finished," said Forbes, "we might start along. The Rajah's at the stables. I thought you might like to walk him down to the course, and get your legs bent over him."

"Thanks," said Hatfield; "I should." He had dressed before lunch, and had a tweed coat over his racing-jacket. Forbes's colors were very gaudy—scarlet and black hoops. As they reached the stables a coach-horn sounded, and Hatfield looked back. The Alden Adamses' drag was swinging through the grounds. The crowd had begun to gather. Already the court before the porte-cochère was filled with traps and with men on hacks who were stopping at the club to see the list of starters. The horn sounded again, and the "four" rumbled past. Hatfield caught a glimpse of the Girl, buttoned up to the chin in a man's mackintosh, but she didn't see him. She was sitting between two loquacious young men who, together with the rest of the party, seemed needlessly jolly. He followed the back of her sailor hat with his eyes till the coach disappeared around the turn that led to the porte-cochère. Suddenly Forbes touched him on the arm, and he felt himself blushing. The Rajah had been led out, and was standing beside him. He turned and clambered into the saddle.

"Take him quietly," said Forbes. "He's feeling a bit beany, and he may bolt. Your stirrups seem about right. I'll see you at the post. I'm going to drive down. There's a boy waiting for you on the course."

Hatfield followed the path around the stables, and turned into the lane that led down to the great meadow where the steeplechase course was laid. Ahead of him was a dotted line of traps and hooded and blanketed horses moving slowly toward the track. A

HIS FIRST RACE 143

Hempstead cart with a lively pony dashed by, and the Rajah shied into the fence. Hatfield lost a stirrup, and the young man in the cart snickered. Hatfield felt that he must be making himself ridiculous. One vehicle after another passed, and he knew that each time the occupants were commenting upon his inexperience. As he reached the meadow he heard the coach-horn again, and turned out. The drag swept by at a canter. The Girl saw him this time, and bowed; but it was a distant, formal little nod, and she knew it. To her, he looked very bored and indifferent. It seemed profitable to her to appear to him much interested in other matters. She did not know she was cruel.

"You're dining with us, you know!" Adams yelled from the box.

Hatfield nodded. "If I'm dining anywhere," he murmured. He followed the drag with his eyes. The people on it were having a very good time, and he compared himself with them—particularly with the two insufferable young men. It struck him as a queer misnomer to call riding steeplechases an amusement. Then he bowed to Galloway, who drove by with the Braybrookes; for Mrs. Galloway wouldn't come when her husband rode. Galloway was joking with Mrs. Braybrooke, and to all appearances he seemed conspicuously gay. Those familiar with his habits, however, knew that after lunch he usually smoked a cigar; now he was sucking his lungs full of cigarette smoke. Hatfield rode toward the judges' stand, where the scales were, and one of Corlies's grooms came up to him.

"Here's the racing-rein, sir," said the man. "Mr. Corlies told me I was to put it on the Rajah. You'll be likely to need it, sir." A little squall burst from the south, driving a fine drizzle across the plain.

"I'll weigh out while you're putting it on," said Hatfield. He took the saddle and breastplate, and went to the scales.

"A hundred and sixty-eight," the clerk said. He was three pounds over, but overweight was allowed. He borrowed a pair of lighter stirrup-irons from a boy on a pony, got his number, and went back to his horse. Forbes's man came along with a bucket, and began to sponge out the Rajah's mouth. Presently Forbes appeared.

"They're about ready," he said. "You know the course. It's the hurdle, the mound, the brush, and the liverpool of the regular course, and then a two-mile flagged loop over natural fences, back on to the course, over the water and the hurdle, and finish down the regular stretch. That's about four miles, or a little more. The Rajah will last, and jump strong. Don't hurry him, but don't bother him by trying to lie too far back. Let him rate along and make the pace, if he wants to and can. The only mean place is in the loop, coming back, where there's something of a drop on the other side of the hedge fence. Get him well in hand there, and don't try to fly it, or you may come to grief. The committee shouldn't put such a thing in the course. But I've put a boy there, in case you have a spill. Keep your whip till the stretch. Hello!" he added, "where did you get that rein?"

"Corlies lent it to me," said Hatfield.

Forbes glanced up curiously.

"Corlies?" he repeated. He looked the rein over, and tested its strength. "It's all right," he muttered,— "of course," he added. "That's queer for Corlies, though. Give me your coat."

Hatfield stripped it off, and rode away shivering in his colors to the place where the parade was forming. The bugle sounded, and they filed past the line of spectators to the post. He fixed his eyes on his horse's neck, but he was conscious that the gaze of the crowd was on him. His face burned and his head began to swim. He clutched the saddle with his knees, and coaxed the fretful Rajah into line. Suddenly some one said, "Go!" and the race had begun.

The sudden speed took his breath away, and he hung back. He saw that the field were going at the first jump, in two lines. He put his weight on the Rajah's mouth, and fell back into the second. He recognized Corlies as he rose to the hurdle ahead. Corlies sat back leisurely, and horse and man went over like a single creature. The rest he saw only as a confused line of bobbing figures. The next instant his own horse, with a rush, sprang into the air, landed, and was bolting after the leaders. He pulled him in as he came up on Galloway's off side. Then his strength seemed to ooze out, and he was panting. A horse's head crept up on his right. He glanced around, and saw Corlies, who forged up. They galloped, with their knees almost brushing.

"Steady," said Corlies, quietly; "there's four miles." The boy shut his lips tight, and nodded.

"Can I last four miles?" he began to ask himself. He was determined that he would, but he did not see how it was to be done; he was pumped already. They approached the bank, and the three took it together. He felt the Rajah's knees rub the top sods, but he gained half a length on Galloway in the leap. He realized then what they meant when they called the horse a "close jumper." Presently a warm glow broke over him, and his breath came more easily. The speed no longer frightened him. It was getting into his blood. His nervous apprehensions vanished. He felt a mad exhilaration coming over him. It was like the fury of the Berserker. "I'm going to win!" he muttered. Then he suddenly understood why men ride steeplechases. He settled comfortably into the saddle, and took an easier hold on his horse's head. The Rajah was working under him like a steel machine. He flew the brush as if shot from a mortar. A wild thrill went through him, and he caught himself laughing hysterically. He turned in the saddle, and looked back at the field. Galloway was pounding along on his left, a length behind. Braybrooke was lapping Galloway, still farther out. Directly in the rear was Colfax, and behind him came the rest in a bunch. On his right, and galloping neck and neck, was Corlies. As they neared the liverpool he became aware that Galloway was drawing up. Corlies called sharply:

"Don't let him head you here!"

Afterward Hatfield found out what this advice meant. At that time he merely acted upon it. He glanced back anxiously, and felt for the cutting-whip, tucked under his leg. But the Rajah was holding Galloway stride for stride, and they flew the liverpool three abreast. The course bore to the right, and led over a board fence into a corn-field. The going grew heavy, and he felt his mount struggling ankle-deep. Instinctively he checked him to a hand-gallop. He knew that he had done right when he saw Corlies take in his rein and keep by his side.

With a whoop Galloway went by, Braybrooke followed, and Colfax came alongside. A clod of mud from Braybrooke's horse plastered Hatfield's cheek. In a moment they rose to the next fence, and were on good turf again. He heard a crash, and, twisting around, saw some one fall. "Some one's down!" he said to Corlies. Corlies nodded. They began to overtake Braybrooke and Galloway. He saw Galloway clap in his heels, and again he felt nervously for his whip; but he remembered his orders, and did not take it out. A series of fierce puffs of wind suddenly checked them appreciably and another rain squall broke down the valley, and met them in the face. The water filled his eyes, and he lost track of distance and direction. He saw two blurred figures ahead, and followed them. Looking down, the earth seemed a brown-green tide that rushed by. Suddenly to the right he made out the flags on the fence he was nearing, and realized that he was out of the course. The Rajah put his head down, and bore still farther to the left. He leaned forward, took the rein up short, and swung him back, barely in time to go over the rails inside the streamer. He lost his stirrups in landing, and groped for the swinging irons. He was half-way across the field before he got them. His thigh muscles were limp, and he was rocking in the saddle. "It must be half over," he thought. They were nearing a hedge faced with a board fence. The Rajah rose, and that instant Hatfield saw the drop on the farther side. He had forgotten Forbes' instructions to shorten his pace. He hunched his shoulders for a fall; but the old horse collected himself, and landed with his fore legs well away. Hatfield went up on his neck, but scrambled back and got his stirrups again.

Braybrooke and Galloway were dropping back. Corlies was still on his quarter, to the right. They rounded the loop, and with the next jump turned on to the steeplechase course again. If the horse lasted, he knew now that it lay between him and Corlies. He gritted his teeth, and tried to steady his seat. But inch by inch Corlies drew up and forged past. Hatfield took the water two lengths behind him, and the Rajah was beginning to lean upon the bit. The spring had gone out of his stride, but he kept to his work. He was four lengths behind when Corlies went at the last hurdle. This was built solidly of new rails. Suddenly Hatfield knew that Corlies's mare had taken off too soon. She seemed to hang a moment, and then to shoot heels over head directly in his path. He put his weight on the Rajah's mouth, and swung him close to the wing on the left. The checked horse floundered into the hurdle, and bucked weakly over. As he landed, Hatfield saw Corlies's mare roll across her rider and scramble up; but Corlies lay motionless on his side in front of the middle of the jump. Hatfield heard Galloway and Braybrooke galloping up. He flung himself to the ground beside the unconscious man.

"Look out!" Galloway yelled. He was taking off on the other side. Braybrooke was beside him. The boy caught Corlies under the armpits, and staggered back, as the two horses landed. He saw the Rajah and the mare go off with them down the stretch. Then he bent over the injured man, and tore open his racing-jacket. Underneath, Corlies wore a flannel waist-coat. Hatfield unbuttoned it and felt for the heart. Some papers in an elastic band slipped out of the inside pocket and fell to the ground. The heart was faintly beating, and Hatfield sat down with the man's head in his lap. He himself was "done." He saw Colfax come over the hurdle, then another and another. Then a man rode around the jump to where he was and dismounted. It was Varick.

"Is he bad?" he panted.

"I don't know," said Hatfield. Presently some men rode up on ponies, and a farmer came with a wagon.

They lifted Corlies in, and went off toward the finish. Hatfield slipped Corlies's papers into his hip pocket, and walked slowly after them with Varick, who was leading his horse.

"You pulled him out, didn't you?" asked Varick. "He had a close call."

Hatfield nodded. "St. Lawrence seems pumped," he said, glancing at Varick's dripping horse. "It was fast, wasn't it?"

Varick grinned dismally. "St. Larry has had enough. That was an awful corn-field."

They went on in silence to the crowd which had gathered about the wagon, and met Colfax on the edge of it.

"Charley Galloway won," he said. He looked at Hatfield. "You gave it away. You might have won as you liked."

"How's Whitney?" asked Varick.

"All right," Colfax answered. "He's come to. The wind was rolled out of him, and a couple of ribs cracked. You can't kill him. Good race, wasn't it? I wish I hadn't drunk so much ale," he added to Hatfield. "I'm far from well."

Then Forbes came up.

"Well, I lost the race for you," said Hatfield. "I'm sorry." He was not sorry, though. He was only surprised at the suggestion that he might have left Corlies there and won it. He was new at steeplechasing.

"It's all in the game," said Forbes. "One's got to learn. He carried you well, didn't he? Here are your coats."

The people and the vehicles were beginning to scatter, and Hatfield got into Varick's trap and drove home. As they turned into the club grounds, Adams's horn sounded, and the drag went by.

"Remember, dinner at eight!" Adams shouted. Then the Girl bowed again—it seemed to Hatfield, quite differently this time. It was a bow that gave him a very comfortable feeling. He caught a second glimpse of the two youths, and was surprised that he had ever envied them. They were only a pair of pasty-faced "dancing men."

AFTER the race, most of the men gathered in the club for drinks and discussion; but Hatfield went to his room. He lighted his fire, and rang for his tub and hot water. Then he took the three letters from his writing-case, and burned them. He was tired, but his nerves were pleasurably drowsy. He sat down and watched the blazing sticks with a delicious animal contentment. His thoughts were agreeable ones. There was a new feeling of confidence in himself, and a consciousness of power that he had never had before. He had a curious sense, too, of having suddenly grown older, and it pleased him.

The evening came on, and he was getting ready for dinner when a servant knocked, and told him that Corlies would like to see him. He recollected the papers which he had forgotten to return, took them from his breeches pocket, and went to the injured man's room. Corlies lay in bed. The doctor had cleaned him up and bandaged his ribs. His left arm was sprained and lay across his breast in a sling. He smiled as Hatfield came in.

"You see, I'm all right," he said. "Sore, though. Much obliged to you. They've just told me about it. You could have won, you know."

The boy laughed. "I don't know about that," he said. "Anyway, I shouldn't have deserved it, if I had won. I was in a horrible funk before the race." He hesitated a moment. "I might as well confess it," he went on; "I even had a farewell letter all written to my mother. By the way," he added, "I opened your shirt when you were down, and these bills and things got loose. I forgot to send them in."

Corlies looked up anxiously. "Oh, thanks," he said. "I was wondering what had become of that." He stretched out his well arm and took the packet. With his fingers he worked off the rubber band, and glancing over the envelopes, laid them on the bedclothes.

"Is everything there?" asked Hatfield.

Corliss nodded and smiled. He seemed relieved. "You rode a good race," he said. "You kept your head."

The boy flushed with pleasure.

"Of course, it was my first," he answered. "I hope next time I won't be so rattled."

"Your *first*," repeated Corlies, musingly. "It was pretty nearly my *last*. I though it was going to be. I had a presentiment that the mare was coming over on me when she hit. But you will ride well," he added. "I shouldn't worry about funking. You know, a man can even be afraid and ride tolerably well." He smiled. "You spoke about the letter you wrote. Well, I've carried a letter in every race I've ridden for twenty years." He felt absent-mindedly for the papers in front of him, blundered, and sent them sliding down the coverlet off the bed. Instinctively Hatfield stooped to gather them up.

"Never mind," said Corlies. "No; don't!" he called sharply.

But the boy already had got them, and was standing, bent over, his eyes fixed on a worn envelop that bore the name "Hatfield." He would have doubted his sight, but the writing was very plain. There in his hand was a letter addressed to his own mother. What did it mean? A train of strange thoughts flashed through his brain; the blood rushed into his cheeks. He straightened up and fixed his eyes, angry and questioning, on Corlies's face. The sick man met his gaze frankly, and for a time they looked into each other's eyes. Suddenly understanding came to Hatfield, and his anger faded into pity, his indignation into respect. He turned his head away, and held out the packet.

With his good hand Corlies motioned it back.

"Read it," he murmured.

The boy shook his head, and dropped the letters on the bed. Then the shadow of a smile, sad and gentle, rested an instant on the sick man's mouth, a strange tenderness flashed in his eyes, and again his face became grave and expressionless.

"Yes," he said slowly; "I thought this time that it was all up. It was an ugly spill." He stopped, and turned his eyes to the ceiling. "It's a good way to go, though," he said presently; "isn't it?—quick, and without any fuss."

"Yes; that's so," said Hatfield. Then he remembered his dinner at the Adamses'. "That is if one wants to go; but I'm hardly ready yet. Is there anything I can do for you?" he added. "You see, I'm dining out, and I'm afraid my trap's waiting. I'll look in, of course, when I come back."

There was no answer. Corlies had closed his eyes, and seemed to be falling into a doze. Then Hatfield drew the shade around the candle, and tiptoed out.

CARTY CARTERET'S SISTER

X

CARTY CARTERET'S SISTER

"ELEANOR," said Miss Carteret, "I'd like a trap at half-past eleven. Mr. Bennings and I want to drive over to Captain Forbes's. And you'll come?" she added to Willie Colfax.

He nodded affably, and helped himself to marmalade. Mr. Bennings looked annoyed.

"We're going to buy horses," she continued. "That is, I'm going to buy *one*. Mr. Bennings, I believe, is going to buy a drove."

Mr. Bennings raised his hand in deprecation.

"Aw—I say, not a drove; just a few likely ones," he remarked.

"Polly Carteret," said Mrs. Braybrooke, "you're an extravagant goose! What in the world will you do with a horse?"

"I shall give him sugar," Miss Carteret replied. "That will be one thing."

Mr. James Braybrooke stared at her, gathered up the sporting-pages of the newspaper, and left the table.

"You're impossible!" said Mrs. Braybrooke. She

went to the window, and looked out. The Braybrookes' breakfast-room commanded a stretch of rolling lawn set with mighty oaks. The Indian-summer sun was streaming down upon it.

"You see, Mr. Bennings," observed Miss Carteret, "this is the way they encourage me to patronize Oakdale horses. When I was little I didn't care much about horses, and Eleanor used to make me feel that my life was a failure. Now I want to buy a horse, and she calls me extravagant."

"It's getting married," volunteered Willie Colfax. "Don't do it. You lose your nerve and grow economical. One's always thinking about the little ones who have to be educated and set up in life. Please, more coffee, Nell," he added.

Mrs. Braybrooke colored.

"Don't irritate your sister," said Miss Carteret. "I'll pour it."

Mr. Bennings seemed to have something on his mind. He held the marmalade-jar suspended in air.

"But—aw, I say," he observed seriously, "really, now, a *good* nag, you know, is not a bad investment."

Mrs. Braybrooke turned from the window, and regarded him with something like a sniff.

"But she doesn't know a good one. Now, I say, if you don't know horses, just be a lady; only don't pretend. And, Polly Carteret, you don't know any more about horses than"—she looked about as if for a comparison, but found none which was adequate—"than THAT!" she exclaimed. "And the way you *talk* is ridiculous."

"Mr. Bennings," said Miss Carteret, mildly, "do you believe her?" Mr. Bennings deemed himself rather discerning about women.

"No, 'pon my word, Mrs. Braybrooke," he replied, "honestly, now, I can't believe that, you know. You misunderstand Miss Carteret; you really do. We had a long conversation last evening, and she impressed me as very well informed—unusually well informed. Perhaps not so keen about racin', you know, but very well up on huntin'-cattle." He set down the marmalade-jar, and glanced at Miss Carteret for a smile of gratitude; and Miss Carteret smiled.

"There!" she said to Mrs. Braybrooke; "I told you I had learned about horses. Don't be so superior."

Mrs. Braybrooke shot a glance at Bennings, and her nostrils quivered.

"When you finish, come into the morning-room," she remarked. "I want to find Jimmy." She went out, followed by her brother, who was trying to lead her into a discussion of some ideas relative to matrimony.

"I say," said Bennings, when they were alone,—he

spoke confidentially,—"you *were* chaffin', don't you know, about buyin' a nag to feed him sugar?"

"I *was* chaffing," replied Miss Carteret. "You 'caught on,' so to speak, very quickly. Seriously, I should never think of buying a horse just to have something to feed sugar to. With so many poor people who can't afford sugar, it wouldn't be ethical."

"That's so," said Bennings; "but at first it *did* sound just a bit odd, you know. It was a capital joke, though," he added; "and I *do* like a joke."

She dropped her eyelids.

"I could see that," she said. "I can't tolerate people who don't like jokes."

"You don't say so!" he exclaimed. "That's very interesting. You know," he continued, "that's the only thing I have against an Englishman. Awfully good sort, but no sense of fun, you know. I've been over there a good deal, but I can't get used to that. I call it the national defect. This chap, you know,—Mark Twain,—he's noticed the same thing about 'em." This was Benning's stock conversation on the English people.

"That's very interesting, too," observed Miss Carteret. "Will you be ready at half-past eleven?"

"At your service—always," he exclaimed, jumping up. Then she went out, and left him to his eggs.

P. St. Clair Bennings had arrived at Oakdale the afternoon before. The last time Braybrooke had gone to town he had met him at the club, and they had lunched together. As it was October, they naturally discussed hunting-stables, and Braybrooke asked him down to look over Forbes's string before it went to the Horse Show. Bennings was glad to come, and he was pleased to find Miss Carteret stopping there, because he ranked women only after horses. Miss Carteret had made rather quick work with him. He already considered her a "devilish fine girl," and an inner voice had begun to ask whether it might not be generous to shorten his visit. When Bennings first came into his money he bravely faced the fact that he could not both hunt and marry, so he put the latter out of his mind. He had sojourned long in Great Britain (as unkind persons intimated, to make amends for having been born in a New Jersey manufacturing town), and, moreover, by nature he had been endowed with an earnest rather than an acute intellect. There was not much more to be said about him. He rode fairly well. His clothes were distinctive. His speech was that version of the cockney speech of England which is peculiar to the "American *malgré lui*."

Miss Carteret was a school friend of Mrs. Braybrooke's. Their mothers had been connected in some way. She lived in Washington, but she had been born on the James River, which accounted for a throaty, Southern quality in her voice. She spoke slowly, and in her accent there was a soft echo of colored mammies which was attractive. Overlooking such artificial classifications as by complexion and by morals, girls seem to fall into two categories. The members of the first inspire esteem and nothing more. A woman belongs to the second when men simultaneously pick up her handkerchief and lurk in wait to put hassocks under her feet. Conversely, a woman's habit of confidently dropping things is also a sign of the type. Miss Carteret continually was shedding her handkerchiefs and other portables, and, as a rule, all the available men were adjacent, and anxious to restore them. She was tall and blonde, with a double allowance of pleasing red hair, and her eyes were of a curious dark-blue color. As she herself had remarked, she was intelligent without being hampered by an education.

THE trap which came to the door at half-past eleven was Willie Colfax's tandem. Colfax had suggested this substitution of vehicles to avoid the possibility of being packed in behind, and Miss Carteret had accepted it gracefully. She liked anything which increased the probability of something happening. "I'm sure Mr. Bennings won't mind," she remarked; "and if he does, he won't say so."

She got into the high cart beside Colfax, and looked down pleasantly.

"I do hope, Mr. Bennings," she said, "that you really don't mind sitting in behind with the man, and riding backward. And if you'll get my parasol—I left it on a chair in the hall; and please ask my maid for my field-glasses; they're in my room. You know," she explained to Willie Colfax, "I'm getting near-sighted, and I'm going to look at these horses critically. Besides, the leather case is rather smart."

"Rubbish!" ejaculated Colfax, jerking the wheeler, who was restless. "Oh, hurry up, Bennings!" he bawled.

Presently Mr. Bennings appeared, somewhat out of breath, and climbed up behind, with the parasol and glasses.

"Now, if you'll hold them," remarked Miss Carteret, "I guess we're all ready." She waved her hand to Mrs. Braybrooke, and they drove off. "Good-by, Eleanor!" she called. "I'm going to buy such a nice horsey!"

Mrs. Braybrooke surveyed her with disapproval.

"Jimmy dear," she remarked, when the cart was out of sight, "please, like a good boy, have something saddled, and ride over there. That girl will do something idiotic, and make us ridiculous."

"Why don't you muzzle her?" said Braybrooke. "She's your friend." Then he went in, and telephoned to the stables.

As the tandem swung into Forbes's smooth driveway, Mr. Bennings caught a fragment of the conversation which was going on behind him. Thus far he had been occupied in keeping in, for the roads were bad, and they had galloped most of the way. "Well, those are my ideas about horses," Miss Carteret was saying. "I believe in judging a horse according to the things you want him for, just as you would judge dogs or furniture. Seriously, don't you?" She laughed a little.

"You'll be the death of me," replied Mr. Colfax. "Brace up, and don't make a holy show of yourself. You can make Nell and Jimmy as hot as you want, only behave when you're with me. You don't seem to have any reverence." Bishop Cunningham once had made this comment to him, and he remembered it. Mr. Colfax's acquaintance with Miss Carteret dated from the nursery, and warranted a certain freedom. "Great Scott!" he exclaimed, catching a glimpse of the veranda, "there's about a million men there."

"Shall we go back?" inquired Miss Carteret.

"Don't be foolish," he muttered. He made a spectacular turn, and laid his thong over the leader. Bennings caught himself when he was nearly out, and twisted around on the seat.

"But it's all right, you know," he remarked. "Forbes is a married man. It will be all right, Miss Carteret."

"Then of course we needn't go back," replied Miss Carteret. "Thank you, Mr. Bennings. I feel much more comfortable. I'm rather glad, now, that they're there. They can help us to choose, can't they?"

"Why, of course," he said doubtfully. "They are all the fellows, you know, from the club. They've come over to see 'em led out."

There was a chorus of "Good mornings" as the cart drew up, and a dozen men in tweed breeches and jackets lifted their hats and took their smoking things out of their mouths.

"Glad to see you," said Forbes, coming down the steps. He had been presented to Miss Carteret before. "The show is waiting. How are you, Bennings? You too, Willie?"

"Quite well, dear boy," replied Mr. Colfax. "Send somebody to stand by my leader while Cook gets the reins. I'm going to send 'em to the stable."

Miss Carteret stood up to be helped out, and the

dozen men came forward to assist. Miss Carteret could radiate, so to speak, her appreciation of the civil intentions of strangers, and all the while be impassive and good form. People who had studied her said she did it with her eyes, and it may have been so. At any rate, it was a gift which did not lessen her powers of arousing interest.

"The Oakdale Raleigh," observed Varick, nodding toward Chalmers, "will spread his coat over the wheels, and you may descend."

Chalmers blushed and performed that service. Thereupon Miss Carteret got down altogether successfully. She wore exceptionally good boots for a woman.

"May I present these fortunate men?" asked Varick. "We shall then suffer Forbes to go ahead with his equine paradox." At this moment a groom appeared, leading a big raw-boned bay gelding, which he proceeded to trot around the circle of turf in front of the house. A serious silence fell upon the company.

"He's not very much to look at yet," Forbes remarked; "but he's clever, and is going to make a serviceable horse in any kind of going. What do you think of him, Bennings?"

"A bit rough—a bit rough, old chap," Mr. Bennings replied regretfully. "Don't you agree with me, Miss Carteret?"

"Oh, quite," said Miss Carteret. "Positively malicious. I don't like his color, either, and he's too thin."

Colfax suddenly guffawed, and the men regarded him curiously, and asked him whether he was in pain.

"By Jove—'*malicious*'!" exclaimed Mr. Bennings. "That's capital! And you *are* correct about his condition. At least, that's my idea," he added, with a deferential glance at the rest of the company. "I must have more flesh at this time of year—ten stone more, at least." Miss Carteret looked at him out of the corner of her eye. "Really, now, Forbes, that fellow wouldn't last the season," he went on. "But his color will assuredly brighten. Oh, yes; his color will brighten."

"Do you think so?" asked Miss Carteret. "I'm very particular about color."

"And quite right—and quite right!" exclaimed Mr. Bennings. "The Duke of Beaufort lays great stress on color. Says you can invariably tell condition by it. Lord Wicke disregards it, but I admit I agree with the duke. It takes a clever eye, though—a devilish clever eye!"

"I'm glad to hear you say that," said Miss Carteret. "You know, people sometimes laugh at me for judging horses by their color." She was on the point of remarking that she preferred circus horses, with black and white geographical divisions, when Forbes spoke:

"I'll have to tell you that if you take anything, I must reserve the right to show in November. I've got them all entered, you see, and they're being schooled for the green classes."

"Of course that's all right, Captain Forbes," Miss Carteret answered, with a smile. "And you can keep all the prizes, too; only you really must give me the blue ribbons. I shall have a glass case made, and pin them up in rows." The men laughed, and Varick remarked that it was a very good way to store blue ribbons, only he had never tried it himself.

"I say," whispered Bennings to Colfax, "she's a tremendous chaffer; ain't she?"

"Is she?" replied Mr. Colfax.

The talk subsided again as a second horse appeared. It was a big well-made chestnut with a free, sweeping action, and a showy way of carrying its head.

"By Jove!" exclaimed Mr. Bennings. "Now, here we are! That's a rare good one—regular old-country type, isn't it?" He looked at Miss Carteret.

She hesitated a moment, and surveyed the animal.

"Without doubt," she replied. "I suppose," she added gravely, "they must call him Jenson or Blackletter."

"Yes, of course," said Bennings. He kept his eyes on the horse. "Now, that one will jump like a buck, I'll wager. Look at his quarters! Ah, what a pair of breeches!" he ejaculated soulfully. "Lovely shoulder, too, isn't it?" Miss Carteret nodded approvingly. "I say, Forbes," he called, "ask your head lad to move him around again, will you? What's the price on him?"

"Fifteen hundred," answered Forbes. "He's up to any weight. You can see that yourself. What do you think of him, Miss Carteret?"

Miss Carteret gasped, but disguised it in a little cough. The folly of spending several satisfactory gowns on one beast struck her forcibly.

"Well," she said, "this is a rather more expensive type than I want."

"You are quite right," observed Mr. Bennings, as Forbes moved off. "You know, there is no sense in paying for weight one doesn't need, is there? What do you ride at?"

Miss Carteret thought earnestly.

"Really," she replied, "I don't know exactly." She was on the point of adding that she had never ridden at anything, but checked herself.

Bennings looked at her critically. "I should say about ten stone," he observed.

"I dare say that's just it," she answered. "In fact, I know it is. I remember, now, distinctly."

"I *have* a rather good eye for weight," he remarked. "Hello! here's Braybrooke. What's up old chap? Thought you weren't coming."

"Changed my mind," replied Mr. Braybrooke. "Good lot, aren't they?" He gave his horse to a groom.

"They've only begun," said Bennings. "I fancy this chestnut, though. He must be better than three quarters bred, and excellent bone, too. By the way, if you'll pardon me, you know, Mrs. Braybrooke certainly *was* mistaken this morning. That girl, you know, has a capital eye, and, by Jove, understands color uncommonly well. She called it on a rangy bay that ought to be fleshed for six months. And you know, old chap, that's a deuced fine point." Braybrooke glanced apprehensively toward the group of men, and fell to studying a cow in the field beyond. "But of course she ought to be a keen one," added Mr. Bennings. "She's Carty Carteret's sister. You know, I was with Carty at Melton last winter, when he went through thirty minutes with a broken shoulder blade."

"Really!" observed Braybrooke. He was still considering the cow.

As the next horse was led out, he caught Miss Carteret's eye, and beckoned her aside. "Have you bought anything yet?" he inquired.

She shook her head.

"Well, as a personal favor, I wish you wouldn't. You see, we've got a stable full that you can ride whenever you want, and you would only pay twelve or fifteen hundred for something that would be very likely too much for you when you got him. If you must own something, pick up a cheap pony to hack about."

"All right," said the girl. "You're really a very nice boy, Jimmy, and I don't like to tease you. But you needn't say anything to Captain Forbes."

Just then Forbes and Varick came up.

"What do you think of this one?" inquired Forbes, nodding toward a well-turned little black mare.

"Perfectly sweet," Miss Carteret answered. "But I think I'll watch the rest from the veranda. It's too hot here." She turned to Varick. "Will you come up and tell me all about them?" she asked.

He looked at her curiously.

"I dare say you know a great more about such things than I do," he said. He dragged a steamer-chair into position. "You see, I'm only an amateur, a dilettante," —he noted the way she was turned out,—"and you— well, you're Carty Carteret's sister."

She threw her head back and laughed.

"Two weeks ago," she said, "I read six pages of a book called 'The Anatomy of the Horse.' That's all I know. You see," she went on confidentially, "Eleanor and Carty have made my life a burden. The more they talked horse, the more I despised the whole thing. But you *are* out of it here if you don't like horses, so when Nell asked me down I thought I'd try a new tack. You see, I've suspected all along that they didn't understand half the things they said. They just mumble gibberish, like that unfortunate Mr. Bennings—now, don't they?"

"I must decline to answer," replied Varick. "It might incriminate me."

"There, I knew it!" she exclaimed triumphantly. "I just decided to cram up a little, and look knowing; and then I got all these clothes. I knew I could fool them. I can't take in Nell and Willie, of course; so I practise on them, and when they tell me I'm foolish I know enough not to say *that* again. It's really been amusing. Mr. Bennings thoroughly believes in me." She stopped, and watched the little knots of men in the roadway. "Are all those grown men honestly poring over that horse?" she asked.

"They are," said Varick. "An occasion like this is a sacrament to them."

"How funny it is, when you think about it!" she exclaimed. "And do they really find out all sorts of things when they feel his legs and look at his teeth?"

"They really do," said Varick. "In a rudimentary way, I can do it myself."

"Well," she sighed, "it's beyond me. It's like a telegraph ticking. I hear it, but I can't understand what it means. I know a white horse from a brown one, and I have a preference for long tails, which I consider sensible. You see, when you are driving, it's the tail you see most of, isn't it? A system of judging horses by their tails would appeal to me. But what difference does it make whether a horse has fluted colonial legs, or smooth round ones? Absolutely none!"

"Please, a little lower," suggested Varick. "Somebody might hear."

She laughed.

"But seriously," she continued, "I *should* like to get a horse with a long tail. My father insists on having his horses docked, and I'm sick of them. They didn't use to do it. My grandfather used to take me driving with a pair of thoroughbreds that had tails that touched the ground, and they could trot—I don't know how fast!—in a minute, I think."

"Do you remember," said Varick, artlessly, "that there was a time—you must remember it—when your mother wore very tight sleeves?"

"Thank you," she replied. "I've trunks full of them. But people are the only animals silly enough to have fashions. It's wicked to put horses on the same basis."

She looked down the lawn toward the gateway, where something passing behind the shrubbery attracted her attention. In a moment a fat, undersized gray horse jogged into view, drawing a shabby Hempstead cart. Presently he subsided into a sober walk. From his rough coat and fetlocks he seemed to be of Percheron origin. As he drew nearer a fly attacked him, and he switched a superb tail.

"There!" exclaimed Miss Carteret. "That is the kind of horse I really want. Just look at that tail!"

"Good heavens," cried Varick, "but you mustn't!" She seemed not to hear him.

"Do you think," she went on, "that no one would take me seriously if I bought that horse?" Varick chuckled. "I have a little plan," she added, and went down the steps.

"Glad to see you are going to join us again," said Mr. Bennings, bowing profusely.

"Mr. Bennings," said Miss Carteret, "if I buy a horse, will you ride him home?"

Mr. Bennings beamed.

"My dear Miss Carteret," he cried, "*anything!* Anywhere!"

"Thank you so much," she said sweetly. She turned away, and went over to Forbes and Galloway.

"Captain Forbes," she said, "Mr. Bennings has promised to ride my horse home. He's been very nice to me, and I really think he would like to do it. Besides, he is a good horseman, and I feel that I can trust him. I want to buy that gray horse in the cart."

Forbes and Galloway looked at each other and then at Mr. Bennings. They showed symptoms of exploding.

"Please be very serious," she said. "What's his name, and how much is he?"

"His name," replied Forbes, gravely, "is Birdofreedom, and he does my marketing. I have never considered offering him for sale. He is worth about fifty dollars to me, though that may be extortionate."

"It is," said Galloway; "say ten."

"No," replied Miss Carteret; "I'm not going to bargain with you. I'll send you a check to-morrow for fifty dollars. Will you have him saddled and brought down when the cart comes? I don't want to keep Mr. Bennings waiting. No," she replied to Forbes's invitation; "we can't stop to lunch. We promised Mrs. Braybrooke we'd be back. Besides, I want her to see my horse. You know, she thinks I don't know anything about horses."

"I say," gasped Galloway, his sides shaking, "Bennings will never get over this!"

"Get over what?" said Miss Carteret, innocently. She nodded to Varick, and he joined her. "I've bought him," she said, "and Mr. Bennings is going to ride him home. You won't tell about our talk, will you?"

Varick replied with difficulty.

"No," he replied, "I am your dumb slave. Hello! there's your trap."

Willie Colfax drove up to the old-fashioned horse-block, and stopped.

"Better hurry up!" he called. "We're late now. Good-by, Forbes; sorry we can't stop."

"Sorry too," said Forbes. He turned to Miss Carteret, and helped her up. "They're getting your horse out as fast as possible. Bennings won't mind waiting. We'll give him something to drink."

"Very well," said Miss Carteret. "Perhaps I would just as soon *not* see Mr. Bennings start off. You won't mind waiting a minute?" she called to him. "You can overtake us, you know, and Jimmy will wait, too. Good-by."

"What was all that?" demanded Willie Colfax. He swung his thong, and the horses went away at a gallop.

Miss Carteret explained. What she said was accurate, as far as it went. She considered it unnecessary, however, to dwell upon her own feelings toward Bird-ofreedom.

"Well," said Mr. Colfax, "you're a peach!"

"And you'll wait and let them catch up?" she asked.

"We certainly must give Nell the procession effect," he observed. Instead of waiting, however, he tore around a two-mile loop, which brought them to the Braybrookes' gateway just as Braybrooke and Mr. Bennings were arriving.

Mrs. Braybrooke was on the steps as they drove up. They were late.

"What's that Mr. Bennings is riding?" she demanded.

"That," said Miss Carteret, proudly, "is my horse."

Birdofreedom approached, and Mrs. Braybrooke studied him.

"Polly Carteret!" she exclaimed,—it was almost a scream,—"what on earth do you mean?—Jimmy!"

"He's virtually sound," said Braybrooke.

His wife turned and stalked into the house.

"There, now, Mr. Bennings," said Miss Carteret, mournfully, "you see how a horse will separate friends!"

"Aw—certainly," said Mr. Bennings. "Will you kindly ring for somebody from the stables?" His manner was stiff. He realized that he had overrated Miss Carteret's eye for horse-flesh. "Just fawncy buyin' such a brute!" he said to himself. "Just fawncy!" The girl was a disappointment. It mortified him to misjudge people, and he went back to town that night.

ACCORDING to the account which Varick afterward gave Miss Carteret of Forbes's lunch-party, it had been notable for two reasons. First, "horse" was neglected in a manner without precedent.

"You see," said Varick, "it was unanimously concluded, something more than a dozen times, that you were a bully girl, and had revenged the American people on that ass Bennings. That took up nearly all the time. And besides the absence of 'horse,' there was an interesting display of woman nature. When Mrs. Forbes heard the story, she remarked in her quiet way: 'Well, I don't see how there was any joke on Mr. Bennings. I just think that girl took a fancy to Birdofreedom, and I'm sorry he's sold. He had *such a lovely tail!*' Naturally the laugh was on Mrs. Forbes." Here both Varick and Miss Carteret smiled. "You know, she distinguishes a horse from a cow, and that's about all. She devotes her life to six children. When we had got through enjoying the joke, Forbes said reproachfully (it mortifies him to have his wife display her ignorance): 'Perhaps you don't know, my dear, that she's Carty Carteret's sister. If you think best, I'll explain about Bennings later.'"

When Varick finished this recital Miss Carteret extended her hand and let him hold it longer than was really necessary. She was a very honorable girl about recognizing her obligations.

"I shall keep away from Mrs. Forbes," she said.

Miss Carteret was much interested in what Varick had told her. It explained certain things which had puzzled her, and she disliked being puzzled. When they had sat down to their own lunch on the day of Birdofreedom's purchase, Braybrooke had been severe and dismal. He had made her feel that she had disgraced the family. But in the middle of the meal he had been called to the telephone, and had come back affable—more than affable, for he was talkative, and called her a "bad girl." She knew then that something had come over the wire which reinstated her. The fact was that Galloway had telephone from Forbes's an invitation to dinner which he had forgotten to deliver; and before he rang off he had added:

"I say, Brooky, the Carteret girl's a queen. I'd give my jumping cow to get as good a one on that beast Bennings. Forbes and Varick have let the thing out."

"What thing?" said Braybrooke.

"Why, buying that plug for a joke, you foolish," said Galloway. "Aren't you 'on' yet? Ta-ta!"

GALLOPS

By DAVID GRAY

Two Volumes in One

Volume II

Short Story Index Reprint Series

BOOKS FOR LIBRARIES PRESS
FREEPORT, NEW YORK

Vol. I First published 1898
Vol. II First published 1903
Reprinted 1969

Standard Book Number: 8369-3003-7

LIBRARY OF CONGRESS CATALOG CARD NUMBER:
73-75778

CONTENTS

		PAGE
I	HER FIRST HORSE SHOW	1
II	ISABELLA	33
III	CROWNINSHIELD'S BRUSH	67
IV	TING-A-LING	83
V	THE BRAYBROOKE BABY'S GODMOTHER	109
VI	THE ECHO HUNT	143
VII	THE REGGIE LIVINGSTONES' COUNTRY LIFE	177

HER FIRST HORSE SHOW

I

HER FIRST HORSE SHOW

SHE folded her program carefully for preservation in her memory-book, and devoured the scene with her eyes. It was hard to believe, but unquestionably Angelica Stanton, in the flesh, was in Madison Square Garden at the horse show. The great arena was crowded; the band was playing, and a four-in-hand was swinging around the tan-bark ring.

What had been her dream since she put away her dolls and the flea-bitten pony was realized. The pony had been succeeded by Lady Washington, and with Lady Washington opened the epoch when she began to hunt with the grown-up people and to reflect upon the outside world. From what she had gathered from the men in the hunting field, the outside world seemed to center in the great horse show, and most of what was interesting and delightful in life took place there.

Besides the obvious profit of witnessing this institution, there had arisen, later on, more serious considerations which led Angelica to take an interest in it. Since the disappearance of Lady Washington and the failure to trace her, Angelica's hope was in the show.

One of the judges who had visited Jim had unwittingly laid the bases of this hope. "All the best performers in America are exhibited there," he had said in the course of an interminable discussion upon the great subject. And was not Lady Washington probably the best? Clearly, therefore, soon or late Lady Washington would be found winning blue ribbons at Madison Square Garden.

To this cheering conclusion the doubting Thomas within her replied that so desirable a miracle could never be; and she cherished the doubt, though rather to provoke contrary fate into refuting it than because it embodied her convictions. She knew that some day Lady Washington must come back.

After Jim had sold Lady Washington, he had been informed by Chloe, the parlor-maid, how Angelica felt, and he repented his act. He had tried to buy the mare back, but the man to whom he had sold her had sold her to a dealer, and he had sold her to somebody who had gone abroad, and no one knew what this person had done with her. So Lady Washington had disappeared, and Angelica mourned for her. Two years passed, two years that were filled with doubt and disappointment. Each autumn Jim went North with his horses, but never suggested taking Angelica. As for

Angelica, the subject was too near her heart for her to broach it. Thus it seemed that life was slipping away, harshly withholding opportunity.

That November, for reasons of his own, Jim decided to take Angelica along with him. When he told her of his intention, she gasped, but made no demonstration. On the threshold of fulfilling her hope she was afraid to exult: she knew how things are snatched away the moment one begins to count upon them; but inwardly she was happy to the point of apprehension. On the trip North she "knocked wood" scrupulously every time she was lured into a day-dream which pictured the finding of Lady Washington, and thus she gave the evil forces of destiny no opening.

The first hour of the show overwhelmed her. It was too splendid and mystifying to be comprehended immediately, or to permit a divided attention. Even Lady Washington dropped out of her thoughts, but only until the jumping classes began. The first hunter that trotted across the tan-bark brought her back to her quest.

But after two days the mystery was no more a mystery, and the splendor had faded out. The joy of it had faded out, too. For two days she had pored over the entry-lists and had studied every horse that entered the ring; but the search for Lady Washington had been a vain one. Furthermore, all the best horses by this time had appeared in some class, and the chances of Lady Washington turning up seemed infinitesimal. Reluctantly she gave up hope. She explained it to herself that probably there had been a moment of vainglorious pride when she had neglected to "knock wood." She would have liked to discuss it with somebody; but Chloe and her colored mammy, who understood such matters, were at the "Pines" in Virginia, and Jim would probably laugh at her; so she maintained silence and kept her despair to herself.

It was the evening of the third day, and she was at the show again, dressed in her habit, because she was going to ride. Her brother was at the other end of the Garden, hidden by a row of horses. He was waiting to show in a class of park hacks. There was nothing in it that looked like Lady Washington, and she turned her eyes away from the ring with a heavy heart. The band had stopped playing, and there was no one to talk to but her aunt's maid, and this maid was not companionable. She fell to watching the people in the boxes; she wished that she knew some of them. There was a box just below her which looked attractive. There were two pretty women in it, and some men who looked as if they were nice; they were laughing and seemed to be having a good time. She wished she was with them, or home, or anywhere else than where she was.

Presently the music struck up again; the hum of the innumerable voices took a higher pitch. The ceaseless current of promenaders staring and bowing at the boxes went slowly around and around. Nobody paid any attention to the horses, but all jostled and chattered and craned their necks to see the people. When her brother's Redgauntlet took the blue ribbon in the heavy-weight green-hunter class, not a person in the whole Garden applauded except herself. She heard a man ask, "What took the blue?" And she heard his friend answer, "Southern horse, I believe; don't know the owner." They didn't even know Jim! She would have left the place and gone back to her aunt's for a comfortable cry, but she was going to ride Hilda in the ladies' saddle class, which came toward the end of the evening.

The next thing on the program were some qualified hunters which might be expected to show some good jumping. This was something to be thankful for, and she turned her attention to the ring.

"I think I'll go down on the floor," she said to the maid. "I'm tired of sitting still."

In theory Miss Angelica Stanton was at the horse show escorted by her brother; but in fact she was in the custody of Caroline, the maid of her aunt Henrietta Cushing, who lived in Washington Square. Miss Cushing was elderly, and she disapproved of the horse show because her father had been a charter member of the Society for the Prevention of Cruelty to Animals, and because to go to it in the afternoon interfered with her drive and with her tea, while to go to it in the evening interfered with her whist, and that was not to be thought of. Consequently, when Angelica arrived, the horse show devolved upon Caroline, who accepted the situation not altogether with resignation. She had done Miss Cushing's curls for twenty years, and had absorbed her views.

Angelica would have preferred stopping at the hotel with Jim; but that, he said, was out of the question. Jim admitted that Aunt Henrietta was never intentionally entertaining, but he said that Angelica needed her womanly influence. Jim had brought up Angelica, and the problem sometimes seemed a serious one. She was now sixteen, and he was satisfied that she was going to be a horsewoman, but at times he doubted whether his training was adequate in other respects, and that was why he had brought her to the horse show and had incarcerated her at Aunt Henrietta's.

The girl led Caroline through the crowd, and took a position at the end, between the first and last jumps. As the horses were shown, they went round the ring, came back, and finished in front of them. It was the best place from which to watch, if one wished to see the jumping.

Angelica admitted to herself that some of the men rode pretty well, but not as well as some of the men rode at their out-of-door shows at home; and the tanbark was not as good as turf. It was a large class, and after eight or ten had been shown, a striking-looking black mare came out of the line and started plunging and rearing toward the first jump. Her rider faced her at the bars, and she minced reluctantly forward. Just before they reached the wings the man struck her. She stopped short and whirled back into the ring.

From the time the black mare appeared Angelica's heart almost stopped beating. "I'm sure of it, I'm sure of it!" she gasped. "Three white feet and the star. Caroline," she said, "that's Lady Washington. He oughtn't to strike her. He mustn't!"

"Hush, miss," said Caroline. "We'll be conspicuous."

The man was bringing the mare back toward the jump. As before, he used his whip, intending to drive her into the wings, and, as before, she stopped, reared angrily, wheeled about, and came back plunging. The man quieted her after a little, and turned her again toward the hurdle. It was his last chance. She came up sulkily, tossing her head and edging away from the bars. As he got near the wings he raised his whip again.

Then the people in that part of the Garden heard a girl's shrill, excited voice cry out: "You musn't hit her! Steady Lady Washington! Drop your curb!"

The black mare's ears went forward at the sound of the voice. The young man on her back put down his uplifted whip and loosened the rein on the bit. He glanced around with an embarrassed smile, and the next instant he was over the jump, and the mare was galloping for the hurdle beyond.

Suddenly Angelica became conscious that several thousand people were staring at her with looks of wonder and amusement. Caroline clutched her arm and dragged her away from the rail. The girl colored, and shook herself free.

"I don't care," she said. "He shouldn't have hit her. She can jump anything if she's ridden right. I knew we'd find her," she muttered excitedly. "I knew it!"

Caroline struggled desperately through the crowd with her charge.

"Whatever will Miss Cushing say!" she gasped.

Angelica forgot the crowd. "I don't care," she said. "If Aunt Henrietta had ever owned Lady Washington she'd have done the same thing. And if you tell her I'll pay you back. She'll know that you let me leave my seat, and she told you not to." This silenced Caroline.

"There! He's fussed her mouth again," she went on. The black mare had refused, and was rearing at the jump next the last. The girl stood on tiptoe and watched impatiently for a moment.

"There she goes," she murmured, with a sigh. The judges had ordered the horse out.

Angelica tagged along disconsolately through the crowd till a conversation between two men who were leaning against the rail caught her ear.

"I wonder who that little girl was," said one. "The mare seemed to know her voice, but Reggie doesn't call her Lady Washington."

"No—Hermione," said the other. "He may have changed it, though," he added. "He gives them all names beginning with H."

"You'll have an easy time beating him in the five-foot-six jumps," said the first man. "It's a good mare, but he can't ride her."

Angelica wondered who they were, but they turned around just then, and she dropped her eyes and hurried after Caroline.

As they made their way through the crowd, a nudge from the maid took her thoughts from Lady

Washington. She had been wondering how she would find the young man who had ridden her. She looked up and saw that a man was bowing to her. It was Mr. "Billy" Livingstone. Mr. Livingstone was nearly sixty, but he had certain qualities of permanent youth which made him "Billy" to three generations.

"Hello, Angelica!" he exclaimed. "When did you turn up? How you've grown!"

"I came up North with Jim," she replied.

"You should have let me know," he said. "You know Jim never writes any one. This is the first time I've been here. I'm just back from the country. Where's your box—that's, whom are you with?"

"I'm here with my maid," said Angelica, with a somewhat conscious dignity. "Jim is with the horses."

Livingstone looked from the slender girl to the substantial Caroline, and the corners of his mouth twitched.

"I prefer to be alone this way," she explained. "It's more independent."

Mr. Livingstone thought a moment. "Of course that's so," he said. "But I think I've got a better plan; let's hunt up Mrs. Dicky Everett."

"Is she an old woman?" asked Angelica.

"Not so terribly old," said Mr. Livingstone. "I suppose you'd call her middle-aged."

"Thirty?" asked Angelica.

"Near it, I'm afraid," he answered.

"Well, I don't know," said Angelica. "That's pretty old. She won't have anything to say to me."

"She knows something about a horse," said Livingstone, "though, of course, she can't ride the way you do. If you find her stupid, I'll take you away; but I want you to come because she will be very nice to me for bringing you."

He turned to Caroline. "I'm a friend of Miss Stanton's brother. Go to your seat, and I'll bring Miss Stanton back to you."

Then he led the way up the stairs, and Angelica followed, wondering what sort of person Mrs. "Dicky" Everett might be.

She cheered herself with the thought that she could not be any older or more depressing than Aunt Henrietta, and if she was fond of horses she might know who owned Lady Washington.

Livingstone consulted his program. "It's down on this side," he said. She followed him mechanically, with her eyes wandering toward the ring, till presently they stopped.

"Hello!" she heard them call to Livingstone, as he stepped in ahead of her, and the next moment she realized that she was in the very box which she had watched from her seat among the chairs.

"I want to present you to my friend Miss Stanton," Livingstone said. He repeated the names, but they made no impression upon her, because there, standing in front of her, was the young man who had ridden Lady Washington.

"You seem to know each other," said Livingstone. "Am I wasting my breath? Is this a joke?"

He looked at Angelica. She was speechless with mixed joy and embarrassment.

"Come here, my dear," said one of the two pretty women, "and sit down beside me. Miss Stanton," she went on to Livingstone, "very kindly tried to teach Reggie how to ride Hermione, and we are glad to have the chance to thank her."

"I don't understand at all," said Livingstone. "But there are so many things that I shall never understand that one more makes no difference."

Angelica's self-confidence began to come back.

"Why, he was riding Lady Washington with a whip," she explained. "And I just called out to him not to. You remember Lady Washington,—she was a four-year-old when you were at the Pines—and you know you never could touch her with a whip."

"I remember very well," said Livingstone. "You flattered me by offering to let me ride her, an offer which, I think, I declined. When did you sell her?"

"Two years ago," said Angelica.

Then the other young woman spoke. "But how did you recognize the horse?" she asked. "You haven't seen it for two years."

"Recognize her!" exclaimed Angelica. "I guess if you had ever owned Lady Washington you would have recognized her. I broke her as a two-year-old, and schooled her myself. Jim says she's the best mare we ever had." Angelica looked at the woman pityingly. She was sweet-looking and had beautiful clothes, but she was evidently a goose.

"Miss Stanton won the high jump with the mare," Livingstone remarked, "at their hunt show down in Virginia."

"It was only six feet," said the girl, "but she can do better than that. Jim wouldn't let me ride her at anything bigger."

"I should hope not," said the lady by whose side she was sitting. Then she asked suddenly, "You are not Jimmie Stanton's sister?"

"Yes," said Angelica.

"I'd like to know why he hasn't brought you to see me!"

"He's awfully busy with the horses," the girl replied. "He has to stop at the Waldorf and see about the show with the men, and he makes me stay with Aunt Henrietta Cushing," She stopped abruptly. She was afraid that what she had said might sound disloyal. "I like to stop with Aunt Henrietta," she added solemnly. "Besides, I've been busy looking for Lady Washington."

The young man whom they called Reggie, together with Mr. Livingstone and the lady beside Angelica, laughed openly at this allusion to Miss Cushing.

"Do you know her?" asked Angelica.

"Oh, everybody knows your Aunt Henrietta," said the lady.

"And loves her," added Livingstone, solemnly.

The lady laughed a little. "You see, she's connected with nearly everybody. She's a sort of connection of Reggie's and mine, so I suppose we're sort of cousins of yours. I hope you will like us."

"I don't know much about my relations on my mother's side," Angelica observed. The distinction between connections and relatives had never been impressed upon her. She was about to add that Jim said that his New York relatives tired him, but caught herself. She paused uneasily.

"Please excuse me," she said, "but I didn't hear Mr. Livingstone introduce me to you."

"Why," said Livingstone, who overheard, "this is

Mrs. Everett. I told you we were coming into her box."

"I thought she must have stepped out," said Angelica. "You told me she was middle-aged."

A peal of laughter followed.

"Angelica! Angelica!" Livingstone exclaimed.

"But you did," said Angelica. "I asked you if she was an old lady, and you said, 'Not so terribly old—middle-aged.' And she's not; she's young."

"Things can never be as they were before," said Livingstone, mournfully, as the laughter died away.

"No," said Mrs. Everett.

There was a pause, and one of the men turned to Reggie. "What are you going to do about the five-foot-six jumps?"

"Let it go," said Reggie.

"It's a pity," said the other. "If you had met Miss Stanton earlier in the evening, I think she could have taught you to ride that mare. I wanted to see you win your bet."

"Bet?" said Livingstone.

"Reggie's such an idiot," said Mrs. Everett. "He bet Tommy Post that Hermione would beat his chestnut in the five-foot-six jumps, and Reggie can't make Hermione jump at all, so he's lost."

"Not yet; I've got a chance," said Reggie, good-naturedly. "Perhaps I'll go in, after all." The other men laughed.

"I should think you had made monkey enough of yourself for one evening," observed Palfrey, who was his best friend and could say such things.

"Five feet six would be easy for Lady Washington," said Angelica. "I can't get used to calling her by that new name." She hesitated a moment with embarrassment, and then she stammered: "Why don't you let *me* ride her?"

The people in the box looked aghast.

"I'm afraid it wouldn't do," said Reggie, seriously. "It's awfully good of you, but, you see, it wouldn't look well to put a lady on that horse. Suppose something should happen?"

"Good of me!" the girl exclaimed. "I'd love it! I want to ride her again so much!"

"Well," said Reggie, "I'll have her at the park for you to-morrow morning. You can ride her whenever you like."

A low cry of alarm ran through the Garden, and the conversation in the box hushed. A tandem cart had tipped over, and the wheeler was kicking it to pieces.

"I don't like that sort of thing," said Mrs. Everett, with a shudder.

They finally righted the trap, and the driver limped off to show that he was not hurt. The great crowd seemed to draw a long breath of relief, and the even hum of voices went on again. The judges began to award the ribbons, and Angelica looked down at her program.

"Dear me!" she exclaimed. "The saddle class I'm going to ride in is next. I'm afraid I'll be late. Good-by."

"Good-by," they all replied.

"Don't you come," she said to Livingstone. "It's just a step."

"I must keep my word with Caroline," he answered, and he took her to her seat.

"She's immense, isn't she?" he said, as he came back. "I'm glad Reggie didn't let her ride that brute. She will be killed one of these days."

"She's going to be a beauty," said Mrs. Everett.

"She looks like her blessed mother," said Livingstone. "I was very fond of her mother. I think that if it hadn't been for Stanton—"

"Stop!" interrupted Mrs. Everett. "Your heart-tragedies are too numerous. Besides, if you *had* married her you wouldn't be here trying to tell us why you didn't." And they all laughed, and cheerfully condemned the judging of the tandem class.

THE negro groom who had come up with the Stanton horses met Angelica as she was going down-stairs into the basement where the stalls were. Jim had not appeared, so Angelica and Caroline had started off alone.

"Hilda's went lame behind, Miss Angie," the man said. "She must have cast huhself. They ain't no use to show huh."

Ordinarily this calamity would have disturbed Angelica, but the discovery of Lady Washington was a joy which could not be dimmed.

"Have you told my brother?" she asked.

"Yes, Miss Angie," said the man. "He was gwine to tell you."

"I want to see her," said Angelica, and they went on toward the stall. But what Angelica most wanted was to get among the horses and look for a certain black mare.

Hilda was very lame, and there was fever in the hock. Angelica patted her neck, and turned away with a side glance at Caroline, who, she feared, would rebel at being led through the horses' quarters. She walked down the row of stalls till she came to the corner, then up through another passage till she stopped at a big box-stall over the side of which stretched a black head set on a long, thoroughbred-looking neck.

The small, fine ears, the width between the eyes, the square little muzzle, were familiar; and there was a white star on the forehead. But Angelica did not enumerate these things. Horses to her had personalities and faces, just as people had them. She recognized Lady Washington as she had recognized Mr. Livingstone. She made a little exclamation, and, standing on tiptoe, put her arms about the mare's neck, and kissed it again and again.

"The dear! She remembers me!" the girl said, wiping her eyes. It's Lady Washington," she explained to Caroline. She reached up to fondle the little muzzle, and the mare nipped playfully.

"Look out, miss," called the stable-boy, who was sitting on a soap-box; "she's mean."

"She's no such thing," said the girl.

"Oh, ain't she?" said the boy.

"Well, if she is, you made her so," retorted Angelica.

The boy grinned. "I ain't only been in the stable two weeks," he said. "She caught me on the second day and nigh broke me leg. You see her act in the ring? Mr. Haughton says he won't ride her no more, and she's entered in the five-foot-six jumps."

The girl looked thoughtfully at the boy and then at the horse. An idea had come to her. She was reflecting upon the last words Mr. Haughton had spoken before she left the box. "*You can ride her whenever you like.*"

"I know," she said aloud. "I'm going to ride her in that class. I'm Miss Stanton. I used to own her, you know. My saddle is down there with Mr. Stanton's horses, and I want you to go and get it."

"Oh, never, Miss Angelica!" exclaimed Caroline. "Dear me, not that!"

"You hush," said Angelica.

The stable-boy looked at her incredulously. "I ain't had no orders, miss," he said. "I'll have to see William. Did Mr. Haughton say you might?"

"Of course he said I might," she replied.

The boy said no more and went off after William.

"Of course he said I might," she repeated half aloud. "Didn't he say I might ride her 'whenever I wanted to'? 'Whenever' is any time, and I want to now." She fortified herself behind this sophistry, but she was all in a flutter lest Jim or Mr. Haughton should appear. The thought, however, of being on Lady Washington's back, and showing people that she wasn't sulky and bad-tempered, was a temptation too strong to be resisted.

The boy came back with the head groom, to whom he had explained the matter.

"Why, miss," said William, "she'd kill you. I wouldn't want to show her myself. Mr. Haughton, miss, must have been joking. Honest, miss, you couldn't ride Hermoine." The man was respectful but firm.

"Think what Miss Cushing would say," said Caroline.

"But I tell you I can," retorted Angelica. She paid no attention to Caroline; her temper flashed up. "You don't seem to understand. I owned that mare when she was Lady Washington, and broke her all myself, and schooled her, too. Mr. Haughton hasn't any 'hands,' and he ought to know better than to raise a whip on her."

William grinned at the unvarnished statement about his master's "hands."

"Are you the young lady what called out to him in the ring?" he asked.

"Yes, I am," said Angelica. "And if he'd done what I told him to she would have won. Here's our Emanuel," she went on. "He'll tell you I can ride her. Emanuel," she demanded, as the negro approached, "haven't I ridden Lady Washington?"

"You jest have, Miss Angie," said Emanuel. "Why," said he, turning to William, "this heah young lady have rode that maah ovah six feet. She done won the high jump at ouah hunt show. That's Lady Washington all right," he went on, looking at the head poked out over the stall. "I got huh maahk on mah ahm foh to remembah huh."

The stable-boy grinned.

"Well, she never bit me," said Angelica.

"The young lady," said William, doubtfully, "wants to ride her in the five-foot-six class. She says Mr. Haughton said she might."

"Oh, Miss Angelica," interposed Caroline, "you'll be kilt!"

"You're a goose," said Angelica. "I've ridden her hundreds of times."

"I don't know how Mistah Jim would like it," said Emanuel; "but she could ride that maah all right, you jest bet."

William was getting interested. He was not so concerned about Mr. Stanton's likes as he was that his stable should take some ribbons.

"Mr. Haughton said you might ride her?" he repeated.

"Of course he did," said Angelica; "I just left him in Mrs. Everett's box, and I've got my own saddle and everything."

"All right, miss," said William. "Get the saddle, Tim."

William did not believe that Mr. Haughton had

given any such orders, but he had gotten into trouble not long before by refusing to give a mount to a friend of Haughton's whom he did not know and who came armed only with verbal authority. He knew that if any harm was done he could hide behind that occurrence.

"I want a double-reined snaffle," said Angelica. "Emanuel," she added, "you have the bit I used to ride her with. Bring my own bridle."

"I'm afraid you won't be able to hold her, miss," muttered William; "but it's as you say. Hurry up with that saddle," he called to the stable-boy. "We ain't got no time to lose. They're callin' the class now. You're number two, miss; I'll get your number for you."

"You'll be kilt! You'll be kilt!" said Caroline, dolefully. "Think what Miss Cushing will say!"

"Caroline," said Angelica, "you don't know anything about horses, so you hush." And then she added under her breath, "If I can only get started before Jim sees me!"

IN THE Everett box they were waiting for the five-foot-six class to begin. They called it the five-foot-six class because there were four jumps that were five feet six inches high; the others were an even five feet. It was the "sensational event" of the evening. Thus far the show had been dull.

"Those saddle-horses were an ordinary lot," observed Reggie.

"This isn't opening very well, either," said Palfrey. The first horse had started out by refusing. Then he floundered into the jump and fell.

"Let's not wait," said Mrs. Everett. But the words were hardly spoken when, with a quick movement, she turned her glasses on the ring. Something unusual was going on at the farther end. A ripple of applause came down the sides of the Garden, and then she saw a black horse, ridden by a girl, come cantering toward the starting-place.

"It's that child on Hermione! You must stop it, Reggie!" she exclaimed excitedly.

Before any one could move, Angelica had turned the horse toward the first jump. It looked terribly high to Mrs. Everett. It was almost even with the head of the man who was standing on the farther side ready to replace the bars if they should be knocked down.

Tossing her head playfully, the black mare galloped steadily for the wings, took off in her stride, and swept over the jump in a long curve. She landed noiselessly on the tan-bark, and was on again. Around the great ring went the horse and the girl, steadily, not too fast, and taking each jump without a mistake. The great crowd remained breathless and expectant. Horse and rider finished in front of the Everett box, and pulled up to a trot, the mare breathing hard with excitement, but well-mannered.

Then a storm of cheers and hand-clapping burst, the like of which was never heard at a New York horse show before.

As the applause died away, Reggie rose and hurried out. "Let's all go," said Mrs. Everett.

Before they got through the crowd the judges had awarded the ribbons. There were only three other horses that went over all the jumps, and none of them made a clean score. There was no question about which was first. The judges ran their hands down the mare's legs in a vain search for lumps. She was short-coupled, with a beautiful shoulder and powerful quarters. She had four crosses of thoroughbred, and showed it.

"She's a picture mare," said one of the judges, and he tied the blue rosette to her bridle himself. Then the great crowd cheered and clapped again, and Angelica rode down to the entrance as calmly as if she were in the habit of taking blue ribbons daily. But inside she was not calm.

"I've got to cry or something," she thought.

At the gate some one came out of the crowd and

took the mare by the head. Angelica looked down, and there were her brother and Reggie and Mrs. Everett's party. The Garden began to swim.

"Oh, Jim!" she murmured, "help me down. It's Lady Washington." Then she threw her arms around his neck and wept.

THEY were at supper in the old Waldorf Palm Room before Angelica was quite certain whether actual facts had been taking place or whether she had been dreaming. It seemed rather too extraordinary and too pleasant to be true. Still, she was sure that she was there, because the people stared at her when she came in dressed in her habit, and whispered to each other about her. Furthermore, a party of the judges came over and asked Mrs. Everett to present them.

There never before was quite such an evening. It was after twelve, at least, and nobody had suggested that she ought to be in bed. One pleasant thing followed another in quick succession, and there seemed no end to them. She was absorbed in an edible rapture which Mrs. Everett called a "cafe parfait" when she became aware that Reggie's friend Mr. Palfrey had started to address the party. She only half listened, because she was wondering why every one except Mrs. Everett and herself had denied himself this delightful sweet. Grown-up people had strange tastes.

Mr. Palfrey began by saying that he thought it was time to propose a toast in honor of Miss Stanton, which might also rechristen Reggie's mare by her first and true name, "Lady Washington." He said that it was plain to him that the mare had resented a strange name out of Greek mythology, and in future would go kindly, particularly if Reggie never tried to ride her again.

He went on with his remarks, and from time to time the people interrupted with laughter; but it was only a meaningless sound in Angelica's ears. The words "Reggie's mare" had come like a blow in the face. She had forgotten about that. Her knees grew weak and a lump swelled in her throat. It was true, of coarse, but for the time being it had passed out of her mind. And now that Lady Washington had won the five-foot-six class and was so much admired, probably Jim could not afford to buy her back. It was doubtful if Mr. Haughton would sell her at any price.

Presently she was aroused by a remark addressed directly to her.

"I think that's a good idea," said Reggie. "Don't you?"

She nodded; but she did not know what the idea was, and she did not trust her voice to ask.

"Only," he continued, turning to Palfrey, "it isn't my mare any more; it's Miss Stanton's. Put that in, Palfrey."

Angelica's mouth opened in wonderment and her heart stood still. She looked about the table blankly.

"It's so," said Reggie; "she's yours."

"But I can't take her," she said falteringly. "She's too valuable. Can I, Jim?"

"But Jim's bought her," said Reggie hurriedly.

Angelica's eyes settled on her brother's face; he said nothing, but began to smile; Reggie was kicking him under the table.

"Yes," said Reggie; "when I saw you ride Lady Washington, that settled it with me. I'm too proud to stand being beaten by a girl; so I made Jim buy her back and promise to give her to you."

"Do you mean it?" said Angelica. "Is Lady Washington really mine?"

"Yes," he said.

She dropped her hands in her lap and sighed wearily. "It doesn't seem possible," she murmured. She paused and seemed to be running over the situation in her mind. Presently she spoke as if unaware that the others were listening. "I knew it would happen, though," she said. "I knew it. I reckon I prayed enough." She smiled as a great thrill of happiness ran through her, and glancing up, saw that all the rest were smiling, too.

"I'm so happy," she said apologetically. Then she bethought herself, and furtively reached down and tapped the frame of her chair with her knuckles.

"Well, here's the toast," said Mr. Palfrey, rising. "To the lady and Lady Washington." And they all rose and drank it standing.

ISABELLA

II

ISABELLA

"THAT'S ALL," said Mr. Parsons Scott. He waved his hand at the groom, directing him to take the horse back to the stable.

"They are a good lot," observed Mr. Carteret. He had been putting in the morning inspecting Mr. Scott's hunters.

Parsons Scott had an office in town, at which an office-boy might sometimes be found. Scott's personal attention was devoted to the purchase, education, and sale of hunters. As a prudent grandparent had provided him with an income, he was able to live in the country with comfort and to maintain the town office and his horse business as well.

"I'm glad you like them," replied Scott, referring to Mr. Carteret's commendation of his horses. Carteret's opinion was expert.

"Yes," repeated Mr. Carteret; "they are a good lot. They are better than Harrington's and better than Brown's. But I really don't think there is anything that will do for me. As I told you, I want something like old Elevator—something that jumps exceptionally big and sure."

"The only other thing which I have is a mare that came yesterday from Canada," observed Scott. "I haven't had her out yet. I got her in trade, and probably something is the matter with her; but they say she can jump. Bring out Isabella!" he called to the groom—"the new chestnut mare."

"Did you give her that name?" inquired Mr. Carteret.

"No," said Scott; "I shouldn't name a horse Isabella."

"I didn't know," observed Mr. Carteret. "I thought you might be growing sentimental. It's a pretty name for a gentle mare."

"Stuff!" said Scott.

"Quite an animal," observed Mr. Carteret, as the mare trotted into the paddock. "Sporty-looking, isn't she? White blaze and stockings and a piece out of her ear. She is uncommonly well made," he went on; "but her head is coarse, and she carries it too knowingly for a picture horse."

"Yes," said Scott. "I am sorry about the nick in her ear. It takes a hundred off her value. But she is a mare with a lot of character—the kind that can look out for herself and you too."

Carteret nodded. "Turn her at the jump," he said to the groom. In the paddock there was a made jump, with wings, over which horses could be chased without riders on their backs. The bars were about five feet high when Carteret spoke.

"That's too high to start with," said Scott. "She's just off the car."

The groom, who had started to drive the horse, stopped.

"Let it down to four feet," Scott continued.

"Yes, sir," he said.

Before he reached the jump Scott called him back. Isabella was trotting leisurely into the wings of her own accord.

"Look!" said Scott.

The mare reached the jump, popped over it, gave a whisk of her closely docked tail, and began to graze.

"That's a very remarkable horse," observed Carteret.

"She likes it," said Scott. "Put the bars up to six feet," he called.

The groom adjusted the bars and herded Isabella around in front of the wings again. She looked languidly at the jump, and started for it at a slow canter. She cleared it as easily as before, and went to cropping tufts of grass again.

Parsons Scott swelled visibly with pride. "She just plays over six feet," he said. "It's chocolate-drops for her, Carty," he continued. "This is a horse."

"I think it is," said Mr. Carteret, rather humbly for him. "Let's try seven feet."

"Please, sir," said the groom, "we can't put the bars up no higher."

"Well, never mind," said Carteret. "Scotty," he continued, "I think this one will do. I might as well tell you the truth. I'm looking for something for a—" He hesitated. "I'm looking for a lady's hunter, and I want a natural big jumper, something that *can't* make a mistake. If this mare is only sound—"

"She is sound," Scott broke in. "I might as well tell you the truth, too. She is a perfect lady's hunter. I got her somewhat reasonably because she kicked a man's buggy to pieces. He was an idiot who left her tied in a village street in fly-time. A traction-engine came past, and the buggy melted away. I shouldn't exactly guarantee her to drive, but you can see yourself she's gentle as a kitten. She's a perfect pet for a girl."

"I didn't say it was for a girl," observed Mr. Carteret.

Scott looked at him, but made no reply. He picked up a green apple that lay by the paddock fence and held it out to the mare. Isabella came forward promptly and took it. "Look!" he said. "She'll eat out of your hand."

"That is very affecting," said Mr. Carteret.

"She will probably come around to driving in time," observed Scott. "Suppose we see her under saddle."

"I should like to see her under saddle," said Mr. Carteret.

Scott spoke to the groom, and he led Isabella into the stable. While they waited, the two sat on the top board of the paddock fence and discussed the question of price.

"I think the mare," observed Scott, "is certainly worth a thousand dollars. She'd bring that on her jumping alone, and—"

"But I tell you that's too much," said Mr. Carteret; "my commission doesn't authorize me to spend so much: and yet, I want the horse."

"I was about to say," continued Scott, "when you interrupted me, that on account of the buggy affair I would sell her for exactly—" He stopped. There was a clatter in the stable, and somersaulting through the air out of the doorway shot Scott's groom, followed by Isabella, who trotted to a spot where the grass was tender and began to graze.

Scott jumped down from the fence. "What have

you got under that mare's saddle?" he bawled at the groom.

"Nothing, sir," said the man, who was picking himself up.

"From the way he came off," observed Mr. Carteret, "there might be a springboard, or almost anything of that kind."

Scott paid no attention to the joke. He went over to Isabella, who fed on, undisturbed at his approach. Taking off the saddle, he looked for nail-points and objects of a sharp or lumpy nature. There was nothing there. Saddle and leather pad were in perfect repair.

"You must have done something to her," said Scott. "I'll ride her myself."

The groom acquiesced obediently. Scott mounted, and Isabella stood meekly till he was on and had both his feet home in the stirrups. "Now," he said, "I shall move her around the paddock, slowly at first."

He spoke to Isabella, telling her to "Get up"; and then, placidly and more in sorrow than in anger, the mare gave three bucks. The first was a large one, but Scott hung on. With the second, which was larger, he was on her withers. On the third buck she shook out all reefs and sent him crashing through the top board of the Paddock fence. He landed outside, surprised but uninjured.

"I have been to all the Wild West Shows," observed Mr. Carteret from the fence; "I think you have the best bucker I ever saw. Are you hurt?"

"I shall fix that mare," said Scott, gloomy with rage. He called to the man: "Bring out a harness-bridle with a check-rein, and some strong cord." He climbed back over the fence. "Look at her!" he said. The mare had gone back to the plot of tender grass. The episode seemed to have stirred no evil passions in her.

"She certainly is a mare of character," observed Mr. Carteret, thoughtfully.

Scott watched her in silence until the groom came out with the bearing-rein and string; then he approached Isabella and proceeded to arrange the apparatus, and Isabella made no remonstrance. "Do you see," said Scott, "how she can get her head down now?"

"No," said Mr. Carteret, doubtfully. There was something in Isabella's resourceful calm which impressed him and made him uncertain of everything.

Scott mounted, and clucked to Isabella to start. Then a curious thing happened. She made no attempt to fight the bearing-rein and buck. She lifted her fore legs and reared rather slowly until she was perpendicular.

"Look out! She's going over!" said Mr. Carteret. As he spoke she dropped over on her back.

Scott had anticipated her action. He slid off before she came down, and rolled himself out of the way. He arose hastily, and, with such dignity as a man can command who has been rolling in the soil of his paddock, said to the groom, "You may take the mare to the stable." Then he climbed to the top of the paddock fence and sat down beside Carteret. "Carty," he said after a long silence, "I had always believed that a horse that was well checked up couldn't rear."

Carteret tapped the fence boards thoughtfully with his rattan stick. "Old man," he said, "as we go on in life we lose many of our young beliefs."

There was a long silence. Scott made no answer. "I think," he observed presently, "that a trap just now turned into the driveway."

They could see the house from where they sat, and they watched and waited. In a few moments they saw Williams, the indoor man, come out and hurry down the walk toward the stables.

"You might brush yourself," suggested Mr. Carteret. "A man who sells horses ought not to be found at his own stables with so much mud on the back of his coat."

"Brush me," said Scott. "Who is it?" he called to the man as he approached.

"Mr. Henderson Lamppie, sir," said the man.

Scott jumped down from the fence and twisted his mustache for a moment. "I don't think I can stand him to-day," he said, as if speaking to himself.

Mr. Carteret also came down from the fence. "Old man," he said, "I ought to be going."

Scott looked at him in surprise. "But you said you'd stop for lunch," he said plaintively, "and it is almost ready."

"I know," said Mr. Carteret; "but I forgot about an appointment. I must hurry."

"Carty," said Scott, "if you leave me alone with Henderson Lamppie, it never can be the same between us."

"Well," said Carteret, "if you put it that way, I shall have to stay; but I may not be very civil."

"You can be what you please," said Scott. "Tell Mr. Lamppie," he said to the man, "that we are at the stables. Put another place at lunch, and make my excuses for not going up to the house to meet him. Carty," added Scott, after the man had gone, "what an odious little beast that fellow is!"

"The most odious," said Mr. Carteret.

"Carty," said Scott, "don't you think it strange that

a girl like Elizabeth Heminway should stand having him about? Those Dago diplomats are bad enough, but Lamppie is worse."

"That thought has occurred to me," said Carteret.

"Carty," said Scott, "I feel that we ought to do something to save Elizabeth Heminway. One of us ought to marry her."

Carteret laughed softly. "That thought, too, has occurred to me," he said; "but not the part of it which introduces you."

"Well, ride up, then," said Scott. "Go out in front. I'll give you the panel first."

"It is foolish," said Carteret, slowly, "to ride for a fall when you know the landing is hard."

"Falls be hanged!" said Scott. "If white men like you are going to funk, probably some Dago or Chinee will marry her, or Lamppie."

"Very probably," said Mr. Carteret. "It is apt to be that way."

"Well, something ought to be done," said Scott.

"That's true," said Carteret.

"We might begin by murdering Lamppie," suggested Scott.

"Why not put him on Isabella?" said Mr. Carteret. "It's more lawful."

"That might be better," said Scott. "He's coming."

Carteret glanced at the approaching figure, and then looked gravely at a mud-puddle about fifty feet beyond the paddock fence. "Do you think," he said, "that she could buck him over the fence into that?"

"I think she could," said Scott; "but probably she wouldn't: she's too contrary."

"Probably not," said Mr. Carteret, with a sigh.

"Hallo, you chaps!" called out Mr. Lamppie, when he came within hearing distance. "I say, Scotty, have you got a good one for me? I'm in a hurry, and can't look the string over, but I want the best you've got—something that can take care of himself."

Scott came down from the fence and greeted Mr. Lamppie. "We have just been looking at the biggest jumper I have. She is likewise, in my opinion, the most capable of looking out for herself."

"Is that so, Carty?" said Mr. Lamppie.

"It is," said Mr. Carteret.

"Trot her out," said Lamppie. "That's what I'm looking for."

Scott called to the stable: "Bring out Isabella again."

"Under saddle, sir?" asked the man.

"I'd rather see her stripped first," said Lamppie. "You see, I can tell at a glance whether there is any use seeing her jump."

The groom came out with Isabella.

"Not a bad-looking mare," said Lamppie. He turned to Carteret. "What do you think, Carty?"

"I don't think," said Mr. Carteret, severely; "I know."

"Quite right," said Lamppie, affably; "you are quite right." Lamppie was uncomfortable when he talked horse before Mr. Carteret, who was eminent in these matters, and he tried to put himself more at ease by being patronizing. "As I said, you are quite right," he went on; "she is dooced good-looking. Now the question is, Can she jump as I like to have them?"

"You are the only person who can decide that," said Scott. The bars were standing at six feet. "Send her over," he said to the groom.

"But, I say," interrupted Lamppie, "you're not going to start her in at six feet?"

"Why not?" said Scott, with surprise in his tone. "She plays over six feet."

The words were scarcely spoken before Isabella cantered into the wings and popped over the jump with several inches to spare.

"That is astounding," said Lamppie, "truly astounding!"

"I'm sorry," said Scott, "that we can't put the bars up higher; but if you want to ride her over the paddock fence, you may. It's not more than seven feet six."

Lamppie looked around, and his eye fell on the broken board in the paddock fence. "You haven't been sending her over that?" he said in amazement.

"That is one of Scott's reckless acts," said Carteret. "He was riding the mare in the paddock, and the first think I knew, by Jove! he'd taken the fence. It's not surprising that he broke the top board, because he held on to her head shockingly. You know, Scott has bad hands."

Lamppie looked at the jump in wonder. "Did the mare go down?" he asked.

"No," said Mr. Carteret; "she never staggered."

"That is the boldest jump," said Lamppie, "that I ever heard about."

"Lamppie, you are right," said Mr. Carteret. "You'd better get up on her back," he continued, "and try her over something yourself. You needn't select such a tall obstacle; but she won't go down with you."

"I'm afraid I haven't time," replied Lamppie, doubtfully. He looked at his watch. "No, I haven't," he added. "I ought to be going now." When Lamppie knew that Mr. Carteret was watching him take a jump, the space between himself and the saddle, which, in fact, was not inconsiderable, seemed at least four feet. He would come down somewhere in front of the saddle, and, to make matters worse, would hoist himself into his seat by the reins. "No," he repeated, "I haven't time; but," he continued, turning to Scott, "I'm going to take that mare on your say-so and at your own price."

"But," said Scott, "I haven't said any 'say-so,' and I don't intend to. You make a mistake to buy a horse without riding her. You see, to be honest, I don't think she'd suit you." There was a moral struggle going on within Scott, and the right triumphed. "She bucks," he said.

Mr. Carteret looked away in disgust.

"Fudge!" said Lamppie, "I don't mind a little playful bucking. It is rather pleasant to go prancing about a bit."

"It is, isn't it?" said Carteret. "It's the luxury of riding." He looked at the broken board in the fence and smiled sweetly at Lamppie.

"She bucks a good deal," said Scott.

Lamppie looked shrewdly at Scott and then at Carteret. "I see his game," he said to himself: "he wants Carty to buy the mare." Then he said aloud: "That's all right; I'll take her."

"Mind, I've warned you," said Scott. "You had better try her first."

"No time, said Lamppie. "I'll send after her to-morrow."

"I think," began Mr. Carteret, slowly, from on top of the fence—"I think, Lamppie," he went on, "that you are funking. She's a bad horse. You'd better try her before you buy."

Lamppie was now sure that Carteret wanted her. He looked knowingly at him and laughed. "Sorry, I took her away from you, Carty," he said. "By-by, boys!" He waved his hand and was off.

"Well," said Mr. Carteret, after he was out of earshot, "*we* didn't have any fun, but Isabella will have some. Why did you try to spoil the sale of your high performer?"

Scott looked dismally at Carteret. "It is all right," he said, "to kill a man fairly, but to sell him dynamite sticks for cream candy is mean."

"You are childish," said Mr. Carteret, "and you will never succeed in the horse business. As it is, do you suppose any one will believe that we have *not* unloaded Isabella on Lamppie? If you must pay the piper, why not dance?"

"I'm afraid there is something in what you say," said Scott, sadly. "But we might have a small drink in celebration because he didn't stop to lunch."

"That is a reasonable excuse," said Mr. Carteret, and they went to the house.

The next day Scott had Isabella led by a groom eleven miles to Lamppie's establishment and delivered in good order. The day following he received Lamppie's check. In the same mail came a letter from a ranch which he supported in Montana. His manager, it appeared, had contracted bad habits, and the property was vanishing. This letter made it necessary for Scott to set out for Montana at once. Accordingly, on the third day after the delivery of Isabella, he started on his journey.

As he was boarding the train the telegraph-operator rushed out with a message. "This has just come," he said.

Scott tore open the telegram. It said:

I. has begun with L. Collar-bone and shoulder-blade this morning.   C. C.

"Whew!" said Scott, softly. He got on the car and ran into Eliot Peabody.

"Has some one left you a fortune?" said Peabody, pleasantly.

"No," said Scott. "Why?"

"You look so happy," answered Peabody.

"It is very bad news," said Scott, "very regrettable." Then he sat down and read the telegram again.

Scott got back a month later, and went to work at his hunters. The first person outside his own establishment whom he saw was Mr. Carteret. Scott was schooling over some low fences, which were happily screened from the house of the man who owned them by a thick wood, when he saw Carteret hacking along the road. He went out to the road and joined him.

"That's a good-looking horse," said Mr. Carteret, by way of a greeting, "but he's got a spavin coming, I'm afraid."

"Nonsense!" said Scott. But he dismounted and anxiously examined the suspected leg. "Well," he said, "if it's a spavin it's a spavin, and it can't be helped."

"When did you get back?" asked Carteret.

"Yesterday," Scott replied.

Carteret looked at him gravely. "Have you heard about the mare?" he said.

"What mare?" said Scott. He was still studying the prospects of spavin.

"The chestnut one, Isabella," said Carteret.

"I got your telegram," said Scott. "It was too bad about Lamppie's collar-bone."

"That was the beginning," observed Carteret.

"Did he ride her again?" asked Scott. "I never thought Lamppie was that kind of fool."

"No," Carteret answered. "She has been working with others. They've had some drag-hounds at Newport—"

"Did they furnish sport?" interrupted Scott.

"I don't know," said Carteret; "I was afraid to go there. But I think Isabella furnished some sport. You see," Mr. Carteret continued, "I was going to Newport just after you left for the West, and then I changed my mind. I got a line from Elizabeth Heminway asking me there to stop with them."

"You did!" exclaimed Scott. "Why didn't you go? How is that girl going to be saved if you refuse to do your duty?"

"Haven't you had a letter from her?" asked Carteret.

"No," said Scott, wonderingly. "Why?"

"Haven't you heard?" said Carteret.

"Heard what?" demanded Scott.

"Why, it seems," said Mr. Carteret, slowly, "that I was not the only person commissioned to look for a lady's hunter. Lamppie was buying a horse for Miss Heminway when *you* sold him Isabella."

Scott's jaw dropped. "I didn't sell him the horse as much as you did," he said.

"That is, of course, untrue," replied Mr. Carteret; "but I am afraid that Lamppie takes your view of it."

"Was her letter severe?" asked Scott.

Carteret shook his head. "That is what scared me," he said. "It was sweet and gentle. I suspect that she wants me to ride that horse."

Scott laughed. "So you didn't go?" he asked.

"I went to Lenox instead," said Carteret. "I was there three days. The second day a man came up from Newport who is attached to the French embassy. He had his arm in a sling and his knee in a rubber bandage. He had been hunting Isabella. I left and went up to Bar Harbor. When the boat got there, they carried somebody ashore who hadn't been visible on the trip. It was what's-his-name,—you know him,—one of the secretaries of the British embassy. He is a good man on a horse. He had been *breaking* Isabella for Miss Heminway. He told me all about it. Isabella caught him with a back roll and loosened his ribs. This chap said that two horse-tamers belonging to some of the Latin legations were also laid up as the result of breaking Isabella to oblige Miss Heminway. I left Bar Harbor in a day or two and went up to town. In the club I met Crewe and the British first secretary. They were talking about a young Spanish man who had been witching Miss Heminway with his horsemanship. He had concussion of the brain, and they doubted whether he'd pull through."

Carteret paused.

"Is that all?" said Scott.

"I think it is enough," said Mr. Carteret. "It has strained diplomatic relations with the powers, and though it has thinned out many undesirable admirers, it has ruined our prospects."

"I am afraid that it has not helped *you*," said Scott. "I am sure that Lamppie remembered that I warned him *not* to buy the mare."

Carteret looked at Scott with contempt.

"I'm coming to lunch," he said, and rode off.

When Carteret arrived, Scott was reading a letter. He looked up as Carteret came in.

"It is all right," he said. "We are forgiven."

"To what do you refer?" asked Mr. Carteret.

Scott handed him the note. "It is a very sweet and noble letter," said he. "She appreciates our innocence in the matter."

"From Elizabeth?" asked Carteret, as he took it.

Scott nodded.

"She says she wants to keep the mare, much as one might preserve an historic battle-ground or the sword that slew a king."

Carteret read the letter. "She asks you down to Long Island for Sunday," he said. "Are you going?"

"I am," said Scott.

"She has asked me also," said Carteret. "I found a note from her when I got home."

"You are going, aren't you?" said Scott.

"I am in doubt," said Carteret, slowly. "I am suspicious. I have known Elizabeth Heminway for a good many years. She is forgiving and noble, but I think she would like to see us riding Isabella."

"Rubbish!" said Scott. "She can't *make* us get up on a horse we don't want to ride, and she can't trick us into it, because we know the mare. She might have her painted, but she can't put back the piece out of her ear."

"No," said Carteret, uneasily; "I suppose not. But Elizabeth is a woman of some intellect. I wouldn't mind the spill, but she would have a crowd around, and I don't fancy being made a Roman holiday for Lamppie and a lot of Dagos."

"You'll go," said Scott.

"I suppose I shall have to," said Mr. Carteret. "Are we going to have any lunch?"

CARTERET and Scott arrived at Miss Heminway's on Saturday afternoon. Miss Heminway lived with an aunt, or rather she had an aunt live with her. Her character and fortune fitted her to lead a somewhat original life and to assume much of the independence of action of a man. She had her own hunters, driving-horses, dogs, zoölogical garden pets, to say nothing of a large and ever-diversified corps of personal attachés. All these she regulated according to her own views.

Carteret and Scott had an extremely happy time. They were the only guests, and the subject of Isabella was not introduced. Once Mr. Lamppie's unfortunate accident slipped into the conversation, but Miss Heminway laughed, and looking meaningly at her friends, said: "I am willing to let bygones be bygones. Are you?"

Carteret and Scott laughed delightedly and said that they were more than willing. What pleased them especially was the double meaning of the remark, which they took to imply that Lamppie was a bygone thing in Miss Heminway's estimation.

Both walked with her, singly and together, on Sunday morning; but in the afternoon their joy clouded. Almost a dozen people came to luncheon, and as many more appeared soon after. As a natural consequence, a kind of horse show ensued on the side lawn where the jumps were. Among those who came was Lamppie. His collar-bone had knit and his shoulder was out of bandages, but he wore a silk handkerchief about his neck as a sling in which he rested his arm. He answered all inquiries as to his condition cheerfully and in detail, but he seemed to receive neither the sympathy nor the notice of Miss Heminway.

Scott observed this promptly.

"She is done with Lamppie," he whispered to Carteret.

"It looks that way," Mr. Carteret answered. He never was very positive in any of his statements about Miss Heminway's probable acts.

After the company had seen Miss Heminway's fourteen hunters, and a new four had been hooked up and sent around the drive, and the ponies had been led out, and the St. Bernard puppies and two raccoons and the Japanese monkey, Mr. Lamppie cheerfully inquired if there were not something more.

"There is one more horse," replied Miss Heminway. "It's a chestnut mare. But I've had her only a week, and I don't know whether she will jump or not. However, we can see."

Miss Heminway spoke to her head man, and in a few moments a stable-boy came across the turf, leading a good-looking, powerfully made chestnut mare. As soon as it came near, Scott nudged Carteret with his elbow, and at the same moment Carteret nudged Scott with his.

"Look," whispered Scott; "they have tried to paint

out the blaze on her face and her two white stockings in front.

"Yes," said Mr. Carteret,—his eyes were very quick,—"and they have tried to sew up the notch in her ear."

The point of one ear was drawn together in an unnatural fashion, and close inspection showed that a piece was gone from the tip and the edges were sewed together. At short range the chestnut dye on the mare's face and legs was apparent to eyes accustomed to horses.

"She's very good-looking," observed Crewe to Miss Heminway.

"I like her," replied Miss Heminway.

"She's devilish good-looking," put in Lamppie.

"The question is," said Miss Heminway, "will she jump? I don't want her to try anything high, but I should like to see her ridden over the bars at about three feet. Danny Foster," she continued, "is the only boy at the stable I let ride her, and he is away this afternoon, so that somebody with good hands will have to ride her for me."

There was a heavy silence.

Miss Heminway looked at Crewe.

"Won't you?" she said.

"Why," said Crewe, "I should be glad to, but I'm

ashamed to ride before Carty and Scott, who are distinctly the only men present with truly good hands. Besides, they are stopping in the house, and riding your horses is by right their—" he hesitated and then said—"privilege."

"I don't care," said Miss Heminway; "only somebody get up and ride."

No one made a move.

"Come, Carty," she said sharply, "ride the mare and stop this nonsense. You are coy as a girl asked to sing."

Carteret pulled his straw hat over his eyes and tapped his leg thoughtfully with his rattan stick. "Elizabeth," he said, "you are a superior woman, but you have missed it this time. In the first place, your Titian red is very badly put on, and your surgery on that ear is abominable; a seamstress could do better."

"What do you mean?" demanded Miss Heminway.

"Don't try to force a poor joke," said Mr. Carteret.

Miss Heminway turned to Scott.

"Will you do me a small favor?" she said.

"Anything in the world," Scott answered, "except ride that mare." He laughed knowingly. A whisper ran through the group of onlookers, and then a laugh. Miss Heminway turned her back upon both Scott and Carteret. Mr. Lamppie was standing before her.

"Mr. Lamppie," she said, "if *you* are not *afraid*, will you kindly show my mare over that jump?"

Lamppie bowed.

"I have only one good arm," he said, "and you know I am not considered much of a horseman by Carty and Scott, but I shall be truly happy to try."

He started for the horse, and at the same moment Scott and Carteret started too.

"Elizabeth," said Mr. Carteret, quietly, "you mustn't let him ride that brute. His shoulder has only just healed."

"Please mind your own affairs," said Miss Heminway, severely.

Scott had rushed forward in the attempt to seize Lamppie before he was in the saddle; but, regardless of what was supposed to be his injured arm, he scrambled up, and kicking his heels into the mare, galloped off.

"Mr. Scott," called Miss Heminway, severely, "will you kindly *not* interfere with Mr. Lamppie?"

Scott turned and meekly rejoined Mr. Carteret.

"Look!" exclaimed Miss Heminway.

"I don't care to look," said Mr. Carteret. His back was turned to the horse. "I don't want to see a murder."

But Scott looked. He saw the chestnut mare carry

Lamppie into the wings of the jump at an even canter, clear the bars in an easy manner, and come jogging back to the spectators.

There was a burst of applause.

"Has she killed him?" asked Mr. Carteret.

"Carty," said Scott, "it is all over with us."

Mr. Carteret turned around. Lamppie was bowing to Miss Heminway.

"Shall I take her over again?" he asked. "She goes like a sweet dream."

"If you will, please," replied Miss Heminway.

Mr. Carteret watched the mare and Lamppie repeat their performance. He lighted a cigarette and inhaled a long puff of smoke. "Lamppie wins by a block," he said softly.

"How do you suppose they did it?" said Scott.

Carteret's reply was interrupted by Lamppie. "I say, Carty," he called out, "don't you chaps want a turn on this mare? She's a lovely ride; nothing to be afraid of."

"I am very much obliged to you," said Mr. Carteret. "I'll not ride."

"Well," said Miss Heminway, sweetly, "if there are no more animals and things to be seen, we might go in and have tea."

The party went into the house, but Carteret and

Scott disappeared. They went out a back door and proceeded to the stables.

It happened that Fredericks, Miss Heminway's head man, had formerly been employed by Mr. Carteret. Carteret had given him up much as an orchid fancier might send a lady his choicest air-plant. When the two men entered the stable, Fredericks greeted them obsequiously. There was a queer look in his eyes, but he was very grave because Carteret was grave.

"Fredericks," said Mr. Carteret, "we want to see that mare."

"Very good, sir," said Fredericks, and he took them down the stable to a box stall. He opened the doors and showed them the mare. A stable-boy was scrubbing her legs with some chemical preparation, and they were becoming white.

"This part of the job," said Carteret, pointing with his stick to the mare's legs, "you did very badly. I should like to know, however, how you got Isabella to go so kindly in so short a time. I consider that a very remarkable achievement, Fredericks."

"Thank you, sir," said Fredericks. He bowed very low, and his cap concealed his face, but it could not conceal the quivering of his large frame. "I beg pardon, sir," he gasped, and fled out of the stall, apparently in a convulsion.

"I am afraid," said Scott, "that if we were Fredericks we should feel as he does. I want to know, though, what he used."

Fredericks returned shortly, much mortified and with many apologies for his breach of manners.

"I'm going to tell you, sir," he said, "if I lose me place. Come this way, sir."

He led them to another box-stall which was at the end of the passage, opened the door, and stood aside for them to pass through. They entered the box, looked at the horse before them, and then at each other.

"Well," said Mr. Carteret, "it is easy when you know how."

They were in the presence of Isabella. In shape, size, and color the other mare was her counterpart; but that this only was Isabella they knew now by her eye, by her expression, and by her simplicity of character. She was trying to get her nose into Scott's pocket, and failing in that, she nipped his hands with her lips.

"She's too fat," said Scott. There was nothing else which occurred to him to say.

"So she is, sir," said Fredericks.

"No exercise," said Carteret; "the diplomats gave out."

"I was three weeks finding that other mare," said Fredericks. "She's pretty near a match, sir."

"Did you cut the tip of her ear and then sew it up?" demanded Carteret.

"Not I, sir," said Fredericks. "No, sir. That was Miss Heminway's friend Dr. Anderson, the surgeon, sir. He did it with instruments and cocaine and surgeon's needles, sir, and Mr. Lamppie helped him, and held the cocaine bottle."

"They all knew about it," said Mr. Carteret. "Thank you, Fredericks; we sha'n't tell on you."

They walked in silence back to the house. At the door Carteret spoke.

"I told you," he said, "that Elizabeth Heminway was a remarkable woman."

"You did," said Scott.

"I knew we ought not to come."

"You said that, too," said Scott.

"And you made me come," said Carteret.

"I did," Scott replied.

"Well," demanded Carteret, "what are you going to do about it?"

"What is there to do about it?" said Scott.

There was a long silence. Carteret tapped his leg thoughtfully with his rattan stick.

"What is there to do about it?" Scott said again.

Carteret made no answer but opened the door and went in, and Scott followed.

CROWNINSHIELD'S BRUSH

III

CROWNINSHIELD'S BRUSH

MR. CROWNINSHIELD left his wife talking with the M. F. H. and walked his horse away from the hounds, for he had been cautioned that it kicked. In doing this he met Mrs. Palfrey, who was riding across the lawn in the other direction. They both stopped.

"I'm glad to see you hunting," she said.

"You're very good," said Crowninshield, dryly.

"And Juggernaut," Mrs. Palfrey continued; "how very fine he looks! Precisely the right flesh for hunting condition."

"Is this Juggernaut?" asked Crowninshield. "I didn't notice. Maria ordered it. Look out! He kicks."

"Oh, no! Juggy wouldn't kick, would he?" said Mrs. Palfrey, cheerfully, to the big black horse. "When we owned him," she went on to Crowninshield, "the only bad trick he had was sulking. He has a light mouth, and if you fuss it he'll sulk. Pity, isn't it, when he's such an unusual performer?"

Just then Juggernaut let fly at an inquisitive hound.

"Oh, naughty!" exclaimed Mrs. Palfrey.

Crowninshield gazed off toward the links.

"It's a beautiful morning for golf," he said slowly.

Young Mr. Carhart, who had just joined them, looked at him with wonder and rode away.

"You mustn't say such things," said Mrs. Palfrey. "The golf people are disagreeable enough without any encouragement. The first thing you know they'll vote to give up the hounds."

"I wish they would," said Crowninshield. "This hunting bores me. I don't like it. I don't like to hurry, and I don't like jumping fences. I'm afraid.

"My wife," he continued, "is kind to dumb animals. She subscribes to an institution for homeless cats. She is a member of an anti-check-rein association. She gets me into the newspapers by stopping teamsters who beat their horses and making them promise to be gentle. Why, then," he demanded, "does she insist upon my hunting, when, if I were a tame ape or a raccoon, my feelings would be respected and I could stop at home?"

"Well," observed Mrs. Palfrey, "Maria hasn't confided in me, but she probably wants you to get over being afraid. I think I should feel that way about Willie. You see, one doesn't expect quite so much from an ape. Crowny," she went on, "why don't you go hard a few times and thrust a little? Jump some fences that will make her anxious about you, and then you can retire."

"That might do," said Crowninshield, "but suppose when I'm thrusting I get rolled out, and have to spend my season of retirement on a water mattress?"

"Of course there's that chance," said Mrs. Palfrey, cheerfully, "but Maria would make it up to you in devotion. She'd feel in a measure responsible for the accident."

"Perhaps," said Crowninshield. The suggestion was apparently occupying his mind, and he said nothing more.

Presently the M. F. H. started down the road, the hounds behind him, and Mrs. Crowninshield rode up.

"He's going to draw the Benton woods," she said. "There's a fox there. They saw it this morning and stopped the earth. Harrison," she observed to Mr. Crowninshield, "keep close to Donahue"—he was the first whip—"till we get out in the open. There's a good deal of trappy country to the west of the woods, and Donahue knows it better than any one else."

"Thank you very much, Maria," said Crowninshield. "If you are in doubt about the country you may follow Donahue or any one else, as you see fit. I intend to ride my own line."

Mrs. Crowninshield looked at her husband with surprise.

"You've hurt his feelings," said Mrs. Palfrey, "and he'll probably do something foolish and break his neck."

"I think I can trust his sober second thought," said Mrs. Crowninshield, but plainly she was a little worried. After a moment she rode up beside her husband. "Are you angry with me?" she asked meekly. She was a very pretty young woman, and when she looked meek she was especially pretty.

"No," he said.

"Then why don't you look pleasant and smile?" she asked.

"Maria," said Crowninshield, "you are a—" He stopped and looked at her sternly and rode ahead.

Mrs. Crowninshield turned to Mrs. Palfrey. "What ideas have you been putting in his head?" she demanded. "I don't want him to kill himself. I have been trying to get him to like it, and to go along respectably. But now his temper is stirred up, and he may do something absurd."

She rode after him, but, as Mrs. Palfrey could see, he repelled her advances with a dignified silence.

The covert into which the hounds were taken was a big oblong wood lot, with a board fence across the farther end and wire fences on the other three sides. They went in through a gate which the farmer unlocked for them.

"This is a bad place to get out of," said the M. F. H. to the two ladies. "The hounds will probably work down toward the board fence, but we've got to go out over it whichever line the fox may take. We can't get over the wire."

He rode off and began casting through a bottom covered with tall dead weeds. As the first hound entered the undergrowth a fox scurried out and went away through the woods. "Gone away!" yelled the whips. In a moment the pack was on the line and gave tongue riotously, and fox, hounds, and horses were off. The field crashed through the woods, down the steep banks of a little stream, up again, and on toward the board fence. Mrs. Crowninshield was riding Ten Pin, who was an excitable brute, and took hold pretty hard at the beginning of the day. She reached the boards among the first and went over. As she landed she looked back through the thick growth of saplings and saw Juggernaut coming along. She pulled up as much as she could in the hope of seeing him jump, but her horse began going sidewise through a thicket, and made it impossible for her to look back. However, she listened, and heard no sound of broken boards, which indicated that Mr. Crowninshield was over without accident. Then Ten Pin put his head down and bored away for half a field, and this for the time being put Mr. Crowninshield out of her thoughts.

The fox was still in view, and the pace was as fast as the hounds could make it. There was every promise of an exceptionally good day. Presently the fox began to swing in a wide circle, and treated the hunt to some of the biggest country in that part of the State. A new picket fence not much less than five feet high was followed by a stiff in-and-out across a narrow lane. Then there was a big rail fence with a ditch on the take-off side. The first whip went down at this, and those who got over had a grateful feeling toward the horses that were carrying them. At a stone wall the M. F. H.'s mount made a mistake and the M. F. H. was left ignominiously chasing his horse and shouting "Whoa!" A series of stiff post-and-rail obstacles followed, which thinned out the field still more.

Ten Pin was still pulling, and Mrs. Crowninshield had not much opportunity to look around for her husband, though she thought about him several times. There was a man on a big black horse riding his own line half a field ahead of her and some distance to the right. She was somewhat near-sighted, and could not make out who the man might be, but her judgment told her that it was not Mr. Crowninshield, although the horse looked like Juggernaut. "I don't think Juggernaut could hold this pace, even if Harrison wanted to," she added mentally, to assure herself.

They went at a line of new rails, and Ten Pin pecked badly, but she kept him up.

"Careful, there!" called the M. F. H., who had caught his horse and had come up, cheerful but out of breath. "Nice run, isn't it? It won't last much longer," he panted. "The fox is making for the woods where we found him. The pace is too hot. We ought to kill there. The earth is stopped; we've gone around in a circle."

"Have you seen Harrison?" Mrs. Crowninshield asked.

"No," said the M. F. H., "I haven't. I lost my glasses at the beginning, and you know I can't see much without them. I'm sure he's all right though." The M. F. H. felt justified in his confidence by a long acquaintance with Mr. Crowninshield, and with his repugnance to all forms of violent exertion. "Look out ahead!" he added.

The hounds swung sharply to the left, and disappeared in a piece of thick woods. The field followed over a rail fence, and the next minute encountered a thicket of wild-grape vines, which took young Carhart off his horse and made the others pull up to disentangle themselves. When they got into the open again the hounds were vanishing over the crest of a little hill.

"Hurry," called the M. F. H. to Mrs. Crowninshield, "or we shall lose them." She urged Ten Pin with the whip, and they swept up the hill with a handful, all that was left of the field, behind them. From the top they saw the tail hounds a field ahead going under the wire fence into the covert where they had found half an hour before, and a man on a black horse disappearing after them into the woods.

"Good Lord," exclaimed the M. F. H., "somebody's jumped that barbed-wire fence! Who is it?"

"I don't know," Mrs. Crowninshield called back. "I can't make out." The black horse looked to her like Juggernaut, but she tried to put that idea out of her head. She was worried none the less. Carhart was behind her, and she could not think of any one else absent-minded enough to jump barbed wire.

"We'll have to go around to the other end where the boards are," called the M. F. H., and he used his spurs. "If the fox gets through the covert and breaks away again, perhaps we'll make up our lost ground."

As they galloped along the edge of the covert they

could faintly hear the hubbub of the hounds deep in the wood. Suddenly it stopped.

"They must have killed," said the M. F. H. He turned around the corner of the wood lot, straightened out his horse at the board fence, and went over. The others followed, and galloping through the woods they came upon the pack jumping excitedly about the figure of a man for a brown thing which he held high above them. When they came closer they could see that the man was Mr. Crowninshield. He was trying to keep off the hounds and to cut off the brush at the same time, which was a difficult thing to do.

"It was Harrison, after all," murmured Mrs. Crowninshield, and grew extremely white.

When Crowninshield saw the M. F. H., he paused with the knife in one hand and the fox's corpse in the other. "I suppose I ought not to be cutting this creature up," he said. "Doesn't it violate hunting etiquette? But the proper official wasn't on hand." He smiled blandly.

The M. F. H. said nothing. He was getting his breath and taking in the situation. Besides, there was nothing to say.

Just then Carhart rode up and regarded Crowninshield solemnly for several moments. Then he dismounted, went over to him, and held out his hand.

"You go too hard for me," he said.

"It was luck," said Crowninshield, modestly.

But Carhart shook his head and turned away. He was deeply impressed.

While Carhart was paying this tribute to Crowninshield, his wife recovered from her agitation, and began examining Juggernaut's legs for traces of barbed wire. Her inspection proved that the horse had escaped without a scratch. "He always was such a clean performer," she murmured. Suddenly a look of wonder came into her face. She went close to the horse and put her hand upon its neck. Then she turned toward Crowninshield and regarded him curiously.

In the meantime the M. F. H. had got his breath.

"I'm going to give your husband," said he, "a short lecture on fox-hunting. Crowny," he went on, drawing up alongside of Mr. Crowninshield, "you've won the right to membership in the idiots' club, of which Carhart is the president. But don't jump any more wire fences, particularly after half an hour's hard galloping. A gentleman should have some regard for his horse. Besides, we don't want to stop hunting to attend funerals."

"All right," said Crowninshield; "I will reform," and a twinkle came into his eye. "I say," he added, "how about this brush?"

"No one ever won a brush more honestly," said the M. F. H. Then he turned away and began calling the hounds.

One by one the field straggled in and heard about Crowninshield's exploit and congratulated him. He bore it with modesty and composure.

"Aren't you a little proud of him?" asked Mrs. Palfrey of Mrs. Crowninshield.

Mrs. Crowninshield nodded, but suppressed her pride admirably.

"I am going to confess," Mrs. Palfrey continued, "that I suggested to Harrison that he should try going a bit hard. I knew he would enjoy it more if he did. But I really didn't expect him to do this."

"Really?" said Mrs. Crowninshield, coldly; and Mrs. Palfrey moved away and joined Carhart.

"Maria doesn't know exactly what to make of it," she whispered.

"No," said Carhart; "very curious that he should never have let himself out before."

"It is," said Mrs. Palfrey. "There go the hounds," she added, and they followed them out to the road.

Most of the field went back to the club, where they lunched together in their riding things, an occasion which took the form of an ovation to Crowninshield. They toasted him and congratulated him, and he charmed them with the sincere modesty with which he deprecated his exploit. Finally they called upon him for a speech.

"Tell us how, being a mere golfer," said the M. F. H., "you happened to do it."

"I will," said Crowninshield. He rose to his feet and produced the brush from his coat pocket. "The principle which I employed in obtaining this coveted trophy is the one laid down by Napoleon as the first rule of war, 'Be at the right place at the right time.'"

There were cries of "Good!" from McMillan, who had been lunching heartily upon liquids and was somewhat over-appreciative.

"But how did you happen to be there?" asked the M. F. H. "How did you get over that wire fence?"

There was a pause, and Crowninshield smiled modestly.

"I didn't get over it," he said. *"I was there. I was there all the time!"*

"Most extraordinary!" gasped McMillan, and became hysterical.

"Go on," said the M. F. H., when he could be heard.

"It was very simple," said Crowninshield. "Juggernaut balked at that first board fence, and I couldn't get him out of the field. I must have fussed his mouth and his disposition. The gate was locked and the farmer who had the key was following the hunt in a buggy. So I had to wait. In about half an hour the hounds came along and I joined in."

"Crowninshield," said the M. F. H., with the first voice that he could command, "you have made this a happy day. You are entitled to your brush."

Crowninshield bowed and beat a retreat to the smoking-room. He had not been there very long before a servant told him that Mrs. Crowninshield had ordered the trap and was ready to go home.

"All right," said Crowninshield. He rose at once, which was not his custom, throwing his cigar into the fire. The fact was that he was uneasy about facing Mrs. Crowninshield alone, she took hunting so seriously. He would have been as well pleased to have her drive home by herself and send the cart back for him.

As they drove away from the club mechanically she took the reins, and then, as if recollecting herself, she gave them to her husband. "You drive," she said.

He looked puzzled, for she usually drove, but he did as she asked.

"Well," he said seriously, after a long pause, "I suppose you're ashamed of me?"

She shook her head and smiled. "No," she answered.

Crowninshield looked at her curiously. Her lip quivered a little. "Didn't you think better of me," he asked, "when you believed that I had jumped that wire fence?"

"No," she said. "Because"—she hesitated a moment—"I knew you hadn't jumped it."

He looked her in the face. "You knew it?" he said slowly. "How?"

"Yes," she answered. "You see, the other horses were wet, and Juggernaut hadn't turned a hair."

There was a long pause.

"Suppose I hadn't told?" he suggested in a low voice.

She reached out her hand and placed it upon his knee. "But you did," she said.

TING-A-LING

IV

TING-A-LING

THEY were sitting on the balcony which distinguished the bridal suite, in the sun of the June morning. Below was the main street, animated mildly with the shopping of a dormant New England community. A few ancient carriages, reliquaries of the first families, mingled with the buggies and the delivery-wagons, and at dignified intervals a horse-car jingled past and disappeared in the vista of elms.

"It's ten minutes past eleven," he observed, looking at his watch. "We have five hours to wait for the fourten train, but I believe we *dine* at twelve."

"Are you hungry?" she asked. "I dare say we could get something even before dinner—perhaps a pie."

They both laughed. "This is an awful place," he said, "isn't it? No more historic New England for me."

They leaned lazily upon the balcony rail, and sat with their heads together, looking down into the street. A grocer's clerk was putting things into a wagon, and they wondered who was going to have asparagus, and how big a family it might be which needed six quarts of strawberries. Presently, with the noises of the street, came the jingling of the periodic horse-car, and they turned and watched it approach.

"That is not a bad-looking horse," he said.

"Look!" she exclaimed. There was a note of pity and indignation in her voice. The car, as it drew near, appeared to bulge with passengers.

"It's rather a joke," he said. "Those are women delegates to the Society for the Prevention of Cruelty to Animals convention."

"It's shameful," she said.

The car stopped on the corner in front of the hotel for another passenger to worm himself into the jam on the rear platform. The horse, a big, showy chestnut, stood panting, his nostrils red and dilated. His neck was white with lather. Wet streaks extended up his ears. His body dripped, and the sweat was running down his legs.

As the two strokes of the conductor's bell gave the signal to start, he plunged forward almost before the driver had loosened the brakes. There was a clatter of hoofs on the cobblestones, and a mighty straining. The heavy car began to move, and the chestnut horse went trotting down the street, tail up and neck arched like a cavalry horse on parade.

"He's game," he said.

She put her hand on his arm. "I can't bear to see it," she whispered.

He looked down at her. Her eyes were brimming.

"Don't be a little goose," he said gently; but there was a queer feeling in his throat. He rose to his feet. "I'll be back in a few minutes," he added. "I want to go down to the office." He bent down and kissed her, and left the balcony.

She waited half an hour, and then went down to the corridor. He was not at the office. She decided to go out. As she was on the hotel steps, she met him coming in, and at the same moment a coach-horn sounded, and they saw a coach and four come around the corner.

He looked back. "O Lord!" he exclaimed, "we're caught. There's your brother, and the Appleton girls, and Frank Crewe, and Winthrop, and most of your bridesmaids. I suppose they are on their way to Lenox."

"What shall we do?" she asked.

A great uproar arose from the people on the coach.

"Hello!" said Curtis.

"Hello!" yelled the people on the coach. Mr. Crewe got possession of the horn and produced fragments of the "Lohengrin Wedding March." The people in the street and the hangers-on about the hotel began to gather around.

Her brother waved his hand from the coach. "Well," he said, "how are you getting on? Quarreled yet? I am sorry, but we are completely out of rice."

"I don't understand," said Curtis, looking at the crowd in dismay. "This is a beautiful country, Willie. Historic battle-fields and all that sort of thing; besides, they breed some good horses all about here. We have been picking up one or two."

"For the bride!" called Winthrop, and he generously threw her an enormous bunch of wild roses which Crewe that morning had patiently pulled from the roadside bushes at the cost of no small suffering, and had presented to the elder Appleton girl.

Curtis ignored the episode. His eye at that moment caught a stable-boy leading a big chestnut horse toward the hotel. "Here's one we've just bought," he said. "I think he's likely to make a jumper." He felt his hand, which was behind him, squeezed surreptitiously, and he was aware of beaming somewhat foolishly. He was glad that the people on the coach had turned their attention to the horse.

"Where did you find that?" asked Winthrop.

Curtis hesitated a moment. "Over that way," he said vaguely, waving his hand over an arc which extended from east to west. "It's a great country for horses."

Her brother had been inspecting the horse in silence. "My son," he said to the stable-boy, "how did you gall that race-horse's shoulder?"

"That's a collar-mark," said the boy. "Pulling a street-car is hard work."

Peals of laughter came from the coach.

"You needn't laugh," said the boy. "He's a horse all right."

She had moved to the horse's head. "I believe you," she said to the boy. "He's game."

"He is, ma'am," said the boy.

"Well, Ting-a-ling," said her brother, addressing the chestnut horse, "we can't stop to admire you all day. You're not a bad-looking horse, but if you are a street-car horse, as unfortunately you are, you have the nature that will jump until you get tired, and then you'll roll over things, and make my sister an attractive widow. I wouldn't have you at any price."

"Then everybody is satisfied," said Curtis.

"I am," she said. She gave him a little look that meant that she was satisfied with him, and Curtis felt that he was beaming again. He turned away.

The horse began to rub his nose against her arm and sniffed.

"He's looking for sugar," said the boy. "I give it to him sometimes."

"You are a very nice boy," she said. "What's your name?"

"Tim," said the boy.

"Let's have him take the horse down for us," she said to her husband. "We might keep him, too."

"All right," he said. "But let's get out of this crowd." They slipped away and hurried around the block.

"You were good to get him," she said in a low tone. "The way he acted made me feel that he wasn't meant for street-car work. What shall we call him?"

"I am afraid that brother Willie has already named him," he answered.

"What?" she demanded.

"Ting-a-ling," he replied.

"But he ought to be called Sultan or Emperor, or something like that," she insisted.

"You and I," he said, "we know what a heart he has; but, after all, he *is* a street-car horse. We'd better accept the facts."

"Well, then it's Ting-a-ling," she said.

IT was November; three years had slipped away. The race for the Hunt Club cup was coming off in the afternoon, and everybody was lunching at the club. She was patiently chaperoning the elder Appleton girl and Frank Crewe at a table on the glass-closed veranda overlooking the polo-field.

"We'll give you some lunch," she said to Winthrop, who was passing.

"I'm with Willie," he answered.

"Willie can come too," she said.

He thanked her and sat down.

"Is Ting-a-ling pretty fit?" he asked.

"I think so," she replied; "but of course he's never been steeplechased, so we don't know what he can do."

"He is certainly a good horse to hounds," said Winthrop.

"He's never been down," she said.

"Please don't say that on the day of the race," he interrupted; "it's unlucky."

Just then Willie joined them.

"Still talking steeplechase," he observed. "I suppose your husband is going to win."

"I don't know about that," she answered; "but he'll beat you."

"I'll bet he won't," he retorted. "It's a sure thing. I am not going to ride. They tell me that I am too fat, but that isn't the reason. I am afraid. Hello! here's the steeplechase jockey," he said to Curtis, who came in.

"Have you provided liberally for me in your will? Haven't I always been a good brother-in-law?"

"Always," said Curtis, "and no doubt you need the money; but I am not making wills today."

"You'd better," said Willie, cheerfully. "I'd hate to have that street-car horse roll you out and have no other consolation than the thought that you had loved me." His tone became less playful. "Bequeath me my nephew, and your widow can take the property."

"If that blessed boy of yours," Crewe said to Mrs. Curtis, "isn't ruined by the indulgence of his foolish old uncle, I shall be much surprised."

"*Taisez-vous!*" retorted Willie, "and get a nephew of your own."

Winthrop turned to Curtis. "How has the horse shown in his training?" he asked.

"He rates pretty well, and I have a good deal of confidence in his jumping," Curtis answered. "He's rather a pet, you know, so that perhaps my judgment is prejudiced."

"He'll go until he gets tired," put in Willie, "and then he'll shut up and go through his fences. Those big half-breds are all alike."

"How do you know he's a half-bred?" said Curtis.

"I don't know that he is anything," Willie retorted. "You got him out of a street-car."

"I think we would better change the subject," said his sister; "you're becoming disagreeable. Remember," she added to the party, "you are all coming in this evening to play bridge. You can't come to dinner, because the cook is sick."

FROM the hill back of the club-house they watched the race. A horse of Winthrop's with Crewe up, made the running for the first mile. Then Curtis took Ting-a-ling out of the bunch, and went away apparently without effort. At the two-mile flag Curtis was a hundred yards in the lead. The other horses seemed to be racing for the place.

"He seems to have things all his own way," said Winthrop to Mrs. Curtis. "My horse is done."

"He *is* going well," she whispered. She was very much excited.

Toward the middle of the third mile the four horses that were running in the second flight drew up, and it became a race again. Her heart almost stopped beating. "Is he tiring?" she murmured. The five went at the board fence near the third-mile flag in a bunch. As they took off, there was crowding on the outside. Then four horses jumped cleanly; one fell, and the four went on again.

A rustle of apprehension ran through the crowd.

"Who's down?" exclaimed the elder Appleton girl in a low tone.

"Is he hurt?" said her sister.

"It's Ting-a-ling!" murmured Mrs. Curtis.

The horse got up, and galloped riderless after the leaders. A moment later the rider got up and started across the field on foot.

"He's not hurt," said Winthrop. "I'm awful sorry. He would have won."

"That's good of you," she replied. But she suspected that he was only softening the bitterness of the disappointment. Willie was right. The horse ran himself tired and stopped. She felt that she was very white and made an effort to talk. "That's your horse ahead with Frank Crewe," she said; "he's got the race."

It was so, and the crowd was already surging down to the finish-flags to congratulate the winner. Mrs. Curtis drove her cart across the meadow to meet the dismounted rider.

Their eyes met as she pulled up.

"It's too bad," she said. "Are you hurt?"

"I think my collar-bone is gone," he answered. "I'll see Tim and send the horse home, and then I'll go to the club and get bandaged."

He gave his orders to the boy.

"You was fouled, sir," said Tim. He was much excited. "I seen Mr. Crewe pull across you about two lengths from the fence."

"Not at all," said Curtis, shortly. "Walk him home at once and do him up."

"Is it so?" she asked. "Were you fouled?"

"I don't think I'd say it," he answered. "I rode very badly. It was my fault. I shouldn't have pulled back into the crowd."

She said nothing. She saw that he was very much disappointed. But the hardest for her to bear was that her confidence in Ting-a-ling was gone.

At the club-house Willie was on the veranda.

"I am awfully sorry," he said. "But, seriously, you had better shoot that horse. You'll not be so lucky another time."

Curtis looked up angrily to reply, and then turned away with his lips tightly closed.

"I'll be ready in half an hour," he said to his wife.

In rather less than that time he came from his dressing-room, his arm in bandages and the hand in a sling. He sent for his trap, and found Mrs. Curtis in the tea-room.

"I think we had better go," he said. "They have just telephoned from the house, saying the baby isn't very well. I told the doctor to come along as soon as he could. Don't say anything to Willie about the little chap," he added. "He'll tag along and make a fuss and irritate me."

She rose and followed him. The trap was at the door, and they drove away.

Earlier, the November afternoon had been flooded with a damp sunshine, and there had been a still and unnatural mildness in the air. Toward four, as they left the club, the sky became overcast, and out of the west a mass of blue-black cloud began to rise and stretch across the horizon. Soon it threw the western part of the plain and the hills beyond into darkness. Overhead it was still light, but the shadow drew on and began to chill the day.

Curtis looked apprehensively toward the west and touched the horse with the whip. His wife had the reins.

"It's growing colder," she said.

He bent forward and tucked the robe about her feet.

Uncertain drafts of wind rattled the brown leaves on the oaks and made the dead goldenrods along the roadside bow excitedly.

"I am afraid that we are going to get wet," he said.

The gusts became stronger. The blackness from the west had spread until it was overhead, and light clouds were moving eastwardly across the face of the sky.

"I felt a drop of rain," she observed.

He urged the horse to a gallop.

"So did I," said he a moment later.

"It will be a good night to stay at home and read," he went on. "Don't you think I am getting to be quite a reader? Two books already this month; one of them had three hundred and twelve pages. But there were a good many pictures," he added conscientiously.

She smiled, but said nothing.

He watched her as they drove along. Presently he broke the silence.

"I wouldn't worry about the baby," he said. "Probably he has a little cold or a stomach-ache. The nurse is terrified if he sneezes."

"That's probably all," she said; "you know what a goose I am."

As they turned into the driveway the rain began to pour down. Under the porte-cochère she got out of the trap and went in while he held the horse.

Presently a man came from the stable, and he too went in. He was taking off his coat when his wife came down from the nursery.

"Well?" he asked.

"He's about the same," she answered. "He seems to have a little fever. What time did the doctor say he would be here?"

"About six," said Curtis. He looked at his watch.

"It will be an hour yet. It's begun to snow," he added.

They went to the library, which looked toward the west, and watched the breaking storm.

"It was too bad about Ting-a-ling," she said after a pause.

"Well," he answered, "we have to take things as they come. I should like to have shown what a horse he is. We shall next year."

"I wish you would promise never to ride him in a race again," she said.

"I don't think you ought to ask that," he answered sharply. "For the horse's sake, I want him to have a chance to redeem himself. Don't you?"

"Isn't it wrong to take unnecessary risks?" she replied.

He made no answer.

The rain had changed to sleet, and the ground was already white. The bare elms on the lawn were creaking dismally. They could see the stiff shrubs in the garden bend to the gusts. The storm beat on the window-panes, and in the fierce blasts the house trembled. As they stood by the window, the man brought lighted lamps, and they realized that the night had set in.

"Suppose we have a look at him," he said. By "him" he meant Ting-a-ling. "Won't you come? If the doctor arrives, they can send for us."

"I'd like to," she said.

On the way out, she went to the pantry and took some lumps of sugar.

The stable servants were at supper, and the stable was still except for the sound of the horses munching at their oats. As he drew the door open the grinding hushed except in the two stalls where the phaëton ponies ate stolidly on. The line of dusky heads was lifted and thrust curiously forward. From the box-stall in the corner came a low whinny, and in the dim light of the wall lamp they saw a long neck stretched out and two pointed ears cocked forward. It was Ting-a-ling.

"You beggar!" said Curtis. "You know what we've got." He went into the stall and stripped off the blankets. She followed him. "Hello!" he exclaimed. His arm was nipped gently. "You have very bad manners." The horse drew back, tossed his head, and pawed.

"Look here," Mrs. Curtis said. She held out a piece of sugar. A soft muzzle touched her hand, the lips opened and scraped across her palm, and there was a crunching sound.

"You baby!" she said, and gave him a second piece. "I'm very fond of you," she added under her breath, "in spite—" She stopped.

"He seems to be feeding well," said Curtis.

He put his hand into the manger. It touched the clean, moistened boards of the bottom.

"You're a pig!" he exclaimed. "He's put away five quarts already," he said to his wife. "Doesn't he look fit?"

They drew back and looked the horse over. The legs were clean, the great muscles stood out on forearm and quarter, the flesh was hard and spare.

"He's a great type," said Curtis, "isn't he? But if he were three-cornered I'd like him just as well. I'm ashamed to care so much for him."

"Do you remember the day we got him?" she asked.

He stepped back and put his arm around her.

"It seems yesterday, dear," he said. "How the years go by!" He put back the blankets, and stood a moment fastening the surcingle.

"Barring accidents, old horse," he muttered, "we'll have your name on the cup yet."

A swelling feeling came into his throat, and he put his face against the sleek neck. He straightened up quickly as he heard the doors slide apart and somebody come in.

"Mr. Curtis," called a voice. It was Tim.

"Hello!" said Curtis.

"The doctor's come," said Tim.

"All right," answered Curtis.

He drew his wife's wraps about her, and they made their way back to the house.

The doctor met them at the door of the nursery.

"This child is sick," he said. "The temperature has gone up in a way I don't like. We've got to operate."

"Operate!" Curtis exclaimed. He put his hand upon the banister. "What do you mean?"

"Yes," said the doctor.

"When?" said Mrs. Curtis.

"Lamplight is bad," said the doctor, "but we must do the best we can. It ought to be done before ten o'clock. I should be afraid to wait longer."

Neither husband nor wife spoke. The doctor looked at his watch.

"Whom would you rather have?" he asked.

"Have?" repeated Curtis. A gust rattled the windows at the end of the hall, and as it died away he heard the *tick-tick* of the sleet on the pane. He looked at the doctor with a white face.

"Can't *you* do it?" he asked. "Suppose we couldn't get any one from town by ten o'clock?"

"We must," said the doctor, cheerfully. "I'm not a surgeon, and there is none in the village. Would you rather have Anderson, or Tate?"

"Dr. Anderson," said Mrs. Curtis.

"He must get the train that leaves town at eight

o'clock," said the doctor. "There is no other until midnight."

"It's a quarter past six now," said Curtis. "That gives us just an hour and three quarters. I'll telephone at once." He left the room and went to the telephone.

After some delay the village operator answered.

"You can't get the city," said the girl; "the wires are down. I have been trying to get them for an hour for the telegraph people. Their line is closed, too."

"When do you expect your wires to be repaired?" he asked.

"Can't say," the operator replied. "Not to-night, though. The linemen can't work to-night."

"Thank you," said Curtis. He hung up the receiver and stood blankly before the instrument. He was about to move away when he heard a footstep. He turned, and his wife was standing beside him.

"He'll come," he answered. "I'm going to the sta-
He put a cigarette in his mouth and struck a match.

"Is anything the matter?" she asked. "Won't he come?"

"He'll come," he answered. "I'm going to the station for him myself. I'll dine when I come back. You and the doctor get the things ready." He went into the smoking-room and walked the length of the room and back. "Six miles, ten, fifteen, and six more downtown," he said aloud. He looked at his watch again. It was twenty minutes past six. "Start at half-past," he went on; "that's twenty-one miles in an hour and a quarter—and these roads!" He went to the wall and rang a bell. "Twenty-one miles in an hour and a quarter," he repeated. "Searchlight can't do it, nor Xerxes, nor Huron, nor the roan mare."

A servant appeared.

"Tell Hobson," he said, "to saddle Ting-a-ling at once. Tell him to hurry, and send Tim here."

Tim came, and Curtis explained.

"Can he do it?" asked Curtis.

"I don't know, sir," said the boy.

"He's got to do it," said Curtis. "Do you understand?"

"Yes, sir."

They hurried to the stable, and found Hobson buckling the throat-latch.

"All ready, sir," he said.

Tim climbed into the saddle and gathered up his reins. Then Hobson threw open the door, and the horse and boy clattered out and disappeared in the storm.

Curtis looked at his watch. It was twenty-eight minutes past six. "Have the bus and a pair at the house at eight," he said, and went back to the house.

He met his wife in the hall.

"Is there any change?" he asked.

She shook her head.

"Suppose he should miss the train?" she suggested.

"He won't," said Curtis.

She sighed, and was silent for a pause. "What a wonderful thing the telephone is!" she said. "What would we have done without it?"

"That's so," said Curtis. "I'm going to the station at eight," he added.

At ten minutes of nine she was standing with her face against the window-pane, when the lights of the station bus in the driveway glimmered through the storm. She went to the head of the stairway and waited breathless.

"Suppose," she thought, "he has missed the train!"

Presently there sounded the crunching of wheels on the gravel under the porte-cochère. This meant that the bus was stopping at the house. Then the door opened.

"Come along," said her husband's voice.

"Thank God!" she murmured. She sat down for a moment, and then went to the nursery, which had been made into a hospital.

There was the tramp of ascending feet on the stairs, and then the surgeon and the village doctor came in and asked her to leave the room.

It seemed a long time, but it was only half an hour, when Dr. Anderson came out.

"It's all right," he said.

"What are the chances?" she asked.

"There aren't any," he replied; "that is, perhaps only one in a million—"

She looked alarmed.

"Of anything unpleasant happening," he went on. "We got it just in time. Your son is better off than other boys who wear their appendices. His is in a bottle."

The door-bell sounded faintly from the rear of the house, and they both listened. A moment later the front door opened, and she heard voices in the lower hall.

"They're a lot of people who've come in to play bridge. I'd forgotten about them," she said. "Will you tell them I'll be down presently?"

She went into the nursery, and Dr. Anderson went down-stairs.

When she came down she found them in the dining-room, watching the surgeon and Curtis eating supper, and asking them questions about the operation.

Her eyes caught Willie's. He was quiet and white.

He drew a chair for her, and she sat down next him. She put her hand in his.

"It's all right," she said.

"It was an awfully close shave," he whispered.

"Yes, it was," she answered.

She turned to Dr. Anderson. "You were good to come," she said. "I wonder what we would have done if you hadn't been at home when Mr. Curtis telephoned?"

"Telephone?" he repeated.

Curtis got up and went to the sideboard for a whisky-decanter.

"Yes, telephone," she said.

The surgeon looked at Curtis.

"Mary," said Curtis, "the telephone wires were down. Tim went to town for the doctor."

She looked around in amazement.

"But we didn't know till nearly half-past six," she exclaimed. She turned to Dr. Anderson. "You caught the eight o'clock train. How did Tim go?"

"On horseback," said Curtis.

"But that's twenty miles!" said Willie.

"Twenty-one," said Curtis; "he went in an hour and a quarter."

There was a silence for a moment. Then she spoke.

"What horse did he ride?" she demanded.

"What horse have we that could have done it?" replied Curtis.

She looked at him for a moment in apprehension. "Is he all right?" she asked.

"I don't know," said Curtis. "Tim came back by train."

"Send for Tim," she said to the butler.

Tim came, and stood fumbling with his cap, which was soggy with melted snow.

"Weren't you frozen?" she asked.

"No, ma'am," the boy answered.

"Tell me about it," she said.

"Tell about it?" repeated the boy. "Why, ma'am——" He grew confused and stopped.

"But tell me——" she hesitated, and her lip trembled—"tell me how Ting-a-ling is."

The boy made no answer, but looked toward the surgeon.

She turned to Dr. Anderson. "What is it?" she demanded.

"I was starting out to dine," said the surgeon, "when a policeman came to the door and said there was a sick horse on the corner, and a boy with him who wanted to see me. I went and found them both there."

"Well?" said Mrs. Curtis.

"Well," said the doctor, "as I reached the corner the cross-town trolley-car was letting off a passenger. When the bell rang to start, the horse in the street lifted his head, scrambled to his feet, staggered a step forward, and came down again. He was dead."

There was a stillness in the room, and the crying of a sick baby sounded faintly from up-stairs. Presently it ceased. For an instant the wife's eyes met those of her husband. Then resting her elbows on the table, she hid her face in her hands.

"God forgive me!" they heard Willie murmur in a queer voice. "That *was* a horse!"

"A street-car horse," said Curtis gently.

No one spoke again, but each rose and left the dining-room.

THE BRAYBROOKE BABY'S GODMOTHER

V

THE BRAYBROOKE BABY'S GODMOTHER

THE bishop put on his glasses and wandered down the car, consulting a ticket and examining the numbers on the revolving-chairs.

"Good morning," said a voice.

He looked down and saw Miss Henrietta Cushing.

"Why, how do you do?" said the bishop, smiling. "This *is* a pleasant surprise." He held up his ticket hopelessly. "Can you help me?" he asked. "I can't make out this number. It might be a nine or a seven or a six."

"Pay no attention to the number," said Miss Cushing; "if the officers of this railway cannot write legibly they must take the consequences. Sit down next to me, and I shall not permit them to turn you out."

"I shall do that," said the bishop, gratefully, and he sat down.

Miss Cushing lived a few doors from the bishop in Gramercy Park, and they were old friends as well as neighbors. She was a little woman. Her hair, parted in the middle and drawn smoothly down in the fashion of another generation, was streaked with gray; but it was thick, and her brow was smooth, her gray eyes were bright, and there was a tinge of pink in her cheeks. She was dressed simply in black, but her clothes were very well made, as women observed, and there was always a remarkable piece of lace about her neck. She was rich even for these days.

Miss Cushing was cousin to most of the distinguished New Yorkers of the days before the plutocracy, but she had no immediate family, and she lived by herself in seclusion. Like many women who have never married, she had elaborate theories in regard to the discipline and bringing up of young children, and spoiled all those with whom she came into contact by a too indulgent tenderness. Her liking for babies amounted to a passion, and she gave large sums secretly to charities of which infants were the beneficiaries. Her dominant feeling, however, was her sympathy for the sufferings of defenseless animals. She gave not only her money for this cause, but her time also, and served on the executive committee of the council of the society.

The bishop settled himself in the chair next to Miss Cushing and relaxed his great frame. A sigh of relief and comfort escaped him.

"I hurried," he said; "I was afraid that I was going to be late."

"Are you on pleasure bent," asked Miss Cushing, "or is this work?"

"There are some duties," replied the bishop, "which are so pleasant as to escape from the category of work by their very nature. It is one of these which is taking me to Oakdale. You see——" he continued, but Miss Cushing interrupted him.

"Oakdale!" she exclaimed. "It must be a great trial and mortification to you to have that place in your diocese." She looked at him with eyes full of sympathy.

"Why?" said the bishop.

"Why?" repeated Miss Cushing. "Have you never been there? Have you never heard of their practices?"

"Practices?" said the bishop.

"Yes," said Miss Cushing; "barbarous practices."

The bishop looked perplexed. "I have been there," he said; "I have been there a good deal. At first the interest in horses and sport rather astonished me,—it is a hunting community,—but——" the bishop hesitated.

"Exactly," said Miss Cushing, showing a gleam of white teeth and then closing her lips very tight; "a fox-hunting community. You are a bishop, and you have been the president of a fellow-society to ours. Do you think it humane or Christian," she continued, "to pursue God's defenseless creatures for hours, yes, for days, till they fall exhausted in the mouths of ravening hounds?"

The bishop looked thoughtfully at Miss Cushing. "Do they do that?" he asked. "Are you sure of your facts?"

"Oh, quite," she replied. She opened a little bag and produced a roll of newspaper clippings inclosed in an elastic band. Removing the band, she flattened out the slips and arranged them for reference.

"Here," she began, "is the interview with a veteran fox-chaser in which he tells about a dog which chased a fox for five days and nights. What do you think of a man who would boast of such a deed?"

"I should think," answered the bishop slowly, "that he was a liar."

"Quite so," said Miss Cushing, who did not catch the bishop's meaning. "He must be depraved."

"But this account," said the bishop, "refers to the South. I am sure that at Oakdale the hunts last but a few hours, and I recall some one telling me that the only fox which they have killed in three years they happened on in a farmer's poultry-yard as they were coming home."

"They have deceived you," said Miss Cushing. "It is very natural. Look!" she continued. She held out a dozen short clippings. "These are recent accounts of the hunts at Oakdale, not the South. In each one it mentions by name the persons who were '*in at the death.*' The death, you understand, means the death of the fox." She selected a clipping and began to read. It concluded: " 'The hounds finished at Smith's Corners. At the death were—' " Miss Cushing stopped as she read the first name, a woman's. "I suppose you know who that is?" she said to the bishop. "What would Tilly say if she knew that her daughter had married into that set, and was watching the death-agonies of a creature that never did any one harm? Our work in the streets and slums is difficult enough as it is; but when the daughters of one's friends are offenders too, it is somewhat discouraging."

"Yes," said the bishop; "your work is not only a good but a difficult one. However," he added, "I believe that the expression 'in at the death' must be used figuratively, because I have heard that all last spring the club hunted nothing but drags."

Miss Cushing looked at him in surprise.

"That is exactly what the club wrote to our secretary!" she exclaimed. "And what pained me very much was that the letter was signed by young James Braybrooke. You know," she added, "that his mother, till her death, was my dear friend."

"Well," said the bishop, somewhat sharply, "why should you be pained by the fact that *he* signed the letter! It said that they had been hunting a drag, just as I told you."

Miss Cushing looked at the bishop in amazement. "Bishop Cunningham," she exclaimed, "your course is a matter for your own conscience, but I shall never consent to make flesh of one and fish of another. While I am in the council, our society shall protect drags as well as foxes."

"Drags as well as foxes?" repeated the bishop.

"Yes," said Miss Cushing, with emphasis.

The bishop looked at her, utterly at a loss. Then a light broke upon him and his face softened.

"Ah, yes," he said mildly; "do you know what a drag is?"

"It is a small creature," Miss Cushing replied. "I have never seen one, as I disapprove of menageries; but I presume that it belongs to the fox family."

"You say that you have never seen one?" observed the bishop.

"Yes," said Miss Cushing; "I have never seen one, but that is not a reason why our society should suffer them to be tortured. It is high time that a stand was taken, when people of our class amuse themselves with cruelty to drags. And I am going to Oakdale to investigate the matter myself and bring the offenders to justice."

"Good!" said the bishop. Then he seized his newspaper and disappeared behind it till a fit of violent coughing should pass away. His massive body shook and Miss Cushing became alarmed. She called the porter. "Bring some water to Bishop Cunningham," she said.

Before the water arrived the bishop had recovered.

"I beg your pardon very humbly," he said; "these attacks come on, and there seems no way of stopping them."

"There is a troche," she said, "which is admirable for bronchial irritation; I cannot recall the name, but I shall send you a package."

"You are very good to me," said the bishop. He wiped his eye-glasses with his handkerchief and settled himself. "So that is your errand to Oakdale?" he began, the corners of his mouth twitching anew.

"Is it coming on again?" inquired Miss Cushing, anxiously.

"I don't think so," said the bishop. He cleared his throat and shut his mouth with a grim expression. Then he turned to his newspaper again. "I'll glance at the morning news," he said, "if you will excuse me."

When the train stopped at Oakdale, the bishop helped Miss Cushing to the station platform, and spoke to a liveried servant who was waiting there to take his bag.

"The trap will drive up, sir," said the man, "as soon as the train pulls out." He said this as he noticed Miss Cushing apparently looking about for a vehicle.

"Are there no cabs here?" asked Miss Cushing, in a tone of surprise.

"No, madam," said the man.

"Haven't you arranged for some one to meet you?" asked the bishop. "You see, the village is two miles farther on, and nobody gets off here except people who are going over toward the club, and those usually arrange to be met."

"Dear me!" said Miss Cushing. "I wonder what I shall do."

"Oh," said the bishop, "you will come over with me."

"That is very kind of you," said Miss Cushing, "and in the circumstances I am afraid that I shall have to trespass upon your kindness."

As the train moved away, a smart-looking pair of horses and a two-seated trap came up to the platform.

"Here we are," said the bishop, gaily, and he helped Miss Cushing in. "This is much better than a cab, and if we are not run away with or shied into a ditch, we shall arrive at the club in half the time in which a livery vehicle would have taken us."

"Yes," said Miss Cushing, "it really has turned out very well."

Just then the footman turned around and spoke to the bishop.

"I beg your pardon, sir; I forgot to tell you that Mr. Braybrooke sent his apologies for not meeting you himself, but there was an unexpected party of gentlemen—" Here the off horse shied at something invisible to man, and nearly succeeded in crowding the near one over a culvert. The footman's attention was occupied in holding on, and when the danger had been averted he had no opportunity for continuing.

"Mr. Braybrooke!" exclaimed Miss Cushing to the bishop. "Are these James Braybrooke's horses? Am I riding in his carriage?" Her tone expressed both horror and indignation.

"Well," said the bishop, "you couldn't stop at the station all day, and it is too far to walk."

"No matter how far it was," said Miss Cushing. "I certainly should have walked, and I shall walk now."

"You will do nothing of the kind," said the bishop, mildly.

"But you must see," said Miss Cushing, "that this

is improper. I have not seen James Braybrooke since he was a baby; yet, for his mother's sake, I would save him from public disgrace if he would abandon his practices. However, I am investigating a case against him, and I cannot accept the hospitality of his carriage."

"Would it not be judicial to suspend judgment until you have investigated?" suggested the bishop.

"Stop the carriage!" demanded Miss Cushing. "I am going to walk."

"From the next hill," said the bishop, "one gets quite the best view of the neighboring country." He put his hand on Miss Cushing's as if to say, "Hush, my child!"

There was no answer to make. Miss Cushing said nothing, but her mouth straightened at the corners. They drove in silence for a few minutes, and then they passed the stone gateway of a country house, and presently the brick one of another.

"Are we very nearly there?" asked Miss Cushing.

"Yes," said the bishop; "I was just about to ask you with whom you were going to stop."

"I shall go to the hotel for lunch," she said; "but I am going to see a woman who lives near the club." She opened her bag and produced a letter. "A Mrs. Patrick Hennessey," she continued.

"I do not recall any such name," the bishop said. "Does the lady belong to your association?"

"No," said Miss Cushing; "but she intends to join, and she is much in sympathy with us."

"Oh, I see," said the bishop. "This is how you got your information."

Miss Cushing looked at him doubtfully. "I ought not to have told you this," she said, "because all complaints are treated as confidential. You will say nothing about it, will you?"

"Assuredly not," said the bishop.

At this moment there appeared a young man on a polo pony, riding toward them. The bishop waved his hand to him, and the young man waved his hat in reply. As the trap came up to him he turned and rode beside it.

"Miss Cushing," said the bishop, "may I present Mr. Braybrooke?"

Miss Cushing bowed stiffly, and Mr. Braybrooke took off his hat again.

"Miss Cushing has come down—" began the bishop.

"We are very glad to see her," interrupted Mr. Braybrooke. "I think," he continued, speaking to Miss Cushing, "that you were a great friend of my mother's."

Miss Cushing bowed again.

"I saw you as you came over the hill," Braybrooke said to the bishop; "we've been having some gymkhanas on the lawn. I am afraid," he added apologetically, "that they are about over."

"That is too bad," said the bishop; "it would have been interesting to see them."

"Perhaps," said Braybrooke, "we can get up an extra race or two, but it is pretty nearly time for lunch. Are you interested in sports?" he asked Miss Cushing. As he spoke they turned into a gateway and rolled up a long private drive.

"Don't think of having anything on my account," said Miss Cushing, "because I could not stop; I really must be going on."

"Why?" said Braybrooke, with a shade of disappointment in his tone. "I hoped that you had come down with Bishop Cunningham to stop the day with us."

"That's very kind of you," said Miss Cushing, uncomfortably, "but I couldn't think of it." She resolved to blurt out the truth. "You see," she began, "I've—"

"Oh, I see," said Braybrooke; "you are lunching with some one else. Where can I send you?"

"This is most embarrassing," said Miss Cushing. "There was no cab at the station, and Bishop Cunningham insisted—"

"Of course," said Braybrooke. "I really wish you would stop with us; but if you are engaged for lunch, the trap will take you over."

Miss Cushing looked helplessly at the bishop.

"You would better stay to lunch," said the bishop.

"You really must," said Braybrooke, "if you have no other engagement."

"No, I couldn't think of that," said Miss Cushing; "but if you could tell me how to get to the nearest hotel in the village I should be very grateful."

Braybrooke looked perplexed, and made no reply.

"If it is any trouble—" said Miss Cushing, quickly.

"It would be no trouble," said Braybrooke, "but there isn't any hotel. I might send you over to the club," he added, "but I don't think that ladies lunch at the club alone. I'll ask Mrs. Braybrooke."

The conversation was interrupted by their arrival at the house. The bishop waved to Mrs. Braybrooke, who was on the veranda to meet them. "We have arrived, my dear," he said, and patted her hand affectionately. "Let me present you to Miss Cushing. She is my very dear friend."

Mrs. Braybrooke smiled. "It is very nice of you to come with the bishop," she said to Miss Cushing, "and it was very nice of him to come, too. This is a great event for us." She smiled again.

A pang of shame pierced Miss Cushing. "What shall I do?" she asked herself. Before an answer came the bishop handed her out upon the veranda.

"You are very good," she said abjectly to Mrs. Braybrooke. She looked at the bishop, but his gaze was directed across the lawn, where there was a tent and a group of men in boots and breeches.

"If you will excuse me a moment," said Braybrooke, "I'll see if we can get up another race." He left the veranda.

"And if you will excuse *me*," said Mrs. Braybrooke, "I shall see if we are not soon going to have lunch; you must be famished." As she spoke she disappeared into the house.

But Miss Cushing knew that it was not to find out when lunch was to be served, but to order an extra place made at the lunch-table. She turned to the bishop.

"I can't—I can't stop and lunch in their house," she gasped.

The bishop looked at her mildly.

"I must explain at once," she went on. "How can I eat the bread of people whom it is my duty to prosecute at law? People whose hands are stained—"

"Wait a minute," interrupted the bishop. "I thought that you had come down here to investigate."

"But the articles!" exclaimed Miss Cushing, clutching the bag in which they were stowed away. "Can you have any real doubt? And then the statements of Mrs. Hennessey."

"But," said the bishop, calmly, "if you are going to make a personal investigation, you ought to make it. Don't you think so?"

"But it can only confirm what we already know," she said helplessly.

"Very well," said the bishop. "What are you going to do?"

"Exactly!" exclaimed Miss Cushing. "What *am* I going to do? Can't you suggest something? If I had not got into that carriage—" she stopped. She was too high-minded to intimate that it was his fault.

The bishop regarded her and deliberated. "Henrietta," he began firmly, "in past years you have had the experience of a woman of the world, and you know that you have no moral right to make a scene or to injure the feelings of others. It is not for me to say what you should do, but I would suggest that you accept the situation until you can escape from it with decency."

"Do you think," demanded Miss Cushing, "that it is right for me to lunch with people whom I propose to prosecute in the courts?"

"What else is there to do?" replied the bishop.

At that moment Mrs. Braybrooke appeared from the house. She spoke to Miss Cushing. "You must come with me," she said; "I want you to see the baby."

"The baby?" repeated Miss Cushing. ("Is there a baby?" she said to herself.)

"Why, yes," said Mrs. Braybrooke, rather at a loss.

"Of course," said Miss Cushing. "I want to see it"; and she followed Mrs. Braybrooke in.

Braybrooke came back as they disappeared. "I suppose," he said to the bishop, in an undertone, "that Miss Cushing didn't expect that we would be having people to lunch, and feels embarrassed. It was awfully nice of her to come down."

"I don't think she did expect to find a party," the bishop replied.

"You see," said Braybrooke, "I feel that it is a good deal for Miss Cushing to come down here just to be present at the baby's christening."

"You are quite right," said the bishop; "but there is somebody coming to announce lunch."

As they took their places in the dining-room the bishop observed that Miss Cushing wore a softer expression and that there was a mild light in her gray eyes. He smiled.

"I am very sorry," said Braybrooke,—Miss Cushing was sitting upon his right,—"that we couldn't get up a race for you. But, you see, the men were hungry and were cross as beasts. Besides, they had sent their horses to be cooled out. But perhaps," he continued, "later, after the show, we can get up something."

"*After the show?*" repeated Miss Cushing, inquiringly.

"I ought to have said after the ceremony," said Braybrooke, apologizing. "I'm awfully careless."

"Oh, the ceremony!" exclaimed Miss Cushing. "Oh, I understand." ("*The ceremony*," she repeated to herself. "What ceremony? What kind of party have I come upon?")

"By the way, did you see it?" asked Braybrooke. He nodded his head upward.

Miss Cushing looked at him inquiringly.

"The baby," he said.

"Oh, yes," said Miss Cushing; "he is charming."

"Whom do you think he looks like?" Braybrooke demanded.

"You," replied Miss Cushing; "he is very like you."

Braybrooke grinned. "I think so, too," he said; "but they say I'm conceited to think so."

Miss Cushing smiled. "He seems fond of the child,"

she said to herself. "He is very like his mother. It is hard to believe that he pursues little drags to death." This reflection recalled her mission, and made her miserable again until Willie Colfax, who sat upon her other hand, engaged her in conversation.

"Do you ride much?" inquired Mr. Colfax, blandly.

Braybrooke, who overheard, shot him an annoyed glance. He knew that his brother-in-law was preparing to sell a horse.

"Each afternoon that is fine," said Miss Cushing, "I go to the park in my victoria."

"I know," observed Mr. Colfax, "but do you ride much? Have you any saddle-horses?"

Miss Cushing looked at him suspiciously, but his expression was sweet and innocent.

"I used to ride when I was a girl," she said, "but that was a long time ago."

Mr. Colfax regarded her incredulously. "You ought to keep it up," he said. "I believe in enjoying things while we can. Still," he continued, "one can get a great deal of pleasure out of a good harness-horse, too. I have rather a good one."

"Really," said Miss Cushing. "I should like to see it. I am fond of horses."

"I'll show him to you," said Mr. Colfax, politely.

Here Braybrooke interrupted him, and the subject was changed.

Miss Cushing enjoyed the lunch-party in spite of her qualms of conscience. It was different from any that she could remember. At times it was rather noisy, but she thought it entertaining. Mr. Colfax's suggestion that she take a place at Oakdale was, of course, out of the question, but it was pleasant to have people express kind wishes. She liked Mr. Colfax.

When lunch was over she had an opportunity to speak to the bishop.

"They have been talking about some ceremony that is to take place," she said. "Do you know what it is?"

The bishop looked surprised. "Haven't you heard?" he said. "They are going to baptize the child."

"And is that what you came down for?" Miss Cushing demanded.

"Yes," replied the bishop.

"But why didn't you tell me?" said Miss Cushing.

"You didn't ask me," the bishop answered.

Miss Cushing looked about her anxiously, and drew a long breath. "I *must* slip away," she said. "Even if I have lunched with these people, I cannot intrude into the circle invited to be present on a solemn occasion of this kind. Besides, I must find Mrs. Hennessey. Yes, I must slip away," she continued. "Directly I get home I shall write and explain, and I do wish that you would write, too."

"I shall write anything you wish," replied the bishop. "However, I don't see how you are going to 'slip away.'"

Miss Cushing looked furtively about, as if considering an exit by one of the windows, when Mrs. Braybrooke approached and spoke to her.

"Do you mind driving to the church with my brother, Mr. Colfax?" she asked. "If you have the least objection, don't hesitate to say so," she continued, "because I don't mind telling him that you can't go. But he asked, as a great favor, to be allowed to take you."

Miss Cushing looked at the bishop. His face was expressionless. She gave a nervous little laugh. "Of course I haven't the *least* objection," she said. "I am much flattered."

"That's so good of you," said Mrs. Braybrooke, with her delightful smile. "It will please Willie, and it will be perfectly safe, because he has Planet." She turned and left them.

Miss Cushing stood facing the bishop. Her bosom heaved, but she said nothing. At first it seemed as if the bishop were about to speak; then his mouth shut tightly.

At this juncture Mr. Colfax appeared.

"My cart is here," he said to Miss Cushing, and bowed.

Without a word Miss Cushing followed. From the veranda she climbed over an enormous wheel, and found herself driving to the church in a primrose-yellow dog-cart behind Planet, who, with extra heavy shoes, was performing showily. She fell to thinking about the situation.

"He's not bad-looking, is he?" began Mr. Colfax.

"I beg your pardon?" said Miss Cushing, aroused from her thoughts.

Mr. Colfax repeated the question.

"He has reference to the baby, I presume," thought Miss Cushing. "He's a sweet dear," she replied.

"He is," said Mr. Colfax; "and though that splint on his off fore leg is conspicuous, he's never gone sore with it. A good blister would take it off."

Miss Cushing looked at him in horror. Then she appreciated that there had been a misunderstanding, and held her peace. As they pulled up in the village street before the church, Mr. Colfax was still discussing Planet, his breeding, conformation, and manners; but it was all lost upon Miss Cushing. During the last ten minutes she had been formulating an artifice which promised to save her from committing the quasi-sacrilege that was imminent. The afternoon was warm, and she planned to linger in the vestibule until all had gone into the church, under the pretext of a headache, which the close air indoors would aggravate. The church inside, as a matter of fact, was damp and pleasantly cool, not having been opened for several days; but well-bred people do not insist too much upon facts.

Miss Cushing's artifice promised success. The entire party passed in together, and no one urged her to enter. Only Mr. Colfax remained outside, raptly watching Planet's action as the groom drove him up and down the village street. But Miss Cushing knew that Mr. Colfax was to be the godfather, and she felt that he, too, would come in a reasonable time before the ceremony was to begin.

To avoid being seen from the street, she withdrew into a corner of the vestibule close to the leather swinging-doors which opened into one of the side aisles. Here she stood, ready to assume an attitude of entering, when, to her alarm, she heard voices of people approaching from the inside. The owners of the voices stopped, apparently close to the doors, and began a conference.

"What did the man say?" she heard a woman's voice demand. She recognized the speaker as Mrs. Braybrooke.

"He said that her leader ran away and smashed things up," a man's voice answered. The man's voice was Braybrooke's.

"Well, couldn't she have come in another trap?" Mrs. Braybrooke demanded.

"The man said that they went into a ditch and put her shoulder out," replied Braybrooke.

"What a pity!" said Mrs. Braybrooke. "Poor Kitty will be laid up again for the hunting."

"That must be the Kitty," said Miss Cushing to herself, "who was going to be godmother." A feeling of relief came over her. "They'll postpone it," she thought.

"Yes," said Braybrooke, on the other side of the doors; "it will very likely lay her up. I wonder if she hurt her horses. Her leader was that mare she was going to sell Mr. Heminway for Anita."

"Well," said Mrs. Braybrooke, "I'm sorry for Kitty, but what are *we* going to do?"

"You might ask Jane to take her place," suggested Braybrooke.

"If I do that," Mrs. Braybrooke replied, "Emily and Josephine will both think it strange that I didn't ask them."

"But you can't ask them all," said Braybrooke. "Haven't they any sense?"

Mrs. Braybrooke ignored his question. "I wish I knew what to do," she said helplessly. "There was, of course, a special reason for having Kitty, but—" She stopped. "It would be much easier," she continued, "to have somebody whom Josephine and Emily and Jane didn't know at all. I wish I could get Sally Thompson here from Washington."

"It's all right to wish," said Braybrooke, "but we've got to get a godmother. The bishop is waiting."

"It's all right for you to say we've got to get somebody," said Mrs. Braybrooke, "but whom can we get?"

"Well," said Braybrooke, "if you want somebody outside of our own crowd, it is easy to choose, because there is only one such here."

For the moment Miss Cushing's heart stopped beating. It was like the age-long moment of a nightmare.

"It was awfully civil of her to come down with the bishop," she heard Braybrooke continue, "just because she was an old friend of my mother's; and if we explained the thing she would probably help us out."

"It was very sweet of her," said Mrs. Braybrooke; "but she has never known *us*, and she might think it was indelicate."

"I don't think so," said Braybrooke. "We didn't think it was indelicate of her to come down without an invitation, did we?"

"No," said Mrs. Braybrooke; "we took it as a compliment."

"She would take it as a compliment, too," Braybrooke replied. "Anyway, it's like being asked to be a groomsman or pall-bearer; one can't refuse."

Miss Cushing heard no more, because she had fled to the church door. In the doorway stood Mr. Colfax, exhaling a last puff from his cigarette.

"Where are you going?" he inquired. "Is anything the matter?"

"Nothing," said Miss Cushing. "I thought it would be cooler outside."

"I think you are mistaken," said Mr. Colfax; "it is much cooler in the church. I haven't been in yet, but I know. It's awfully hot in the street. Are you feeling ill?"

"Well," said Miss Cushing, vaguely, "you see, I don't feel exactly ill." She paused.

"I'm sorry," said Mr. Colfax, sympathetically. "I'd better tell Mrs. Braybrooke."

"Oh, don't!" exclaimed Miss Cushing. "Please don't!"

"But," said Mr. Colfax, "my sister would be angry with me if I didn't."

"Oh," said Miss Cushing, "I feel very much better. In fact, I feel quite well."

Mr. Colfax looked at her with polite doubt, but she made a gesture of protest.

"Then," said he, "shall we go in?"

Miss Cushing did not answer him, because the leather doors opened into the vestibule and Mr. and Mrs. Braybrooke came through them.

"I say," said Braybrooke, "we've been hunting everywhere for you two."

Miss Cushing folded her hands and waited in silence.

"I was just coming in," said Mr. Colfax, and he threw away his cigarette.

When Miss Cushing arrived at the Braybrookes' house after the ceremony, Mr. Colfax handed her out of the cart.

"I think we are a pretty fine team at a christening," he observed.

Miss Cushing smiled in a dazed sort of way and nodded her head. She looked toward the bishop, who was standing in the doorway. The bishop caught her look, but pretended not to, and disappeared into the house. He did not feel that he had anything to say at that moment which would be helpful.

Miss Cushing went into the house, too, in a mechanical way. Her ideas and feelings were so confused that she had no ideas left, and her feelings were rapidly reaching the point of outburst. In fact, she did not know whether to laugh or cry, and she was ready to do either. Inside everybody was gathering in the big library, and she could see the servants bringing trays on which were champagne-glasses. Mr. Colfax followed her and found a chair for her, and presently she was surrounded by a group of men. Besides Mr. Colfax were Mr. Carteret, Mr. Varick, and other members of the hunt. The bishop and Braybrooke, who were passing, stopped and joined the circle.

"There is the greater responsibility upon Miss Cushing," Mr. Carteret was saying, "because so little can be expected from the infant's godfather."

Miss Cushing did not have to reply, because everybody laughed, even Mr. Colfax.

"Then you ought to come down soon," Mr. Colfax said to Miss Cushing, "and begin your work. It might amuse you to come down next Monday. We run a drag. Have you ever seen a drag hunt?"

Miss Cushing stiffened up in her chair. The opportunity for her to declare herself and satisfy her conscience had come.

"Mr. Colfax," she said solemnly, "do you believe it right to pursue a harmless little animal with fierce hounds?"

A heavy silence hung over the room.

"Animal?" said Mr. Colfax.

"Yes," said Miss Cushing; "I said animal."

"But it's a drag," said Mr. Colfax aghast.

"You intimate that a drag is not an animal. Please explain," said Miss Cushing.

Then Mr. Colfax explained. The men shut their mouths tightly, and each looked straight ahead of him at some selected point on the opposite wall.

In the silence that followed after Mr. Colfax had finished, the people in the room heard Miss Cushing murmur to herself, "Well, well, well!"

She said nothing else.

After a pause the bishop began to speak. "Miss Cushing," he said, "is very tender-hearted, and when she reads in the newspapers of drag-hunting, and notes the list of those who are 'in at the death,' her heart is full of pity and sympathy for what she had quite naturally supposed to be an animate quarry. Moreover, she is an officer of a very admirable society for the prevention of cruelty to dumb creatures, and it is her duty to interfere whenever she may chance to observe it. Hence this misapprehension."

Braybrooke made a low exclamation. "Miss Cushing," he said, "I really am awfully glad to find this out."

Miss Cushing looked at him inquiringly. "Why?" she said.

"Because I have a case for you," he replied. "You see, our laundress at the kennels poured a kettle of hot water over one of the hounds."

"Atrocious!" exclaimed Miss Cushing. "Give me her name!"

"I don't want her punished," said Braybrooke, "but I want her prevented from doing it again. Can your society do that? You see, she sometimes drinks too much."

"I shall have our agent sent down at once," said Miss Cushing. "Give me her name."

"She is a Mrs. Hennessey," said Braybrooke; "I think Patrick is her husband's name."

"Hennessey!" exclaimed Miss Cushing.

"Yes," Braybrooke replied.

At this moment the circle of men parted to admit Mrs. Braybrooke.

"You mustn't monopolize *all* the men," she said, with a smile, to Miss Cushing. "Besides——" She stopped and half turned as the rattle of glasses on the metal tray sounded behind her.

"I say," said Willie Colfax, "I think you people ought to drink the health of the godparents."

"I think," said the bishop, "that it would be eminently proper to toast the godmother, particularly as the circumstances, I might say, are somewhat unusual."

"They prove," observed Braybrooke, quite reverently, "that the Lord will provide, don't they?"

"They do," said the bishop. Then they drank Miss Cushing's health.

"And now," said Miss Cushing, beaming, "I propose a toast to my godson. I neglected to bring his porringer with me, but I shall attend to that later." And they drank that toast, too.

A servant approached the bishop and spoke a few words in a whisper.

"Henrietta," said the bishop, "it seems that we must rush for our train. The carriage has been waiting some time."

They hurried out in a confusion of handshakings and got into the trap.

"Good-by, everybody!" cried Miss Cushing, and they all answered "Good-by," and waved their hands, except Mr. Colfax, who stood on the veranda with a bottle of champagne, and called after them: "Come back! You've forgotten to drink to the godfather!"

When the trap turned into the highway, the bishop looked thoughtfully at Miss Cushing. "Well," he said, "you have discovered a case."

Miss Cushing shot him a quiet glance, and gazed off over the pasture-lands, on which stretched the long afternoon shadows of the elms.

The bishop saw that she was smiling, and made no reply. He, too, looked off over the meadows.

THE ECHO HUNT

VI

THE ECHO HUNT

WHARTON came in from the stables, and met his wife in the hallway. He stopped and smiled.

"There's a great game on out there," he said, making a gesture toward the terrace behind the house.

"The children?" she asked.

He nodded. "It's something that has developed since I've been away—hunters and hounds and steeple-chasers. You ought to see Bub," he added.

"Is he bad?" she asked.

"I suppose so," said Wharton; "but that wasn't what I meant. It's his costume. He's magnificent."

She smiled.

"Do you know where they have picked up their horse-talk?" he went on.

"I suppose from Williams and the men at the stables," she answered.

He shook his head.

"I don't think so," he said. "They have a lot of English expressions that no one about here uses. Williams never took care of hunters before he came to us."

"Then I don't know," she said; "they haven't used them before me. Are they still at it?"

"I fancy so," he replied. "Come and see. We can watch them from behind the kitchen lattice."

She threw a golf-cape over her shoulders and followed him. There were three children on the terrace, surrounded with the sticks, the fragments of things, the broken tops that furnish the child's play-world. In the center was a hurdle made of three laths which were supported at the ends with bricks.

"They seem to be schooling over that jump," whispered Wharton. "Look at your baby."

Bub, who was mounted on a broom-handle, was galloping in circles, apparently warming up for a go at the hurdle. Over his normal clothes he wore what seemed to be a square of red flannel, in which a hole had been cut for the head. It was belted at the waist with a strap, and was trimmed off above the knees to give the effect of a huntsman's coat. His feet were in his own rubber boots, which, however, were adorned with brown-paper tops. From the ankle of one dangled a rusty spur. On his head, or rather inclosing his head, was a man's cork polo-helmet.

"Where do you suppose he got those things?" said Mrs. Wharton.

"Give it up," said Wharton. "Probably the coat is Elinora's handiwork. He's an M. F. H., or something, turned out in pink."

"Hush!" whispered Mrs. Wharton. The two older children were talking.

"It's my turn," said Elinora. She was mounted astride a small spotted rocking-horse from which the rockers had disappeared.

"But truly, Elinora," said John, "Shamrock isn't up to your weight." John looked at the rocking-horse and then at Elinora. "I don't think," he observed doubtfully, "that that horse would carry thirteen stone to hounds."

"Thirteen stone!" whispered Wharton. "Did you hear?"

"Yes, he would," replied Elinora. "Didn't he take the prize at the Dublin show?"

John still looked doubtful. "Let me go first," he said.

"No," said Elinora; "it's my turn."

"Well," said John, "but please be careful this time, and don't drag your hind legs."

He looked apprehensively at the rocking-horse and then at the hurdle.

"I'll try," said Elinora.

"I'll take a rail off," suggested John.

The top lath was a foot from the ground.

"No; don't!" said Elinora.

She seized her mount by mane and tail, and after a few preliminary rearings and curvets, cantered cautiously at the obstacle, checked, lifted the fore legs over, and then leaped with her own. However, when she raised the rocking-horse's front legs it depressed those behind. There was the sound of tumbling bricks. The hurdle was wrecked.

"Oh, Elinora!" said John, sadly. "Whirlwind could have jumped it."

"I am sorry," said Elinora.

But Bob only yelled and made his broomstick prance.

"Destruction appeals to Bubby," whispered his father behind the lattice.

"He's only six," said Mrs. Wharton.

"I told you," said John, mournfully, as he set to repairing the hurdle, "Shamrock is too green, or something. You've put a leg on him. You'd better do it up in wet blandages."

"*Bandages*," said Elinora, "not *blandages*."

She became absorbed in examining the legs of the rocking-horse, and John restored the hurdle.

"Do you really think," inquired Elinora, "that we ought to do his leg up?"

John rode over and laid his mount on the ground. It was a stick with a wooden horse's head on the end of it. Then he gravely ran his hand down the rocking-horse's hind legs.

"There's fever in them," he said. "I really think he ought to be fired," he added, with more interest. "Let's do it with matches."

"No," said Elinora; "it's cruel." She looked regretfully at some charred marks which a piece of red-hot barrel hoop had made on Shamrock's front legs.

John picked up his mount. "I wish Whirlwind had legs," he observed; "but he added resignedly, "he can beat you, and he can jump higher, too."

"There's the bandages," said Elinora. She produced a dust-cloth, tore it in strips, and gave one of them to John.

"You do the other leg," she said.

"That's why the parlor-maid's dust-cloths have been disappearing," whispered Mrs. Wharton.

"No," said John; "I haven't time. I've got to jump Whirlwind."

He turned away and began a preliminary gallop before going at the hurdle.

Bub had watched the treatment of Shamrock's legs till John turned away; then facing his broomstick at the jump, he charged it, took off too far away, floundered through the laths, and rolled over on his head.

Mrs. Wharton started, but her husband caught her arm.

"He's not hurt," he said.

"Oh, Bubby," exclaimed John, "why don't you behave? Didn't we say you were too little to jump anything but small drains?"

Bub rose and looked apprehensively at John. He saw that there was no imminent danger, and the anxiety faded from his face.

"I'm the first whip," he said stolidly. He glanced at his costume as if for confirmation, and his eyes lingered proudly on the spur.

"You're a naughty boy," said John. "Don't you ever touch that hurdle again."

Bub kicked contemptuously at the laths.

A flash came into John's eyes.

"What shall I do with my little son?" murmured Mrs. Wharton behind the lattice.

John stepped forward, but stopped as he heard a shout from Elinora.

"The hounds are out!" screamed Elinora.

The beagle, the family fox-terrier, and a setter pup suddenly emerged from the dog-house near the stables and tore across the terrace. Elinora went after them, shouting; "Gone away!" She was followed by

John. As they disappeared around the corner of the house, Bub again kicked at the hurdle. Then he followed.

"Well," said Wharton, behind the lattice, "what do you think of your children?"

She shook her head and smiled. "If they were to be horse-dealers or stable-boys, I should feel encouraged," she said. "Where do you suppose they picked up all those ideas?"

"That's what I asked you."

"In the mornings they go off to the woods on the hill," she observed, "and in the afternoons they play on the terrace, but very rarely about the stables."

"Have you taken them to the kennels?" he asked.

"No," she answered; "not this year."

"It's odd," he said, and they went into the house.

THE next day Wharton went hunting. The hounds found a fox, and followed him six miles to the stream that flowed at the foot of the hill back of Wharton's house. Here the pack checked. The huntsman came up and cast down the stream in the direction of a ford.

"That fellow is wrong," said Wharton to himself.

There was an English girl out that day whom Wharton had just met. He liked her. She was handsome, and she went well. He rode along beside her.

"The huntsman is making a mistake," he said; "if you come with me I think we shall have the hounds to ourselves when they pick the line up again. A few hundred yards up-stream there is a fallen tree that bridges the water. I suspect that the fox has crossed on it. It leads to the usual runway on the other side. Farther up, half a mile or more, is another ford. Beyond the ford the valley turns sharply to the left and winds around that hill. If we get on the hillside we command each of the two lines that the fox can take. When the hounds come along, they will cross on the log, but the field must go around by the ford, and we shall have ten minutes' start."

"You're very well posted in woodcraft," she said, smiling.

"No," answered Wharton; "but this is my own country. My house is over the hill. The hounds are to meet there on Saturday. I hope you will be out."

"I hope to be," she said. "Shall we slip away from the field?"

He nodded, and they turned their horses up the stream, rode past the fallen tree, crossed at the upper ford, and slowly ascended the wooded hillside. From time to time they could see the huntsman on his gray horse working the pack in the bottom-land, and when the covert hid him they could hear his horn.

"Look," said Wharton. "He has given up his ford theory. He thinks now that the fox doubled back. Presently he'll find out that that is wrong, too, and then he'll swing around through the woods and work up the stream."

"You are really very wonderful," she said, laughing.

He bowed.

"As I told you," he answered, "I happen to know this bit of country. I'll show you a jump I once saw a woman take. We'll have time."

"She was a stranger," Wharton went on, "and she rode hard. We were coming over this hill very fast, and she went at that rail fence you see ahead."

"That's not such a very nasty-looking fence," observed Miss Melville.

"No," said Wharton; "but there is a twelve-foot drop on the other side into a road. I measured it afterward. Come and look at it."

The girl shuddered and turned her head.

"I don't want to see it," she said.

"Do you expect to see her ghost cantering down the road?" asked Wharton. "I fancy that is what ought to happen if we were in a real English wood. This would be an especially good spot for ghosts," he added, "on account of the echoes that come around the shoulder of the hill. On the other side, where we were first, we could hear the horn. On this side one can't hear it, but we shall get the echo presently."

"Really," said the girl, "I don't believe in ghosts, but I should like to hear the echo."

"Well," said Wharton,—they were standing by the fence,—"the strange thing about this jump—" He broke off as the sound of voices came from the road below. "The strange thing—" he repeated absently, and stopped again. He motioned her to be silent, and slipped off his horse.

Just then, faint but clear, came the echoed "t-o-o-t, t-o-o-t!"—the long-drawn note of the horn when the huntsman is calling in the hounds.

"Is that an echo?" asked Miss Melville.

Wharton nodded. The next moment he started and turned his head intently.

"Did you hear that?" said a voice in the road. It was a child's voice; Wharton recognized it as Elinora's.

Then another child's voice sounded, clumsily imitating the echo.

"That's Bub," said Wharton under his breath. He turned toward Miss Melville, who was farther away from the fence.

"Those are my children," he whispered; "I'll give

them a surprise. "Will you hold my horse a minute?"

He was stretching out his hand with the bridle-rein, when a new voice came from the road. Miss Melville started, and the color left her face.

"The Echo Hunt is having sport to-day," the voice said. It was a man's low-pitched voice, and spoke with an English intonation.

"You bet we are!" a child answered. That was John.

A pleasant laugh came in the man's voice. "I must bet, must I, you little Yankee! I've never needed that advice."

The man laughed again. Wharton looked at Miss Melville. Her bosom rose and fell excitedly.

"What's the matter?" he asked.

She shook her head. "Nothing," she answered. Wharton gave her the rein, tiptoed to the fence, and looked over the rails. Down in the road, in a low phaëton drawn by a fat gray pony, sat a strange man surrounded by the Wharton children. The man seemed about forty. His face was covered with a sandy beard. He wore clothes of brown homespun and dogskin gloves, and on his head was a tweed cap.

The echo sounded again.

"Hush!" said Elinora.

The man pulled up the pony, which had started to walk, and listened.

"They seem to be working this way," he said. "We'll get a burst yet."

"Where ought Bub to go?" asked John.

The man looked across toward the opposite hillside and pointed to a patch of woods.

"I think," he said, "that a knowing huntsman like John would send the first whip to the far side of that bit of covert. Then, you see, if he steals away—"

"I thought," interrupted Elinora, "that we were hunting the stump-tailed—" she hesitated.

"Quite right! It is *she*, the stump-tailed vixen," said the man. "Listen," he added. The echo brought a faint, short "toot," and then, after a pause, another and then another.

"They've gone into covert," he went on. "Perhaps they'll happen on the old girl curled up in a hollow log. Then we'll hear something."

"What?" asked Bub.

"You wait," said the man.

They waited in silence for a few moments, but the echo did not come again.

Wharton turned and looked for Miss Melville. She was walking his horse deeper in the woods. Her back was turned to him.

"I ought to go," he thought. Then he heard Elinora's voice, and he peered through the rails again.

"Tell us," said Elinora, "about the race—you know what-you-may-call-'em handicap—and about Whirlwind."

"The Tunbridgeshire?" said the man.

"Yes," said Elinora.

"Please do," said John; "and how you lost your leg."

Bub, who was sitting between the man's knees, patted his left leg with an expression of awful satisfaction.

"Well," the man began, "there was the favorite, Morning-star; and Egyptian; and Glengarry, that ran second the year before in the National; and Whirlwind. And there was a field of others—near a dozen—with no class or heart."

"What's that?" said Elinora.

"They weren't race-horses," he said.

"And you lay back on Whirlwind till the second time at the Liverpool," put in John. "Now go on."

"You little beggars," exclaimed the man, "you know the story by heart!"

"Not the part where you lost your leg," protested John.

"Yes, you do," said the man; "I'll not tell you another word."

"Oh, please!" said John.

"Not a word," said the man.

There was silence for a moment; then John spoke. "It must be fine," he said, "to have a wooden leg like yours if you were captured by the Indians. When they tortured you, you could just laugh at them."

"Yes," said the man, pleasantly, "that would be a ripping joke on the redskins—a ripping joke," he repeated. Then he caught the gaze of Elinora's eyes looking up into his face, and he turned his own away.

"It must be awful," she said; "and you can't ever ride again?" Her lip trembled.

"Why, yes," said the man, cheerily; "can't I ride in a phaëton, and be the M. F. H. of the Echo Hunt?"

"You told us to say *drive* in a phaëton," said John.

"So I did," said the man, and he laughed. "I've got something more to tell you about Whirlwind—something new," he went on. "He's going to start again day after to-morrow in the Woolwich steeplechase. A friend of mine has him now, you know, and I received a letter a few days ago, saying that he was quite fit. And so I have cabled over a bit of a stake on him. Not much, you know,—one shouldn't bet beyond one's means,—but just a bit for the fun of it. If you can't bet that way, you never should bet at all. Promise me you'll remember that when you have a stable."

"I'll promise," said John.

"That's a good youngster," said the man. Then he leaned back and laughed his low, pleasant laugh. He stopped suddenly. Elinora's eyes were looking up into his face again.

"The old horse starts at very good odds," he said. "If we win a bit, it will come handy to winter the stock." He spoke as if he had a great breeding-farm. Then he looked at the gray pony and laughed again. As his laughter died away Wharton heard the echo rising again.

"Hello!" cried the man in the phaëton. "Listen!"

There sounded a "toot-toot-toot! toot-toot-toot!" and again "toot-toot-toot!" and again the series of short-cut notes.

"They're off!" he said. Then, faint and clear in the silence that followed, the echo brought the chorus of the hounds.

"There's music for you!" he exclaimed.

He straightened himself, and shook the reins over the pony.

"Tally-ho!" he shouted. "Gone away, Echo Hunt!"

"Gone away!" screamed the children. The man waved the whip, and the pony broke into a canter. "Sit tight!" he called, and they swung around the bend in the road and disappeared.

WHARTON stood by the fence a moment.

"That must be the chap who took the cottage over the hill," he said to himself. "I'll hunt him up this afternoon and ask him to dine."

He turned and walked toward Miss Melville, who was coming back with his horse.

"Who was that shouting?" she asked.

"An Englishman who has the cottage around the hill," he answered. "Why?"

"His voice gave me a great shock," said the girl. "It was like the voice of a friend of mine."

"Ah-ha!" said Wharton, gaily; "who knows—perhaps?"

"No," she said quickly; "my friend is dead."

The tears came slowly into her eyes.

"I beg your pardon," he said, and turned away. "I am an ass," he added to himself.

He watched a great cottonwood leaf circle down through the still air and settle on the ground. Overhead the tree-tops traced themselves in silhouette against the windless blue, and here and there in the vistas of the wood a flood of October sunshine came through to glorify some frost-painted maple. Suddenly, coming from the far distance into the stillness, he heard the hounds in cry. This time it was not echo. The sound grew stronger as he listened.

"They're coming," he said. "They'll cross below us." He turned, took his horse, mounted, and led the way through the trees at a gallop.

As Wharton turned into his driveway that afternoon, walking a very tired horse, his wife, who was driving in a buckboard, overtook him. She pulled the ponies down to a walk.

"Hello!" he said. "We had a great run; and say," he added, "I've made a discovery."

"That's nice," she answered. "I've had a good day myself."

He looked at her. "What's up?" he asked.

"Tell me your discovery," she answered.

"I've found out who it is," he said, "that has been playing with the children."

"Well?" she said.

"It's the Englishman who took Wheelwright's cottage over the hill. He seems like a nice chap. Would you mind having him to dinner?"

"I should be glad," she answered. She said nothing more, and flicked a fly off the near pony's withers.

"You don't seem to think much of my discovery," he observed.

"Well, you see," she answered, "I've made a discovery of my own. Look!" She threw the robe back, and disclosed a tea-service which covered the bottom of the trap.

"It isn't plate," she said; "it's old English silver. It's what I've been looking for for years."

"Oh, silver, is it?" said Wharton. "This is a fortunate discovery for me. A kettle, two tea-pots, besides all the bowls and pitchers—good heavens, Elizabeth!"

"Now calm yourself," she said. "I've got it actually for less than what a set of good Sheffield plate would cost. Some family in the hills that had it for years are going away, or something, and they put it on sale this morning with the furniture- and undertaker-man in the village. Suppose somebody else had happened to see it first!"

"I'm disgusted with you," said Wharton. "A bargain turns a woman into a bird of prey. I should hope you would think a little of the people who parted with it for *virtually nothing*. Very likely it's an heirloom."

"I suppose it is," she said. "There's a coat-of-arms on each piece. I'm sorry for them," she added; "but I'm glad I got it, if they had to part with it." She drew the robe up and covered her purchase again. "How did you happen to find out," she continued, changing the subject, "that it was our neighbor who has been educating the children? He's been in the cottage six weeks, ever since you went shooting out West, and I've never laid eyes on him."

"I'll tell you when we get into the house," he answered.

They had reached the porte-cochère, and her groom took the ponies while he waited for a man from the stables to come for his hunter. When the butler came out of the house to take in the silver he was still waiting. The man handed him a telegram.

Wharton tore it open and read it.

"Confound it!" he said.

His wife looked at him apprehensively.

"It's nothing but business," he said. "I've got to go to New York on the afternoon train, and I don't know when I shall get back. Henderson," he added to the man, "pack my bag for three days."

WHARTON got back Saturday morning as the people were beginning to arrive for his hunt breakfast. He changed hurriedly into riding-clothes, and went down to greet his guests. He said "Good morning" to the M. F. H., brought in some farmers' wives who were sitting shyly in their buggies, saw to it that the huntsman and whips got ale and sandwiches, and then went to the dining-room. There he saw Wheelwright and

Miss Melville eating breakfast together in a corner.

He caught Henderson as he moved through the crowd and asked him for some coffee. Then he joined the party in the corner.

"I was telling Miss Melville," said Wheelwright, "that we ought to find that fox you hunted on Wednesday. He went to earth not far from here."

"That's so," said Wharton.

"We had better follow Mr. Wharton," said Miss Melville. "I think he has an understanding with the foxes, and knows where they are going beforehand. On Wednesday—"

"Please don't tell that to Wheelwright," interrupted Wharton, "because he knows the country about here, too, and he'll explain how there wasn't anything remarkable about our cast. If he had been out on Wednesday, he would have come along, too, and very likely would have taken you away from me. He is considered much more attractive than I."

Miss Melville laughed. "That may be two for Mr. Wheelwright," she said, "but it's certainly one for yourself."

"Of course," said Wharton, "I'll admit I'm moderately attractive."

"The man's here with your coffee," said Wheelwright.

Wharton turned and took the plate and coffee-cup. Instead of leaving, Henderson held out a package wrapped in white tissue-paper, and a long envelop.

"These were just left for you, sir," he said.

Wharton glanced at the envelop. The handwriting was unfamiliar.

"I don't want these things," he said. "Put them with my mail in the smoking-room."

The man turned away.

"Wait," Wharton called; "I'll take the letter. Will you excuse me," he said to Miss Melville, "if I open it?"

She smiled. "We will," she answered; "that is, if you will tell Mr. Wheelwright and me who is sending you packages wrapped in white tissue-paper."

Wharton set his plate on the mantel-shelf, tore off the end of the envelop, and drew out a sheet of letter-paper. He glanced at the signature, and read the first few sentences.

"This is from your tenant, I fancy," he said to Wheelwright; "the chap who has your cottage over the hill."

"I got a note from him myself last night," said Wheelwright. "He's going away."

"Yes; so he says," murmured Wharton, reading on. He raised his eyes from the letter. "Your suspicions," he said to Miss Melville, "are unjust. That package contains presents"—he glanced down again at the letter—" 'for Miss Elinora and the Messrs. Wharton of the Echo Hunt.' "

"What does that mean?" asked Wheelwright.

"It's a game he had with them," said Wharton.

He read to the end, and ran his fingers into the large envelop, and drew out one of note-paper size.

"He wants me to register a letter for him," he said. "Why doesn't he register his own letters?"

The envelop came out back uppermost, and was unsealed. Wharton turned it over. There were three five-cent stamps on it. As he read the address, some one passing through the crowd jostled his elbow and shook the letter from his hand. It struck the floor, and there was a ring of metal, and a small object slipped out upon the polished wood.

"Money, money!" exclaimed Miss Melville.

"Yes," said Wharton; "protect me from Wheelwright."

He bent hurriedly down and began groping for the thing that had slipped out. His fingers closed on it under the flounce of a woman's skirt. It was not a coin. He glanced down at it. There was a Victoria Cross in his hand. He slipped it back into the envelop, and as he rose he wet the mucilage and sealed the letter.

"My tenant," said Wheelwright, "must be very much of a gentleman or have great confidence in you."

"He never saw me," said Wharton. He half turned away from the two, and stood staring vacantly into the crowd with the newly sealed envelop covered in his hand.

"That accounts for it," said Wheelwright.

Miss Melville laughed. "I am going over to speak to Mrs. Wharton," she said. "She is pouring tea by the window."

"Yes," said Wharton, mechanically; "she'll be glad to see you."

The girl moved away.

"I say, Wheelwright," he said in an undertone, "this is a curious thing."

"What?" said Wheelwright.

Wharton held out the letter.

Wheelwright gave a low exclamation. It was addressed to Miss M. J. Melville, Ormsly Hill, Leicestershire, England.

"That isn't our Miss Melville," said Wheelright.

"Yes, it is," said Wharton. "Her name is Mary J. Melville, and her father's place is Ormsly in Leicestershire."

"Well," said Wheelwright, "why don't you deliver it to her?"

"I suppose I shall," said Wharton; "but it's a little strange. Besides, I was asked to post it."

He worked his way through the crowd around the center-table to the bow-window where Mrs. Wharton was pouring tea. Miss Melville was standing beside her.

"Have you had some tea?" he asked.

"Thanks; I don't care for any," she answered.

Mrs. Wharton looked up at her husband. "I've found out about the coat-of-arms," she said, nodding to the tea-service before her. "Miss Melville recognized it." She mentioned the family name which the Englishman had signed in the letter to Wharton.

"That's very curious," Wharton murmured.

Miss Melville overhead him.

"It is odd," she said. "They are neighbors of ours in Leicestershire. There was a branch of the family which came out to this country in the eighteenth century. It must have belonged to them."

"Very likely," said Wharton. He stood a moment in silence. He was thinking. Then he looked at her sharply, and she dropped her eyes. "Don't you want to come out and see my garden?" he asked. "There is not much left of it so late in the autumn, but my intentions have been good. Formal gardening is one of my fads."

"I should like to see it," she answered.

He opened the French window, and they stepped out on the terrace.

"It is odd," he said, "that we should have a tea-service with the coat-of-arms of one of your neighbors upon it."

"Yes," she said; "it almost makes me believe in ghosts, in spite of what I said the other day." She turned her eyes away, as if she would have recalled the words.

"I was thinking of that, too," he answered. "Sometimes I think I do believe in them," he went on. "Such strange things happen—such strange coincidences. And there must be happy ghosts—the ghosts that manage unexpected meetings of old friends, and make us cling to our faith in romance."

"I never thought of that," she said. "I'm afraid I'm not very romantic. Life upsets the story-books."

"As a rule," he answered; "but every now and then life arranges some strange true story which no story-book writer would dare to use."

She shook her head. "Perhaps," she said; "but it's best to try to be content with facts."

"For a queen of the hunt," said Wharton, "you are a deep philosopher."

"Hunting," she answered, "is something besides sport. It fills one's lungs with fresh air and keeps one's ideas sensible. And even if one loses the hounds, one loses other things as well."

Wharton nodded. "But perhaps," he said, "some day you will agree with me." He slipped his hand into his breast pocket and took the letter in his fingers. "Suppose——" he said; then he hesitated and stopped.

She looked at him wonderingly.

"Suppose——" he repeated.

He stopped the second time as Elinora appeared around the house, galloping upon Bub's broomstick, followed by John on his own favorite, and by Bub, who brought up the rear. All were screaming loudly.

"I won!" shouted Elinora. "I beat John! John fell down at the ditch!"

"I should say he did," observed Wharton. "He's a sight."

John's hands and knees were covered with clay, and his shoes were incased in it.

"Are these the children who were in the road that day?" asked Miss Melville.

"Yes," said Wharton. "Just now everything is hunting and steeplechasing."

Miss Melville smiled. "Have you been having a race?" she asked Elinora.

"It's the Echo Hunt Steeplechase Handicap," said Elinora, proudly.

"She doesn't know what a handicap is," whispered Wharton, "but it sounds well."

Miss Melville paid no attention to him, but spoke again to Elinora.

"That's very fine," she said. "What are you riding?"

"The Lamb," replied Elinora. "It's Bub's; but Shamrock has real legs, and I can't ride him fast."

"I see," said Miss Melville. "The Lamb was a great horse. He won the Grand National twice."

"Oh, yes," said Elinora; "we know that."

"Of course," said Miss Melville, gravely. "What is your brother riding? It's too bad he came down."

"Whirlwind," said John.

"Whirlwind?" repeated Miss Melville. She looked at Wharton curiously.

"Well?" he said. But he knew what was in her mind.

She made no answer.

"He fell in the mud," said John, "or I'd have won. And I had a bit of a stake on him, too."

Wharton smiled at his son, and the words of the man in the phaëton came back to him.

"So you had a bit on Whirlwind?" he said. "What is a bit, John?"

"Why," said John, "you mustn't bet more than you

can afford; but it's all right to risk a bit, you know."

His manner and intonation were so like the Englishman's that Wharton laughed.

"That's so," he said.

At that moment the fox-terrier looked around the corner of the house.

"There's Blink," said John. They turned toward the dog, and Blink hastily retired, with the three after him.

"I don't think," said Wharton, "that Blink appreciates being one of the hounds."

Miss Melville smiled. "They've left their horses," she said. "I once knew a steeplechase horse named Whirlwind."

"Really?" said Wharton.

He happened to look toward the house and saw Henderson coming out of the French window.

"I fancy I'm wanted," he said.

The man approached.

"I beg pardon, sir," said Henderson. He held out a telegram which had been opened.

"The negro man who left the packages just now came back with this. He said he found it on the floor of the cottage, sir."

Wharton took the telegram and Henderson left.

"I don't see why he should bring this to me," he

said. He drew out the despatch. It was a cable from England. There were four words: "Whirlwind fell at water."

"I beg your pardon," said Wharton to Miss Melville. He stuffed the despatch into his breeches pocket. "Shall we go in?" he asked.

"I think we had better," she answered.

He opened the window, and she passed in. As he followed, his eyes fell on the tea-service.

"That's the bit on Whirlwind," he said to himself.

Miss Melville was speaking to Mrs. Wharton, who was still at the tea-table.

Wharton looked at the girl and thought.

Just then Wheelwright came up. "Have you given her the letter?" he asked Wharton.

"No," said Wharton, "not yet. I want to get hold of that chap," he went on. "I think that would be the best way. We must find out where he's gone, and wire him. Perhaps, though," he added doubtfully, "I ought to give her the letter first."

There was a cracking of whips outside in the driveway on the other side of the house, and the sound of the whippers-in shouting at straggling hounds. Miss Melville turned.

"The hounds are starting," she said.

As she spoke, the setter pup, the beagle, and Blink

the fox-terrier passed unwillingly across the terrace, dragged by John and Elinora. Bub brought up the rear, flourishing a broken buggy-whip. She stepped into the window.

"Good sport, Echo Hunt!" she called. "Have a good day! Have a great many good days!" she murmured. She turned back into the room. "I suppose we'd better mount," she added to Wharton.

"Yes," said Wharton. "I think we had."

She said "Good-by" to Mrs. Wharton. The people were streaming out to see the hounds, and she followed.

Wharton hung back a few steps. He took the letter from his pocket. "What do you think?" he asked Wheelwright. "Had I better give it to her, or shall we find him?"

"I met his negro servant a few minutes ago, when I went to the stables," said Wheelwright.

"Did you find out where he has gone?" asked Wharton.

Wheelwright dropped his voice. "He's dead."

Wharton was silent. He looked at Wheelwright with a question in his eyes.

Wheelwright nodded.

They were at the door, and Miss Melville was waiting.

"Here is Lady Gay," she said. "I ought to have a good day on that mare."

"She'll carry you well," said Wharton. He slipped the letter into his pocket. "Yes," he added, "we ought to have a good day."

THE REGGIE LIVINGSTONES' COUNTRY LIFE

VII

THE REGGIE LIVINGSTONES' COUNTRY LIFE

Mrs. Innis joined Mrs. Courtlandt Dashwood on the veranda of the club-house.

"I've just had a letter from dear Rosina," said Mrs. Innis. She had the letter in her hand, and began to take it out of the envelope.

"Who is 'dear Rosina'?" asked Mrs. Dashwood.

"Why, you remember Rosina Russell?" said Mrs. Innis, in a tone of mild reproof.

"Oh, yes," said Mrs. Dashwood; "she was that Boston girl who married Reggie Livingstone. What's the matter with her?"

"She will do so much for our life here," replied Mrs. Innis. "You know, my dear, we *do* get narrow and material, and, I am afraid, rather stably; and she has a beautiful mind, and fine sympathies for art and poetry. I stopped with them in Rome, and saw the old things they had collected. She is very Preraphaelite."

"Well," said Mrs. Dashwood, "is she coming here?"

"That is just the thing she writes about," Mrs. Innis replied. She unfolded the letter and began to read:

"We are tired of wandering, even though our path has been through the treasure-houses of the past. I suspect that Reginald is anxious to see his friends again, and I cannot but believe that it is best at once to begin our life in America. I consider it very important that we should begin that life under conditions of calm and sweetness. Reginald, of course, has always lived in New York, but I cannot look forward to the unwholesome, feverish, yes, wicked life which goes on there. I know that it is best for us to find some peaceful spot in some beautiful country-side, with a few agreeable people near by, and there to build a house and settle down. I write to ask you about Oakdale, because, from what I know of it, the place seems suitable. Reginald is fond of out-of-door sports, and I truly love horses, though I do not know much about them."

Mrs. Innis paused because Mrs. Dashwood had rushed down upon the lawn. She noticed that Lobster, her white bull-terrier, was behind an ornamental shrub killing the club's Persian cat. She returned presently with Lobster on a leading-string, and Mrs. Innis continued:

"Moreover, there are several of Reginald's old friends living there, though perhaps it would be as well if we should lose sight of some of them."

"I suppose she means Courty," observed Mrs. Dashwood.

Mrs. Innis made no comment, but read on:

"And yet this is perhaps a selfish view to take of the matter. Reginald's influence would doubtless be felt, and his taste for the higher things would be communicated to the companions of his idle bachelor days—days which I know he deeply regrets."

"His nose is badly scratched," observed Mrs. Dashwood, who had been examining Lobster's wounds. "The nasty cat! I ought to take him home to put something on it."

"But don't you think they would be a great addition?" said Mrs. Innis.

"I dare say," said Mrs. Dashwood. "I wonder if Reggie is much changed. You poor dear!" she remarked to Lobster, "I wish I had let you finish it." She rose as she spoke, and ordered her horses.

Mrs. Innis went into the women's room and wrote twelve pages to Mrs. Reginald Livingstone in Florence.

The following autumn, somewhat as a consequence of this correspondence, the Reggie Livingstones were installed in Mr. Carteret Carteret's house, one mile from the club. He was intending to hunt in England that season, and the Livingstones were glad to take his house because they were still warring with the architect about plans. In addition to a building-site near the club, they had purchased the small farm that lay behind. Mrs. Livingstone considered the tilling of the soil and the companionship, as she expressed it, of sweet-breathing Alderney cows to be a source of inspiration and beautiful thoughts. In fact, during the voyage across the Atlantic, when she was bored with the sea, and while stopping at a New York hotel, when she was bored by the town bustle, country life had become a passion. She could hardly wait to enter upon it, and she passed much of her time drawing pencil sketches of walled gardens and hen-houses with Romanesque pilasters.

One evening a fortnight after the Livingstones' installation in the country, and after the community had reassembled for the October hunting, Mrs. Livingstone was in her drawing-room, surrounded by the guests who were sitting through the after-dinner period of a woman's dinner-party. Livingstone's men friends were giving him a dinner of welcome at the club, and it had occurred to Mrs. Livingstone to ask their wives and a few others to dine with her.

"I'm so glad you like us," Mrs. Innis was saying, "because, you know, in a certain sense I feel responsible for bringing you here."

"You are all delightful, dear!" replied Mrs. Livingstone, soulfully, "and the country is beautiful beyond words. I am also very much pleased with this little place of Mr. Carteret's. The dear flowers are simply charming." She turned to Mrs. Dashwood, who appeared either to be bored or very sleepy. "Don't you think so?"

"I think," said Mrs. Dashwood, "that a garden is a bore. When the sun or the frost isn't killing everything, the dogs are, or somebody's horses get into it. It is much better to get your flowers from town by express four times a week."

Mrs. Livingstone's countenance showed that she dissented from this view. However, she had a theory about mastering persons by discovering their nobler interests, so that she continued the discussion.

"If you don't care about watching the growth and development of flowers," she said, "perhaps you would be interested in vegetables. The vegetable-garden here is remarkable."

"It is the same with vegetables as with flowers,"

said Mrs. Dashwood. "They raise them better and cheaper in New Jersey."

"But," protested Mrs. Livingstone, "think of the sentiment and poetry which attach to the fruits of one's own garden. Was it not Horace who wrote an ode to the white turnips raised by Lucullus?"

"How delightful!" exclaimed Mrs. Innis.

"I do not care for turnips," said Mrs. Dashwood. "I believe, however, that they are very wholesome for sheep."

Mrs. Livingstone turned from Mrs. Dashwood to Mrs. Innis. "You and I will garden together, dear."

"Yes, indeed," said Mrs. Innis.

At this not only Mrs. Dashwood but others smiled. Mrs. Innis was remarkable for never doing any of those things except in imagination.

There was a pause in the conversation.

"Well," observed Mrs. Dashwood, loudly, "aren't we going to play bridge?" She had been waiting half an hour for the tables to be brought in.

Mrs. Livingstone made no reply. She seemed not to have heard, though that was scarcely possible. She smiled faintly with what she considered her "sweet expression."

"Yes," she said dreamily to Mrs. Innis, "you and I will have a garden with jonquils and lilies and fritillaria and rosemary and all the delightful old flowers—"

"What is fritillaria?" Mrs. Varick inquired.

"Why, don't you know?" said Mrs. Livingstone. "It is that lovely—" she hesitated, as if seeking the descriptive words.

"Aren't we going to play bridge?" asked Mrs. Dashwood.

Mrs. Livingstone abandoned her search after the descriptive words.

"I am sorry, Mrs. Dashwood," she said coldly, "but I believe that there are no cards in the house. Neither Mr. Livingstone nor myself ever plays. We have ideals which forbid it. While not assuming to criticize others, I must say that I disapprove of playing any game for stakes, however small."

Mrs. Innis's skill at bridge was noteworthy, and her winnings were almost scandalous, but her sympathies were catholic and quick.

"I admire you very much for saying that," she said. "I am sure we play too much, and need just such an influence as yours."

"Of course," said Mrs. Dashwood, "I believe in people living up to their principles, if they have any."

Mrs. Livingstone did not exactly understand what Mrs. Dashwood meant. "I am glad that you agree with me," she said. She considered that a safe remark.

Mrs. Dashwood began to play with the fox-terrier, and made no reply.

"We were talking about gardening and country life," Mrs. Livingstone continued, addressing the company through Mrs. Innis. "Don't you think that a beautiful environment such as we have here must make our lives finer and more beautiful?"

"It must, of course," said Mrs. Innis. "And you remember you promised to have a class and to let us come and be taught about books and art."

Mrs. Livingstone looked down meekly.

"I should be a very poor teacher," she said, "I know so little; but we could study together."

"You know a great deal," said Mrs. Innis. "When shall we begin?"

Mrs. Livingstone thought for a moment. "Wednesdays at ten would suit me best, if it is agreeable to you."

There was no dissent.

"Wednesday suits every one," said Mrs. Innis. "We will begin day after to-morrow. As I've said before, it will make our life so much more profitable and amusing."

Mrs. Livingstone looked doubtful at the last word. She had something in mind to say, however, and she let Mrs. Innis's rather extraordinary point of view pass.

"There is just one thing regarding this place," she began, "about which I am in doubt; that is the hunting. It is certainly a question whether such strong excitement is a good thing, to say nothing of the risks which accompany it. Ought a married man to assume those risks merely in the course of his pleasure, and ought a wife—to be more explicit, ought I to allow Mr. Livingstone to take them?"

There was no answer to this question, which was addressed generally.

Mrs. Livingstone turned to Mrs. Innis.

"Would you let him hunt if he were yours?"

"That is a very hard question," replied Mrs. Innis. "In the first place, you see, I can't imagine him being mine." She blushed, and several of her friends smiled; but Mrs. Livingstone did not notice either the blush or the smiles. "In the second place," Mrs. Innis continued, "when poor dear Mr. Innis was alive, I tried never to allow myself a wish of my own." She sighed, and the friends who had smiled before smiled again.

"That was unselfish of you," said Mrs. Livingstone, "but quite wrong, I am sure, if your wishes were for his good."

She turned to Mrs. Dashwood.

"What would you do," she asked, "about Reggie's hunting?"

"I shouldn't do anything," replied Mrs. Dashwood, still playing with the terrier. "It wouldn't do any good. I've found out that when Courtlandt wishes to hunt or drink or gamble, he does it without consulting me."

"Mr. Livingstone," said his wife, coldly, "neither drinks nor gambles, so that it is unnecessary to consider those subjects. As to hunting, I believe that he would give it up if I asked it."

"He might," said Mrs. Dashwood, "if he wasn't keen about it, or if you cut down his allowance."

"I think," replied Mrs. Livingstone, with reproof in her tone, "that you are seriously in error. A woman should, as they say, manage her husband only by appealing to his strength and manliness, by sharing and sympathizing with his interests."

"You are quite right, my dear," said Mrs. Innis. "Don't let her make you worldly or lose your faith in men. After all," she added, with a shrug of her shoulders, "there is no one else to marry us, is there?"

"I am sure that I am right," said Mrs. Livingstone. "Community of interest is what makes marriage happy. That is why we have come to the country. We both are wrapped up in country life. It is a very wholesome taste to have in common. Town life is full of temptations, but here in the country it is quite different."

"Yes," said Mrs. Dashwood, "different and worse."

"I am afraid, my dear Mrs. Dashwood," said Mrs. Livingstone, "that you are something of a pessimist, aren't you?"

"No," said Mrs. Dashwood; "only I've lived here ten years. But I wouldn't live anywhere else," she added. "I like to ride to hounds."

Mrs. Livingstone looked puzzled. She started to speak, but Mrs. Dashwood interrupted by asking if she might have her horses ordered.

"But you are not going alone?" she said. "Isn't Mr. Dashwood coming for you?"

"I hope not," said Mrs. Dashwood; "not at this time of night."

Mrs. Livingstone recoiled in shocked amazement.

"You mustn't pay any attention to Effie," said Mrs. Innis, soothingly. "It is her pose to be cynical. The real reason why she is going home without Mr. Dashwood is that she has me on her hands, and the brougham holds only two."

"But are you all going?" exclaimed Mrs. Livingstone, as her guests rose. "Aren't any of you going to wait till the dinner at the club is over?"

"My dear," said Mrs. Varick, "they won't be leaving the club for hours. It is much more sensible for us to go to bed than to sit up and wait. You had better do the same thing."

As the last of her guests drove away, Mrs. Livingstone slipped out and stood on the steps in the porte-cochère. The crunching of the wheels on the gravel ceased. She waited for a time, listening for an approaching vehicle, but none came. She was very tired, and presently she went in and went to bed. But she did not go to sleep for a long time. New and disturbing doubts worried her.

At eleven o'clock the next morning Mr. Livingstone had shown no signs of getting up. His door was locked, and when his man knocked at nine, the only response was a mumbled something which he did not understand, but interpreted as a request to be left undisturbed. Mrs. Livingstone was growing uneasy. Her husband always rose at nine, and not unnaturally she feared that he was ill. She was wondering whether she ought to send for the doctor, when the footman appeared and informed her that some one was at the door with a horse and wished to speak to Mr. Livingstone.

She went to the door, and found a groom in the porte-cochère with a horse.

"What do you want?" she asked.

"Please, madam," said the groom, "Mr. Galloway

told me to deliver this horse to Mr. Livingstone and to give him this note."

"You may give me the note," she said, "and you had better take the horse to the stable."

She glanced at the handwriting, which was unfamiliar, and went into the house and listened. There were no sounds of Mr. Livingstone's awakening.

"It may be something important," she said half aloud. "I suppose I *ought* to open it." She hesitated for a moment, then she tore open the enevelope.

"DEAR REGGIE [she read]: Here is old Blue Chip, who stands you for one stack of the same, as per last evening's sale. I hope you feel better than I do.
Galloway."

She looked perplexed. She began to read the note a second time, when she heard a bell ring and immediately afterward the sound of the unlocking of a door. It was a wooden house, and people moving and speaking in the upper story could be heard from below. Presently she heard a servant knock and her husband order a bottle of mineral water.

"Do you wish your breakfast in your room, sir?" asked the man.

"I don't wish any breakfast," replied Mr. Livingstone. "Is there any grapefruit in the house?"

"I'll see, sir," said the man.

"If there is none," said Mr. Livingstone, "bring some lemons with the water, and bring a quart bottle."

Mrs. Livingstone listened with growing anxiety. Her husband rarely ate grapefruit, and invariably did eat a hearty breakfast. Moreover, his voice was hoarse.

"Reggie," she called up, "are you ill?"

"No," replied Mr. Livingstone.

"You are very hoarse," she commented. "You must have caught cold coming home."

"I did," said Mr. Livingstone.

"You know, I told you to take a muffler."

There was no answer.

"Don't you feel well?" she inquired.

"I feel like a little skylark," he replied hoarsely.

"I am so glad," she said sympathetically. "Reggie," she continued, mounting the stairs, "a horse came for you a little while ago—and a note. You were asleep, and it looked like something important, so I opened it."

"A horse?" he said, with a note of surprise in his voice. "Let's see the note."

She handed him the envelop, and he took out the sheet of paper and read it.

"This is some idiot joke of Galloway's," he observed.

"What does he mean?" asked Mrs. Livingstone.

"Blue Chip is the name of a horse," he replied.

"And I suppose the 'one stack' refers to the haystack which it will eat up," she suggested.

"You are a wonderful woman!" replied Mr. Livingstone. He patted her shoulder. "Run away, and let me get my bath."

"But is this the horse you were going to get for me?" she asked.

"Of course," he answered, and disappeared into his bedroom.

Mrs. Livingstone went down-stairs with the intention of going to the stables to inspect her new horse. She put on a hat and stepped through the door, when she saw two men coming up the drive, one pulling and the other pushing what is known as a breaking-cart. She waited till they approached, for she noticed that one of the shafts was broken and that the brass dash-rail was bent out of shape. Moreover, several spokes were missing from one of the wheels.

"Has there been an accident?" she asked anxiously. She glanced fearfully out toward the road, expecting to see a motionless form borne in.

"No, ma'am," answered the man in the shafts; "that is, not recent." He took a note from his pocket. "This is for Mr. Livingstone," he said.

"You may give it to me," she replied. The man handed her the note, and she turned to enter the house.

"Shall we take it to the stable?" the man called to her.

"Take what to the stable?" she said, stopping.

"Why, the cart, ma'am," said the man.

"Is *that* cart for Mr. Livingstone?" she asked.

"Yes, ma'am," answered the man.

"Very well," she said. "Take it to the stable."

She went in and mounted the stairs.

"Reginald," she called, "here is another note for you, and there is a broken cart outside that two men have just taken to the stable."

One half of Mr. Livingstone's face was still unshaven and lathered, but he came to the door with an anxious look, and took the note.

"Good heavens, Rosina!" he exclaimed, "can't you keep these things till I get dressed? I have a headache, and very likely a temperature."

"You said you felt like a lark," observed Mrs. Livingstone.

"Well, don't argue about it," he replied. He tore open the envelop, and read the contents aloud. It said:

"Here is the breaking, or broken, cart that went for the odd reds. I forgot to send it over with Blue Chip.

By the way, this is the best way to drive the old horse —about half an hour ahead of the trap. It saves repairs.

Galloway."

"Is this another of Mr. Galloway's jokes?" asked Mrs. Livingstone.

"Hang Galloway!" said Mr. Livingstone. "He ought to be more considerate so early in the morning."

"Please don't swear," said Mrs. Livingstone. "It distresses me; and, besides, it isn't early in the morning."

"Angel," said Mr. Livingstone, desperately, "please let me shave." And he withdrew.

"But I don't understand about the 'odd reds,' " she called after him, "unless it means the odd spokes that were left in the wheels. They were red."

"That's it," he called back, and shut the door of his dressing-room.

Mrs. Livingstone was curious to inspect her new horse. Mr. Galloway's second note was not reassuring, and when she had said that she loved horses she meant safe, trustworthy horses with kind eyes and indolent temperaments. If it were safest to put Blue Chip half an hour ahead of the trap, she wished to make no experiments at closer range. She decided to consult Barnes, the coachman.

As she was leaving the house she chanced to look toward the gateway, and a spectacle met her eyes which put Blue Chip out of her mind. It was a procession coming up the driveway toward the front door. First there was a man driving a wheelless board platform, known in the country as a stone-boat. There was an old plow on the stone-boat; also a small black pig, which was tied to the plow. Next there was a stable-boy with a calf; after him a groom with a hugely fat pie-bald pony. The groom also led a goat. Behind him came another groom riding a horse that limped in various legs. All four were bandaged, so that the exact nature of the infirmity was not obvious. Next came a farm-wagon loaded with what might be called an assorted cargo. Her eye caught two sheep, a harrow, a coop of chickens, and some distended grain-sacks.

As the head of the line approached, Mrs. Livingstone advanced to meet it. "What is all this?" she inquired of the farm-hand on the stone-boat.

"I was told to leave some things for Mr. Livingstone, ma'am," replied the man. "There's a plow, and a shote, and the stone-boat." He handed her a note.

"Well," she said, "and all the rest of you? What do you want?"

The old farmer on the seat of the box-wagon replied:

"I got a load of stuff from Mr. Colfax's place fer Mr. Livingstone, and I guess the rest of these fellers has stuff fer him, too. Besides them sheep and the harrer," he continued, casting his eyes over the wagon, "I got a coop of games, a coyote pup, four beagle-dogs, one bag of clover-seed, two bushels of early rose seed-potatoes, and one bag of prepared trout food. It's all in this invitory." He handed down a note to the groom on the lame horse, and he passed it along to the groom with the pony and the goat, and eventually it reached Mrs. Livingstone, together with other notes that came from the various other persons in the line.

"Where shall I leave your stuff, miss?" inquired the farmer.

Mrs. Livingstone looked up blankly from the collection of notes in her hand.

"Please wait," she said, "till I speak with Mr. Livingstone." She went indoors and up-stairs to her husband's room. There was no answer to her knock, and she went in. Then she heard a splashing in his bathroom. "Reginald!" she called.

The splashing ceased.

"Reginald!" she called again.

"I'm in the tub!" came the reply.

"But there is a procession waiting outside, and here are a lot more notes."

"A lot more what?" said the voice in the bath-room.

"Notes," she repeated. "Letters from people who have sent you things."

"Oh, bother!" said the voice. Presently the door was unlocked and a wet arm extended.

"Give me the notes," said Mr. Livingstone. Then the door closed again. "I shall be down in a few minutes," he added. "Tell them to wait."

Mrs. Livingstone told the men to wait, and then she went into the library and sat down. She was troubled—she could not explain why. There was something irregular about the way the day had begun. She thought it best to calm her mind, and she took from the table a book of verses by a Bulgarian poetess and began to read. There was little which seemed to mean anything in the verses, but they sounded well, and she decided to read them to the class next day. They were much out of the common, and that is a great deal with poetry, even if it means nothing. She was reading in a low tone to herself:

" 'My heart, the fragrance of the rose,
    The lark's song, and the passion of yesterday—'

"How beautiful!" she murmured, "how true!" She closed the book with her finger at the page, and gazed tenderly across at a Braun photograph on the opposite wall depicting a Botticelli young lady with a scrawny neck. As her eyes returned to the book, her range of vision embraced the bow-window which looked out upon the tennis lawn and the garden. She gave a little scream and clasped the book to her bosom. She saw two horses side by side in the air entering the garden over the wall and high box hedge and about to land on the violet-frames. The sound of breaking glass which instantly followed told her that they had landed. The riders, whom she recognized as Messrs. Dashwood and Colfax, immediately dismounted and began examining their horses' legs. The examination seemed satisfactory, for they presently remounted, without casting a glance at the frames. When they galloped on to the tennis lawn, Mrs. Livingstone threw the Bulgarian poetess on the table and dashed to the window. She could see the deep hoof-prints in the tender turf. The French windows were partly open, and she was about to request them to keep off the tennis lawn when she heard her husband calling from the window above.

"Hello, you chaps!" he shouted.

His hail was answered by Mr. Dashwood:

"What do you mean by putting glass on the landing side of a hedge?"

Mrs. Livingstone gasped.

"I didn't put it there," replied Mr. Livingstone, "but I wish I had. Tomorrow I shall fix it up with barbed wire."

"You will be put out of the hunt if you do," said Mr. Dashwood.

"It was rather a good jump, don't you think?" observed Willie Colfax. "We got a tenner apiece out of Carty. He didn't think we'd have it."

"Where is Carty?" asked Mr. Livingstone.

"He's coming around by the gate," said Mr. Colfax. "He's on a horse that's just been taken up."

"He'll be annoyed about the way you've torn up the garden and the lawn."

"No, he won't," said Mr. Dashwood. "He said that you were a responsible tenant. He didn't care."

Mrs. Livingstone, listening in the library, dropped into a chair. It was difficult for her to believe her ears.

"How do you feel this morning?" inquired Mr. Colfax.

"Ripping," replied Mr. Livingstone.

Mr. Dashwood looked up and smiled incredulously. "You were nosing in rather big last night," he observed. "I felt anxious about you."

"That was awfully good of you," said Mr. Livingstone. "How are you to-day?"

Mr. Dashwood gazed across the landscape, and absently lifted his hat and bared his head to the breeze.

"Have our things come?" he asked after a pause.

"They are on the other side of the house," said Mr. Livingstone. "I think it was low of you to sell me all those things, and lower yet to deliver them."

"They were no good to us," said Mr. Colfax.

"Go around and send your horses to the stable," said Mr. Livingstone. "I'm coming down."

Mrs. Livingstone got up from her chair in the library and left the room. Feelings of surprise and indignation were mastering her.

As Mr. Livingstone came down-stairs he met his wife in the hallway. "What is the matter?" he asked.

"Nothing," she replied in a tone that meant quite the reverse.

"Aren't you going to look at our new possessions?" he suggested.

"I don't think I care for those men," said Mrs. Livingstone.

"Nonsense!" said Mr. Livingstone, cheerfully. "What does it matter about a little broken glass?"

"It isn't the broken glass," said Mrs. Livingstone; "and please don't say 'Nonsense.' It distresses me."

"Come along!" said her husband, and he led the way out into the porte-cochère. As she appeared behind him, Mr. Dashwood and Mr. Colfax both bowed with much manner and said, "Good morning, Mrs. Livingstone."

Mr. Carteret, who rode up at that moment also bowed and said, "Good morning."

Mrs. Livingstone returned their salutes with one dignified inclination of her head.

"It is a very lovely morning," continued Mr. Dashwood. "Beautiful color on the hills, and all that sort of thing."

"Yes," said Mrs. Livingstone; "it is almost a profanation to do anything on such a morning except to admire the view, is it not?"

"You are quite right," replied Mr. Dashwood. "Mrs. Dashwood enjoyed your party very much last evening."

"I am glad that Mrs. Dashwood enjoyed herself," said Mrs. Livingstone.

There was an uncomfortable pause, which was broken by Mr. Colfax. "There is Effie now, with Mrs. Innis," he said. He waved his hat, and Mrs. Dashwood, who was driving along the road in a cart, turned into the Livingstones' driveway. As she saw the array of things marshaled before the front door and the company assembled there, an uncharitable gleam lighted her very handsome eyes.

"Good morning," said Mrs. Dashwood as she drove

up. There was a cordiality in her tone which jarred on Mrs. Livingstone's feminine intuitions.

"Good morning, dear," said Mrs. Innis. "We saw Willie wave to us, and we drove in to say what a good time we had last evening."

"Won't you send your cart to the stable?" said Mrs. Livingstone.

"Thank you, no; we can stop only a minute," said Mrs. Dashwood.

"My dear!" exclaimed Mrs. Innis, "what does *all this* mean?" She motioned toward the procession, which she seemed to have just noticed. "Have you been to an auction?"

"I really don't know what it does mean," said Mrs. Livingstone, stiffly. "I was about to inquire."

Mr. Dashwood and Mr. Colfax grinned, and Mr. Livingstone looked dignified and uncomfortable. Mr. Carteret preserved his usual uninquisitive calm.

"What have *you* been doing?" said Mrs. Dashwood to her husband.

"Nothing," said Mr. Dashwood.

"We jumped the garden hedge," said Mr. Colfax. "It was rather profitable." He looked at Mr. Carteret.

"Yes," said Mr. Livingstone, "and landed in Mrs. Livingstone's violet-frames."

Mrs. Livingstone cast a side glance at Mrs. Dashwood and tried to stop her husband.

"It was of no consequence," she said.

"Courtlandt, you ought to be ashamed of yourself," said Mrs. Dashwood. "But I told you how it would be with a garden," she continued to Mrs. Livingstone. "It is much better to get your flowers from town."

Mrs. Livingstone made no reply.

"But I want to know about these things," said Mrs. Innis, who was studying the procession.

"These are some treasures which Reggie acquired last evening," replied Mr. Colfax. "You know, Reggie is going in for country life. Rather a fine lot, aren't they?"

"No," said Mrs. Innis; "it looks to me like trash."

"How can you say such things?" said Mr. Colfax. "Look at that horse!"

"He's lame in only two legs," observed Mr. Carteret.

"Well, that was Courty's horse," said Mr. Colfax.

"Was that pony yours?" asked Mrs. Innis.

"No," said Mr. Colfax; "that was Varick's. I must say, it was hardly right to unload that on Reggie. Besides having the heaves, it bites. It nearly took his four-year-old's hand off. It isn't a safe pony for children."

"So I suppose he thought that Mr. Livingstone

would enjoy riding him," said Mrs. Livingstone.

"There is also another way of looking at it," said Mr. Colfax, cheerfully. "When you go in for country life, you ought to take the bitter with the sweet. A bad pony about the place adds a spice to things."

"Really?" said Mrs. Livingstone. She was holding herself together with determination. The broken violet-frames, the ruined tennis lawn were easier to bear than Mrs. Dashwood.

"But which are your things?" Mrs. Innis asked of Mr. Colfax.

"Mine," he answered, "are that superior lot in the box-wagon."

She beckoned to Mr. Carteret.

"What is in the wagon?" she asked.

He moved his horse to the side of the wagon.

"There are two sheep," he began.

"They have the foot-rot," said Mrs. Dashwood.

"Would you expect me to draft the sound ones?" asked Mr. Colfax.

"A coop of game chickens," Carteret continued.

"They won't stand," said Mrs. Dashwood.

"A broken harrow," Mr. Carteret went on, "the coyote that killed Mrs. Carstair's peacocks, and two couples of beagles that are down on their feet. They also look as if they had mange."

"They have," said Mr. Colfax.

"What is in these sacks?" inquired Mr. Carteret.

"Clover-seed, potatoes, and trout food," replied Mr. Colfax.

"The trout food, I presume," said Mr. Carteret, "is three years old, dating from the time when you were going to stock your pond, but left the cans of young fish at the station."

"That is true," said Mr. Colfax.

"What is the matter with the clover-seed and potatoes?" Mr. Carteret looked up at the farmer on the box as he spoke.

The old man chuckled.

"It hain't my business to say, Mr. Carteret."

"This seems to be all, Mrs. Innis," said Mr. Carteret.

"Well," said Mrs. Innis, "if the other things are like these, you all ought to be ashamed of yourselves. The idea of giving a lot of rubbish to an old friend who has just come here to live!"

"*Give!*" exclaimed Mr. Colfax, indignantly. "Who said anything about *giving* these things?"

"Do you mean to say you sold them?" said Mrs. Innis.

"Well, it's the same thing; Reggie won them from us at poker."

"At cards?" exclaimed Mrs. Livingstone. She looked at her husband in horror.

"At cards?" repeated Mrs. Dashwood, with polite surprise in her tone. "I think we had better be going." She said this to Mrs. Innis, but Mrs. Livingstone heard.

At that moment the coyote, who had been innocently gnawing his rope, found himself unattached and charged the coop of game chickens. A wild clamor and cackling ensued. The farmer turned back into the wagon with his whip; the coyote jumped out and ran between the legs of the lame horse. As the horse winded the wolf, he gave a snort and dashed across the flower-beds, leaving the groom on his back in a bed of China asters.

The coyote hurried off on another line through the vegetable-garden, pursued by the beagles, which had also escaped and were yapping cheerily.

"Keep them off the flower-beds," called Mrs. Livingstone.

"We'll have a run!" cried Mr. Colfax. "Tally-ho! Gone away!" he bawled, and jumped on his horse.

Mr. Dashwood also mounted. "Forward on!" he yelled, and the two galloped after the beagles.

"They've gone through the vegetables!" cried Mrs. Livingstone.

"They will have a good gallop," said Mr. Carteret, wistfully. "I wish that I wasn't on a horse just off grass."

"But the flowers and the vegetables!" wailed Mrs. Livingstone.

"Never mind, dear," said Mrs. Dashwood; "you can get better ones by express from town. You know I told you how it would be. Good-by; we are going to follow on the road." She whipped up, and went down the drive at a gallop.

"Good-by, dear!" called back Mrs. Innis.

The piebald pony had become aroused by the excitement and began bucking. He ended, however, by biting the stable-boy. The boy put his hand to his injured shoulder, and both pony and goat got away.

"Look! Look! The pony!" cried Mrs. Livingstone. "Look! It's in the geraniums!"

"Hang the geraniums, and the pony too!" said Mr. Livingstone.

"Don't say that!" cried his wife. "It distresses me. Stop the pony!"

"I say," called Mr. Livingstone, "can't some of you catch that pony?"

The stable-boy started after it through the geraniums, and the pony fled to a more distant bed of asters.

Mrs. Livingstone stood white and rigid in the doorway, regarding these events. Suddenly she turned wildly upon Mr. Carteret.

"Take them all away! You must take them!" she commanded.

"Take what?" said Mr. Carteret, startled by her abruptness.

"All these things. They are the fruits of gambling, and they have ruined the lawn."

"But, my dear Mrs. Livingstone," Mr. Carteret began. Then he stopped. Hysterical women disturbed him, and even the remote possibility of possessing a horse like that which had broken loose made matters worse.

"You must take them!" she exclaimed. "They have ruined the garden; they have trampled on the flowers—"

"But the gardeners in a few days—" he interrupted.

"But *we* can't keep them," she said excitedly. "Don't you see? You must take them. *We* have ideals."

"Oh," said Mr. Carteret, as if that explained matters; "but, don't you see, I can't take them: I'm sailing for England."

"My dear," said Mr. Livingstone to his wife, "you are excited."

She gave him a glance, and turned to Mr. Carteret.

"If you can't take them yourself, then you must tell us how to dispose of them; we are your tenants."

To Mr. Carteret this was a new requirement in a landlord, but he saw that it was useless to argue. An inspiration came to him. "There's the curate, you know, in the village. He's been used all his life to havings things that other people don't want, and he's an awfully decent little chap." He started his horse down the driveway and lifted his cap. "Good morning," he called back. "I'm sorry I have to hurry off, but, you see, I'm sailing soon. The curate will be glad to have the calf," he added. He kicked his horse into a canter and fled.

"Take all these things to the curate," said Mrs. Livingstone to the men who remained in the line.

"But, Rosina," said Mr. Livingstone, "you can't send this stuff without some explanation."

"You may explain," said Mrs. Livingstone, and went into the house.

THAT afternoon the Livingstones' stable-men were busy delivering notes to the members of the class which announced that Mrs. Livingstone was indisposed and would be unable to have the class on Wednesday. The next afternoon she took the train for town with Mr. Livingstone, and it shortly became known that they had taken a house in Boston for the winter. The farm and the building-site were offered for sale, and, with Mr. Carteret's permission, his house was relet to some rich people from the West who were anxious to get into the hunting set.

"I was afraid they wouldn't like it," observed Mrs. Innis. They were talking the matter over at tea on the club veranda. "But it is experiments like this that keep life interesting, isn't it?" she added.

"I'm rather sorry for Reggie," said Mrs. Dashwood.